D1389154

LAST RITES

By Shaun Hutson

Assassin
Body Count
Breeding Ground
Captives
Compulsion
Deadhead
Death Day
Dying Words
Erebus
Exit Wounds
Heathen
Hell to Pay
Hybrid
Knife Edge
Last Rites
Lucy's Child
Necessary Evil
Nemesis
Purity
Relics
Renegades
Shadows
Slugs
Spawn
Stolen Angels
Twisted Souls
Unmarked Graves
Victims
Warhol's Prophecy
White Ghost

Shaun Hutson Omnibus 1
Shaun Hutson Omnibus 2

SHAUN HUTSON
LAST RITES

www.orbitbooks.net

ORBIT

First published in Great Britain in 2009 by Orbit

Copyright © 2009 by Shaun Hutson

A CIP catalogue record for this book
is available from the British Library.

ISBN 978-1-84149-765-5

Typeset in Bembo by Palimpsest Book Production Limited,
Grangemouth, Stirlingshire
Printed and bound in the UK by CPI Mackays, Chatham ME5 8TD

Papers used by Orbit are natural, renewable and recyclable
products sourced from well-managed forests and certified
in accordance with the rules of the Forest Stewardship Council.

Mixed Sources
Product group from well-managed
forests and other controlled sources
www.fsc.org Cert no. SGS-COC-004081
© 1996 Forest Stewardship Council
FSC

Orbit
An imprint of
Little, Brown Book Group
100 Victoria Embankment
London EC4Y 0DY

An Hachette UK Company
www.hachette.co.uk

www.orbitbooks.net

*This book is dedicated, with great respect,
to the memory of Mr Bob Tanner.*

Acknowledgements

This, for those of you who are interested, is my thirtieth published novel under my own name (I'm not including the thirty odd under pseudonyms) so I suppose it's something of a landmark. It seems strange that such a landmark (or travesty in the view of some, I'm sure) should have come to pass with so little help from others. I struggled through this one just about on my own. So, not the customary three page list of people, places and things that normally clog up the opening pages of one of my offerings. Instead, just a polite thank you to a select few.

Many thanks to my agent, Brie Burkeman for her continuing battle. Without her help and insight you wouldn't be reading this book.

Every other name that follows should know why they're included, especially by now.

Barbara Daniel, Carol Donnelly, Andy Edwards, James and Melinda Whale, Jo Roberts, Jason, Jonathan and Maria Figgis, Rod Smallwood, Val Janes, Steve, Bruce, Dave, Adrian, Janick, Nicko, Ian Austin, Leslie and Sue Tebbs, Brian, Martin Phillips and Graeme Sayer.

I continue to thank Cineworld UK, especially those

at Cineworld Milton Keynes. Mark Johnson, Debbie, Martin, Paula, Gareth, Dan, Richard, Helen and anyone else who's either been unwittingly left out or who's since left.

I would also like to thank Liverpool Football Club. Aaron, Steve, Paul, Tommy, Dave, Pete, Kevin, Brian and Neil as well as Stewards Pete, John and Vinnie.

I wish there were a more adequate word to use than thanks when it comes to my mum and dad but, unfortunately, as there isn't it will have to do. I hope they realise how much it means.

The same goes for my wife and daughter. Words can never describe how much they mean to me. I hope they too realise it.

And, as ever, lastly and most importantly, I thank you lot, my readers.

Let's go.

'The grave's a fine and private place,
But none, I think, do there embrace.'

Andrew Marvell

Exploration

The underground passageway was narrow. Barely high enough for the man to walk in without stooping and hardly wide enough for him to extend both arms on either side of him. Every now and then, the blade of the shovel he carried scraped against the bricks and a loud clang would reverberate throughout the tunnel. Whenever this happened the man cursed under his breath, waited a moment then walked on, the metallic sound ringing in his ears.

The floor beneath his feet was slippery. Some of it was stone, the majority just earth, moistened by the recent rainfall that had seeped through the ground and puddled in a number of places in the subterranean walkways.

The wetness brought with it a cloying, almost overpowering smell of soggy earth but also of something else not so easily identifiable.

Something rank and rancid.

Something ancient and long buried.

The man shuddered and moved on, the beam of the torch he carried cutting through the gloom effectively enough. He was breathing heavily despite the fact that he'd only been walking for ten minutes or less. It wasn't the distance that was tiring him. It was the difficulty of the terrain and of having to walk bent over like some arthritic old-age pensioner that was causing him to suck in deep lungfuls of reeking air.

He wondered if there were rats down here with him. It was a perfect environment for them. Spiders too had infested the underground tunnels, spinning thick webs in so many places that he was forced to part their dusty webs with his hand if he saw them in time. Sometimes the webs would brush against his face, sticking to his hair or the stubble on his face and then he would have to pause and pull the strands free, spluttering as he did so. The tunnels beneath the ground were pitch black and had been abandoned many years ago. Shunned by the sensible and the sane. Only frequented occasionally by men like himself.

He wondered how many there'd been before him. How many had travelled this febrile and exhausting route in search of what he now sought? How many had ventured into this underground labyrinth with the same objective?

How many had left, he pondered briefly, and the thought was enough to raise the hairs at the back of his neck. He stood still for a moment, trying to get his bearings, anxious to avoid taking a wrong turning in the impenetrable gloom. If he strayed from the path he now walked then he knew he had little hope of ever finding his way back to the surface. Another thought that made him swallow hard.

Could he, he wondered, simply lose his way down here? Wander helplessly for hours on end, turning this way and that, unable to see clearly until he became irretrievably lost?

The possibility didn't bear thinking about so he chose to push those thoughts far to the back of his mind, not daring to entertain them for too long.

His torch beam flickered and he felt a stab of almost un-controllable panic. For an instant he was plunged into the most total blackness he'd ever experienced in his life. So complete and consuming that he couldn't see a hand in front of him.

2

He shook the torch and, to his great relief, it glowed brightly once again. The man was angry with himself because he had no extra batteries with him and he didn't want to be without the light, not down here. Not now. He shone the torch ahead of him and its powerful beam picked out the crumbling stonework that surrounded him. There was a particularly wide expanse of filthy water about ten feet ahead of him and he sighed at the thought of trekking through more of the freezing liquid. The last puddle he'd trudged through had soaked his trousers as high as his ankle. He hoped this latest obstacle wasn't as deep.

He turned and glanced behind him, ears and eyes alert for the slightest sound or movement.

For what seemed like an eternity he stood there, back pressed to the closest wall, satisfied he was still alone in the tunnels, at least for the time being. He nodded to himself for reassurance and sucked in another deep breath.

He moved on.

1

North London

The bones in his nose splintered like glass.

From the sheer force of the impact Peter Mason guessed that the cause of the damage was a foot, driven into his face with lethal power and savagery. His mind had only seconds to appreciate this latest injury when another thunderous blow cracked two of his ribs. He gasped, trying to suck in air, attempting to get to his feet. He had to get up, he knew that. Had to raise himself up from the concrete, away from the kicking feet that swung at him as if he were some kind of human football.

As he tried to rise, blood from the cuts on his forehead ran into his eyes and he blinked rapidly to try and clear his vision. Mason got as far as his knees, flailing blindly with both hands to ward off his attackers. He felt another crushing blow to the back of his neck and pitched forward, scraping his chin and the palms of one hand on the concrete.

'Cunt,' he heard hissed from somewhere above him.

He raised one arm to protect his head but it merely exposed his torso and he felt more kicks to his stomach and back.

5

'Fucking cunt,' another voice snarled.

And they were at him again, raining blows towards his head and the arms he protected it with. Another kick caught him in the back of the skull and, for precious seconds, Mason thought he was losing consciousness. He curled up, protecting his head with both hands now, attempting to roll into a foetal position to minimise the area of his body that they had to aim at but, more importantly, to protect his head.

More kicks slammed into his clutching hands, splitting the skin and jarring his knuckles but he clung on desperately. Apart from the odd powerful and painful kick to his stomach and lower back, they seemed to be concentrating on his head now, doubling their efforts as they saw him pulling himself more tightly into a ball before them.

Another kick sent white hot pain through his left elbow. The one after that almost splintered his right wrist. He gritted his teeth, knowing that he must remain in this position if he was to have any chance of survival. If they managed to get to his exposed head for any length of time then he would have no chance.

He heard their words, cursing and deriding him even over the impact of their blows. Some of the words were said breathlessly. Perhaps they were tiring with the sheer concerted effort of beating him for so long. His watch was already shattered on his right wrist and, even if he'd been able to see it, Mason may have been surprised to discover that they had been striking him for less than a minute. It felt like an eternity and he feared that they would somehow retain their strength for longer than he could. After all, there were five of them. Buoyed by youth, adrenalin and fury, they could keep up this assault all night. Couldn't they?

6

He tried to tuck his knees in tighter to his stomach but his strength was failing. One of them kicked him hard in the small of the back and pain lanced across his pelvis and buttocks. He wondered if the blow had broken his spine. Almost involuntarily, he allowed his legs to stretch before him and, immediately, one of them aimed a kick at his briefly exposed genitals. It missed and connected with his right thigh, thudding into the muscle there and numbing the limb.

Another stamped on him. This time on his arm, trying again to force him into loosening his grip on his own head. Attempting to make him expose his face and skull to their ferocity. The pain was excruciating but Mason somehow held on. He could taste blood in his mouth but he wasn't sure if it was coming from his split lips, the cuts on his face or whether he already had internal damage.

Punctured lung? Ruptured spleen? Pulverised liver or kidneys? There was so much they could already have done to him.

But, as their kicks intensified on his arms and hands, he was in no doubt that they wanted to vent their full energy on his face and skull. It was like a beacon for them. If they could force him to relinquish protection there then they could finish the job. Mason hung on with even greater defiance at this realisation.

Kicked to death.

The words flashed through his brain just as another foot connected savagely with his hands. Another came down onto the side of his head and caught his ear, almost tearing off the lobe. He felt fresh blood burst warmly onto the side of his face, some of it spattering the pavement next to him. He heard a shout of triumph from above him, felt another withering kick to his already throbbing elbow.

7

His grip loosened slightly and they seemed to sense their triumph. Like hunting dogs seeing the last faltering steps of an exhausted prey, they redoubled their efforts and Mason groaned in agony as two kicks caught him on the crown of his skull. His head swam and he realised that he was about to black out but he knew that once that happened he was dead. Without the paltry protection for his head that he'd managed to maintain, they would kill him. It was as simple as that. They would kick him to a pulp. Drive feet against his face and head until the bone simply caved in. Mason tried one last time to roll over, to get to his feet.

It was useless. Another blow slammed into him, bending one of his fingers back so far it threatened to snap off. He thought he heard the bone snap but still he tried to shield himself with arms that were almost pulverised by the incessant impacts. A foot stamped on his head, the entire weight of the one who struck landing on his cranium now and that thought stuck in his mind and stayed there.

They were jumping on him now.

Rising from the ground a foot or so and landing with all their weight on his battered body and head.

Unconsciousness began to flood in upon him. More blood splashed the concrete beneath his head. He saw one of them running towards him, preparing to kick his head as surely as if he were about to blast a football into an empty net.

Mason knew this was the end.

2

Blinding white light.

Peter Mason closed his eyes again to shield them from the cold glow above him.

Stay away from the light.

Was that what it was? This searing luminescence above him, was it beckoning him towards eternity?

Mason was aware of agonising pain all over his body. It felt as if his limbs had been inflated. As if every millimetre of skin was a thousand times more sensitive and that every exposed portion of flesh was being jabbed constantly with red-hot forks.

He was also aware of movement. For fleeting moments he thought he was floating. His body was moving along without his feet touching the ground. And, all the time, that blinding white light remained above him.

So, this was what death felt like.

Apart from the pain it wasn't so dreadful, he thought. But he didn't want to die. He didn't want to be enveloped by the light. He wanted to walk. To live. He wanted the pain to stop.

He tried to turn his head but couldn't. His neck was broken, that was the only answer.

'Can you hear me?'

The words floated through the haze of pain but they didn't really register.

'Can you feel that?'

Mason couldn't feel anything at all except pain.

'What about that?'

Nothing, he thought.

'Don't worry.'

Who was speaking to him? He wondered for a second if it was God.

Then he blacked out again.

Where were the clouds, Mason thought. If this was heaven shouldn't there be clouds? And angels? And Jesus? And everything else that he'd been told to expect when he was a kid. He could see people in white but he was sure they weren't angels. They had no wings.

Always a giveaway. No wings.

And they weren't floating or playing harps. Two of them were looking at him and they were speaking but Mason couldn't hear what they were saying.

He wanted to ask them where the clouds were. Where Jesus was. Where his own mum and dad were for that matter. Weren't you supposed to meet up with your dead relatives when you went to heaven?

What a fucking cop out. No angels. No clouds. No mum or dad. No Jesus. Not even any pearly gates. Did all those fucking painters lie? Were the clouds and the angels just a figment of Michelangelo's imagination? There was nothing to mark this out as heaven.

Just pain.

★   ★   ★

10

Perhaps it was the other place. Not heaven.

Downstairs.

In which case, why wasn't it hot? Why weren't demons jabbing pitchforks up his arse? Why couldn't he see the Lake of Fire? Where were the rest of the damned? Shouldn't they be hanging up in chains like rotting Christmas decorations? Where was Hitler? Where was Stalin? Where was Attila the Hun?

He must be well pissed off. What's the good of having a nickname like 'The scourge of God' and not even being in the welcoming committee? Welcome to hell, Attila can't make it. He's playing poker with Jeffrey Dahmer, Heinrich Himmler and Torquemada. Sorry.

Hell. Welcome to it.

Yeah, you fucking are. Looks like Hieronymus Bosch and Dante were liars too.

Mason closed his eyes again.

How long had he been asleep? It was the first thing that Mason thought as he opened his eyes. He had several seconds of blissful comfort and then the pain came rushing in at him from all sides. He sighed and, for a moment, he feared he was going to be sick. Mason prepared to tilt his head to one side, not wanting to vomit all over himself but he couldn't move his head. The feeling passed and he sucked in a deep breath that hurt his chest.

His mouth was dry, his lips cracked. Someone was standing close to him, looking at him. Mason felt something being pushed towards his mouth and it took him a moment to realise it was a straw. He managed to guide the plastic tube into his mouth using his tongue then he sucked as hard as he could. The water filled his mouth and ran down his throat and he wanted to cough but the pain was worse when he did. He closed his eyes tightly.

11

'Just sleep now,' the figure before him said gently and Mason felt the straw being pulled from his mouth.

Sleep.

It seemed hard to do anything other than that.

Darkness flooded in once more.

3

Walston, Buckinghamshire

The cat was overweight. Years of overfeeding had soft-
ened its naturally feline shape, bloated it. The indulgence
of its owners had done nothing for its health but the cat
ate what was pushed before it unthinkingly and it enjoyed
the pampering. The nightly excursions into the back
garden of the house where it lived and the fields beyond
was one of the few acknowledgements of its natural
status. A brief reminder of thousands of years of instinct.
It didn't run free through the gardens of the houses or
the fields that backed on to them, it waddled as best it
could with its oversized frame, the small red collar around
its thick neck almost hidden by folds of skin and black
and white fur.

It wanted to hunt. To chase the mice that scurried
through the fields and gardens when night came, but its
shape prevented that. It made a few half-hearted advances
towards birds when it was allowed out during the day
and it had once actually managed to catch a mouse. It
had strutted defiantly back to its home, the dead rodent
gripped in its teeth and the cat had dropped the tiny
lifeless form on the kitchen floor but its owner had

screamed and scolded it. Still the cat prowled during the hours of darkness, perhaps remembering its hunting triumph. But now it seemed content to wander around outside the back door for fifteen minutes or less then squeeze itself back inside through the flap in the door that was barely large enough to accommodate its overfed frame.

But, on this particular night, it spotted movement beneath the hedge at the bottom of the garden and it moved with an elegance that years of indulgence had been unable to remove. On fat legs it glided through the flowerbeds towards the source of the movement. The cat paused, ensuring that its prey had not spotted it.

The mouse continued to clean itself, its snout twitching. It didn't seem to have noticed the cat which now moved closer, its eyes fixed on the rodent.

The cat continued to advance, paws pressing sound-lessly across the dark earth, its passage further hidden by the small shed that stood between it and the mouse.

The rodent pricked up its ears and looked around and the cat paused again, sinking lower to the ground but its belly dragged in the dirt and it straightened up again as it continued to close the distance between itself and the mouse.

The rodent returned to cleaning itself, turning away from the houses and from the cat.

A strong breeze blew across the garden, rustling the privet hedge and bringing several scents to the nostrils of both cat and mouse. The mouse stiffened, rising up on its hind legs, perhaps catching the smell of its hunter. The cat, for its own part, showed its teeth and prepared to run at the mouse. There was another gust of wind and the mouse scuttled away towards the hedge. The cat followed, moving as quickly as it could, diving at the rodent, hauling itself through the hedge in pursuit of its prey. It hissed and swiped a paw in the direction of the fleeing mouse but missed and could only watch as the tiny creature disappeared into the tall grass of the field beyond.

Panting from its exertions and wanting only to be back in its basket now, the cat turned and prepared to haul itself wearily through the hedge.

The hand that grabbed it gripped hard just behind its head, lifting the cat into the air, jamming it into the stinking confines of a hessian sack. The cat barely had time to swipe at its attacker before it was pushed into the blackness, hissing and spitting.

It tried to wriggle free of the sack but the top was hastily twisted shut. The cat struggled even more violently because it detected scents it didn't like. The rubber odour of the thick glove that had grasped it and another that caused its hackles to rise.

The smell of blood.

4

North London

Mason guessed that the nurse was in her late twenties. She had dishwater-blonde hair fixed in a bun beneath her white cap and a light blue plastic overall covering her white uniform. She was reading his chart as she stood at the bottom of his hospital bed, chewing distractedly on the end of a Bic. She glanced at her watch then scribbled something on the chart before replacing it and glancing at him. She smiled when she saw that his eyes were open.

'Hello,' she said, softly, her smile widening. She took a couple of steps towards him and reached for his right wrist, pressing two fingers against it as she felt for a pulse. She glanced down at her watch again, checking his heartbeat. She nodded to herself then ran her gaze appraisingly over him.

'I won't ask how you're feeling,' she continued, the smile still in place. 'Pretty sore I should think.'

'I've felt better,' Mason croaked, his throat dry. The words sounded thin and reedy, as if they were spoken by a man being throttled. He tried to swallow but couldn't. The nurse pushed a beaker of water towards

16

him and steadied the straw while he drank a couple of mouthfuls.

He nodded as best he could when he'd finished and she replaced the beaker on the bedside table. Mason moved his eyes slowly, taking in the details of his surroundings. He was in a room on his own, apart from the nurse. The walls were the colour of eggshells, some of the paint peeling around the door that led in and out of the room. It was very quiet. Both inside the room and beyond.

'Where am I?' Mason asked, wincing as he tried to move his right arm and felt pain lancing up the limb from the elbow. There was a drip in the crook of the arm, held in place by several pieces of tape. Mason looked at the tube there and saw a droplet of clear fluid trickle down from one of the plastic bags suspended above him.

'St Luke's Hospital, Camden Town,' she told him. 'It was the nearest A and E to where you were attacked.'

'Attacked,' he repeated, quietly.

'Can you remember anything about it?' the nurse enquired.

'Not much.'

'It'll come back to you. You're lucky to be alive considering the extent of your injuries.'

'How long have I been here?'

'Eight days,' she said, flatly. 'You've been in a coma for six of them.'

Mason felt a chill run the length of his bruised spine.

'Six days,' he gasped. 'Jesus. What did they do to me?'

The nurse was about to answer when the door behind her opened and Mason saw a dark-haired man with greying temples enter. He looked at Mason then at the nurse.

'Mr Mason's just woken up, Doctor Parry,' she informed the newcomer.

'Thank you, nurse. That's good.' The doctor smiled. 'We were wondering how long you were going to keep us waiting, Mr Mason.' He pulled a penlight from the top pocket of his white coat and advanced towards Mason, aiming the thin beam at his grey eyes. Mason winced but the doctor persisted, inspecting both eyes closely.

'You're a lucky man,' the doctor murmured.

'So everyone keeps telling me,' Mason offered. 'Since when was six days in a coma lucky?'

'You could have died,' the doctor murmured. 'Given the two options I'd say that qualified as lucky, wouldn't you?' He switched off the penlight and stepped back slightly.

'What kind of injuries have I got?' Mason asked.

'Do you want the full list?' Parry enquired.

'No,' Mason decided. 'I can live without it.'

'The worst damage was to your skull and your neck,' the doctor told him. He pointed with one long index finger. 'Needless to say there were countless cuts and abrasions, some worse than others. It could have been much worse though.'

'Who found me?' Mason wanted to know.

'Apparently, a car drove down the street where you were being attacked,' Parry informed him. 'Your attackers ran off. The driver of the car called an ambulance. I'm sure the police will give you a much more detailed account if that's what you want. They'll be back when they know you're lucid.'

'Is there going to be any long-term damage, Doctor?' Mason enquired.

'Apart from some scars, no,' Parry assured him. 'We'll monitor you closely in the next couple of days but, with any luck, you should be fit enough to get out of bed by the end of the week.'

'Why can't I move my neck?' Mason wanted to know.

'Because of the brace that's holding it steady,' Parry informed him. 'That'll be coming off soon. We just need to run a few tests on you. Otherwise, you can devote your time to resting.'

'Resting? I've been in a coma for six days. I'd rather get up and walk about.'

'All in good time, Mr Mason.' Parry smiled, turning towards the door. He swept out without another word.

The nurse moved forward and helped Mason as he struggled to sit up.

'Is there anything I can get you?' she asked.

'I'd love a cup of tea,' he told her, smiling. 'Is that allowed?'

'I'll see what I can do,' she told him, heading towards the door.

'While you're at it,' he called after her, 'I could murder a cigarette.'

'I'll be back with the tea,' she told him.

The door slid shut behind her. The silence descended once more. Mason closed his eyes.

5

Walston, Buckinghamshire

The hand that pulled the cat from the sack gripped the animal tightly at the back of the neck.

Disorientated by so long in the stuffy, dark confines of the sack, the cat hissed as it was pulled free, attempting to scratch the person that held it, anxious to be free of the clutching grip. However, once it was free of the hessian, it merely hung there limply for a moment, its tail flicking lazily. Then it seemed to recover its anger and struck out at its captor.

The one who held it ensured that the cat was at arm's length, minimising any chance of being scratched by its claws. The overweight feline hissed but the sound was one of fear as much as of defiance. The smell of blood was still strong in its nostrils and the hand holding it felt it buck angrily in a vain attempt to escape.

Quite clearly the cat was in no position to free itself from the vice-like grip but the one who held it also knew that speed was of the essence if the required tasks were to be completed.

Still holding the cat by the scruff of the neck, the other hand now reached to one side, fingers closing over the secateurs. The cat writhed more frantically for a moment, perhaps seeing the dull light glint on the blades of the cutters. If it had known what was coming next, it would have redoubled its efforts.

The twin blades were driven forward piercing the swollen stomach and ripping upwards, gutting the animal, exposing its intestines and allowing them to spill from the rent like the tentacles of some blood-drenched octopus. Still the animal struggled, even when an ungloved hand pushed through the crimson cavity of its opened chest and gripped its heart.

The organ was pulled free with relative ease, obstructed only by some muscle and ligament around the pulsing prize. At last the cat's movements became weaker and, as its mouth lolled open, the secateurs cut effortlessly through its tongue, slicing the pink sliver free. It fell into the dust close to the puddle of blood that now surrounded the feline's form.

Whispered words filled the silence. Words of encouragement and delight. The cat's body twitched involuntarily.

Flaying it would be relatively easy now. Cutting into the skin then peeling it away from the flesh and muscles. First, the still gleaming eyes must be taken. Gouged and extricated from their sockets and, if possible, kept intact.

The hand wielding the secateurs began to cut once more.

6

North London

Mason was having trouble keeping track of time. Despite his desire to be up and about, he found that he kept drifting off to sleep almost without realising it. The nurse had told him it was something to do with his body needing to heal itself and he accepted that. He was relieved when they removed the drip from his arm and presented him with something more substantial than saline solution and glucose. There wasn't much taste to the food they brought him but it was better than liquid, Mason mused.

His body felt stiff rather than painful now and that was something else he was grateful for. With each passing hour, it seemed that his joints and limbs became more supple. He had less and less need for painkillers, sometimes even refusing them when they were offered just to prove to himself that he was indeed getting better. Mason told himself it was nothing to do with being heroic. Heroism had never been a strong point in his character but he felt more convinced of his own returning health and strength when he could beat off a headache or backache just by riding out the discomfort.

Boredom was the biggest adversary. Confined to bed for twenty-four hours a day, he looked at the floor of the room longingly, wanting so badly to haul himself from between the sheets and plant his feet on the tiles beneath. Surely it couldn't hurt, could it? A steady, careful shuffle from one side of the room to the other. Where was the harm in that?

Mason pulled the sheets back, glancing towards the door of the room in the process. He didn't want one of the nurses walking in and catching him.

(Catching you. What's the problem? You're going to walk across the room, not piss in the corridor.)

They might decide to delay his eventual escape from the confines of the bed as a punishment.

And what if you fall?

Mason hesitated.

What if you bang your head or snap another bone? You'll be in here even longer.

He sucked in a deep breath, his eyes still fixed on the floor. Come on. All you have to do is swing your legs out of bed, plant your feet on the tiles and walk. How hard is that going to be?

Mason flexed his toes and tensed his leg muscles, ready to complete the task. He pushed himself up on one heavily strapped elbow and swallowed hard.

Go on. Get up.

The nurse had told him he'd been in a coma for six days, that was scarcely enough time for muscle wastage to set in, was it? It wasn't as if he was going to put one foot down, lower his weight upon it then collapse due to the lack of strength in his calves and thighs. Mason edged a little closer to the edge of the bed, pushing the sheets a little further. He glanced down at his legs and saw several bruises and small cuts on the ankles and above but nothing too bad. Nothing to prevent the simple task of getting out of bed.

He sat up, his feet pressed lightly against the tiles beneath. His head was aching slightly but he ignored the discomfort, more intent on standing up and walking. He balled his hands into fists and prepared to push himself upright.

Come on. Do it now. Even if your legs give out, the worst that will happen is that you'll fall backwards onto the bed. If that happens you can pull yourself back under the covers and no one will ever know you fucked it up. Go on.

He sucked in a deep breath, closed his eyes and shuffled forward to the edge of the bed, preparing to stand up.

Mason never noticed that the door of his room had opened. Only when the woman who paused there finally walked in and spoke did he snap his head around in her direction.

'They said you were resting,' she told him, quietly, closing the door behind her.

Mason looked impassively at the woman for a moment then eased himself backwards a little more.

Only as she took a couple of steps towards the bed did he smile and lie back against his pillows.

'Hello, Natalie,' he breathed. 'Have a seat.' He indicated the brown plastic chair close to his bed.

His wife kissed him lightly on the lips then sat down.

Realisation

The underground walkway was becoming narrower.

As the spade clanged against the stonework yet again, the man was sure that the subterranean passage was now much more confined and restricted than it had been when he'd first entered it. Almost without him realising, the tunnel had telescoped until he now found that he had to take every step hunched over. His neck and his back ached from the effort and he was finding it more difficult to breathe. Despite the chill that infected the tunnels, he was sweating too.

He shone the torch ahead, wondering if the tunnel was simply going to end in two or three hundred yards. Would it grow so narrow that it finally closed completely? He wondered what the reason was for this. Something above ground that had necessitated this constriction possibly. Perhaps when the tunnel had been dug it had been unavoidable. He pressed on, hoping that the space would open out again soon. He felt even more claustrophobic now. As if the walls themselves were closing around him like a brick fist, determined to crush the life from him. The smell inside the tunnel was far more intense as well. The stink of dampness and decay had been eclipsed by a more pungent and stomach-churning odour that caused him to gag.

25

He paused, trying to breathe through his mouth instead but the foul air made his throat and chest sore.

He shone the torch upwards and saw that the ceiling of the passage was glistening. Frowning, he swept the beam back and forth over the gleaming brickwork there, convinced now that what coated the roof of the passage wasn't just water.

When the tips of his fingers touched the gleaming wetness he gasped.

It wasn't water, that much he'd been right about. It was slime.

Like the thick secretion of some enormous snail. But this was darker and more noxious. It was more like liquid excrement.

He snatched his hand away, wiping the muck off on his trousers with a mixture of disgust and revulsion. However, as his initial feelings passed, his mind began to fill with other thoughts and one in particular struck him and refused to be banished.

Where had the slime come from? What had left it behind?

He swallowed hard, determined to press on but feeling light-headed because of the vile stench that seemed to be seeping into the very pores of his skin.

From somewhere, and at first he wasn't sure whether it was behind or ahead of him, he heard a sound. A splashing sound, as if someone was moving quickly through water. The sound echoed inside the tunnel for a moment then died away and the man flicked off the torch momentarily, standing in the pitch black, trying to pinpoint the direction of the noise.

When it came again he realised that it was coming from behind him and he now knew for sure what he had feared for some time.

He wasn't alone inside the tunnels.

7

Walston, Buckinghamshire

Anne Bailey switched off the engine of the car and sat motionless behind the steering wheel. She exhaled wearily, the noise still reverberating in her ears. A broken exhaust, her husband had told her. He was sure that there was a hole in it. In some pipe that he'd mentioned but that she couldn't remember the name of. It was 'blowing' he'd said. All Anne knew was that the bloody thing had to be fixed and quickly. Not only did it make the vehicle unbearably noisy to drive but, she understood, it also made it dangerous. Carbon monoxide fumes seeping into the car, something like that, she recalled.

As she hauled herself out of the car she knew that the exhaust would have to be fixed, but where the money to carry out the repairs was going to come from, she had no idea. A couple of hundred, her husband had said. He'd also told her that he knew someone who might be able to fix it for half that price but Anne wasn't too sure about that. She wanted it fixed properly, by a mechanic in a garage. However, if the work was going to cost two hundred pounds or more then perhaps this acquaintance of her husband's was the only answer.

A hundred was bad enough but they'd have to find it from somewhere. Either that or she'd have to give up the car and she didn't fancy doing that with the amount of walking she had to do in a day. Perhaps, Anne thought, she could clean the house of the man who was offering to help. She already cleaned eight houses in the town so another one wouldn't be a problem. She didn't enjoy cleaning (apart from having a sly look through the drawers and wardrobes of her employers when she was cleaning their bedrooms) but she had no choice. She couldn't work in a supermarket or shop because she couldn't master the electronic tills. Besides, at her age, very few people were interested in her limited skills. She'd never picked things up very quickly even as a girl and now, at sixty-eight, it was even more taxing for her. She had to earn money some way and there was very little that she could do other than domestic work. She had to supplement her husband's meagre pension somehow. It was all they could do to pay the rent every month and he was no use. What could he do? Anything too strenuous and he'd be dead. Three heart attacks in the last four years had almost killed him as it was. So, Anne cleaned because she had to. Her customers were nice people and they all paid her cash in hand which helped. No problems about declaring to the tax man. All apart from a woman who worked at an accountant's. She paid by cheque. Naturally, Anne thought irritably.

Even the vicar paid her in cash, she mused as she crossed the small car park towards the gate that led to the churchyard. Beyond it, the church poked its spire towards the overcast sky, threatening to tear open the low hanging clouds.

St Jude's was one of the oldest churches in Walston. At least six hundred years old as far as Anne was aware.

Not like these new places of worship that reminded her more of observatories than houses of God. There were two like it in the town. Both with large glass domes where their steeples should have been. Anne hated the look of them. She hated their newness. Just like she hated most things that were modern. To Anne they implied change and she didn't care much for change either. She preferred more traditional things and that included churches. St Jude's with its tower and spire, its ivy-covered walls and its stained-glass windows was how she remembered the churches in her youth.

She felt a strong breeze blow across the churchyard and she pulled up the collar of her coat as she walked. Anne paused to pick up a sweet wrapper that was stuck among some weeds at the side of the path. She muttered something under her breath and stuffed the paper into one of her pockets. Fancy dropping litter in a graveyard, she tutted to herself, how disrespectful. Probably some young child. The offspring of one of the many teenage mothers that lived in Walston, she assumed. No respect. None from the parents and none from the children. That was the world now as far as Anne was concerned. No one had any respect any more.

She continued along the stone path around the church, turning to her right to reach the main door of the old building.

What was left of the cat was nailed to the wooden partition.

All four of its legs had been splayed, a long metal spike driven through each paw so that the cat was spreadeagled against the metal-braced door of the church. Anne shot out a hand to steady herself, her head spinning as she gazed at the butchered remains. She realised in an instant that the cat had been skinned. It took a second longer

for her to notice that both its eyes had been torn from their sockets. She opened her mouth to scream but no sound would come. There were some spots of congealed blood on the door and also on the stone flags beneath. There were some ants busying themselves around the rust-coloured spatters.

Anne staggered backwards, preparing to turn away. She knew she had to get help. Get the vicar. Call the police. Call someone. However, as she readied herself to head back along the pathway, she noticed that the door of the church was slightly open. Perhaps the vicar was already inside, perhaps he'd seen what had happened. She had to check. Had to go inside the church. She had to pass the door with the crucified cat nailed to it.

In spite of herself, Anne took a step forward.

8

North London

Natalie Mason placed the bunch of grapes and two apples in the plastic bowl on the bedside cabinet. She picked one of the grapes and popped it into her mouth.

'That's traditional, isn't it?' Mason said, taking a grape for himself. 'Bringing fruit for the sick.'

'The hospital rang me yesterday and told me you were out of the coma,' Natalie informed him.

'But you didn't want to come until today?'

'Don't start, Peter,' she breathed. 'I got here as soon as I could.'

'Other stuff to do?' he asked, a trace of sarcasm in his tone. 'More important things?'

'I'd been here four times before but you were still unconscious. I didn't know if you were going to slip back into a coma again.'

'So you didn't want to waste your time?'

She stood up and shook her head.

'If you're going to be like this then I might as well go,' she told him.

'No, no,' he urged. 'I'm sorry. Sit down.'

Natalie hesitated a moment then did as he asked. She

crossed one leg over the other and Mason ran an approving gaze over the slender limbs, encased in skin-tight denim. Her short leather jacket was open to reveal the lilac blouse beneath. She wore a silver crucifix around her neck that hung tantalisingly between her breasts. Her freshly washed light brown hair bore blonde streaks and her make-up, as ever, was sparingly but immaculately applied.

'You look great,' he told her by way of a peace offering.

'You look like shit,' she said, flatly.

'That's one of the things I always loved about you, Nat. Your honesty.' He took another grape. 'I look better than I did when they brought me in.'

'I know, I saw you when you were hooked up to all the machines,' she sighed. 'Have they told you when you can leave?'

'The end of the week if I'm lucky.'

'Are you going back to your flat?'

'Unless you want me to move back in with you.'

She smiled and shook her head.

'I'm concerned about you, Pete,' she grinned. 'But not *that* concerned.' She took another grape and popped it into her mouth. 'I don't think that would be wise, do you?'

'You're probably right. You usually are.'

'If you give me a key to your place I can go and fetch some clean clothes for you.'

'Thanks. I appreciate that.'

There was a long silence and she moved her chair a little closer to his bed.

'Do you know who attacked you?' she asked, quietly.

'I didn't get a clear view but I'm pretty sure,' he told her.

'Why did they do it, Pete?' she wanted to know.

'Because that's all they know,' Mason snapped. 'Because they're scum. Because most of the kids in that fucking school are little bastards. Because the school itself is a shit hole.'

'But they tried to kill you. What the hell made them do that?'

'I'd put two of them on detention that day.'

'And that's it? That was their motive? They tried to kill you because you put two of them on detention?'

'That's all kids like that need,' he sighed. 'Them and three of their mates must have followed me.'

'Have the police spoken to you yet? I'd have thought they'd have been here as soon as you regained consciousness.'

Mason shook his head.

'Two months ago another teacher, a supply teacher, was stabbed three times in class and the little bastard who did it got six months in borstal. Nobody gives a shit any more, Nat. So, once the court case is over I just want to get out of here and get away.'

'Away where?'

'Anywhere. Out of London. I'll move. Get a job in another part of the country. There's nothing to keep me here, is there?' He looked pointedly at Natalie.

She reached out and touched his hand lightly.

'Not even me?' she asked, smiling thinly.

'The reasons we separated haven't changed. *We* haven't changed.' He gripped her hand and held it. 'I wish we had.'

Natalie nodded almost imperceptibly, her eyes focusing on a large purplish-coloured bruise on his right forearm. She thought how much pain he must have been in. How close to death he'd actually come. She looked at his face, her own features now expressionless once again.

'I put flowers on Chloe's grave yesterday,' she finally said, softly.

Mason nodded.

'When was the last time you went there, Pete?' she continued.

'I can't remember,' he told her dismissively, easing his grip on her hand.

'Why not? Was it that long ago?'

'I visit when I can.' He shrugged.

'I don't like going there either, Pete. It brings back memories for me as well, you know, but I focus on the memories of when she was alive, when she was happy. Before she was ill.'

'Good for you,' he said, trying to hide the edge to his voice but failing.

'I still do it,' Natalie breathed. 'I do it because she was our daughter and I loved her.'

'I loved her too,' Mason snapped. 'Visiting her grave more often doesn't give you the monopoly on grief, Natalie.' He swallowed hard. 'I can't bear to stand by that grave and think about her. I never could, you know that. That doesn't make me any less of a man. It doesn't mean I didn't care about Chloe when she was alive but all I see when I stand next to that grave is her lying on that fucking bed in the hospital waiting to die. I can't see her running about playing. I can't see her smile. All I see is how she suffered at the end.'

'Running away from the pain isn't going to stop it, Pete.'

'It's my way of dealing with it.'

'That's your way of dealing with everything. You'd rather run or hide from problems.'

'Did you come here to see how I was or to lecture me about my lack of moral fibre? Or were you just worried that if I died, you'd have two graves to put flowers on instead of one?'

'Fuck you, Pete,' Natalie hissed, getting to her feet.

Mason thought about trying to stop her but decided against it. He watched as she walked across to the door.

'Let me know when you decide to move out of London,' she muttered. 'I'll come and wave you off.'

Mason held her gaze for a moment then she pushed the door and stepped through into the corridor beyond. He heard her footsteps receding away in the stillness.

'Shit,' he murmured, under his breath.

Inside the room, it was quiet once again.

9

Walston, Buckinghamshire

Anne Bailey's footsteps echoed on the cold stone floor of the church as she inched her way inside, careful not to brush against the bloodied carcass of the flayed cat. She was breathing quickly and heavily, her heart thumping a little too hard in her chest. Anne leaned against the nearest pew and tried to slow her breathing.

If only she had her mobile with her, she thought. She could have called the police from outside the church but she rarely carried the phone. Her daughter had bought it for her for her last birthday and Anne had protested at the time. What need did she have for a machine that could text? When would she ever do that? How often would she actually use the phone? It was all she could do to press the tiny digits with her swollen fingertips. Now, however, she would have given anything to have had the device in the pocket of her coat.

For a second she thought about calling out the vicar's name. If he was inside the church then he would come running. But another thought struck her. What if whoever had done this to the cat was still close by? Might they come running too? She turned and looked around her.

There were so many dark corners inside the church. So many places where someone could hide. They might even be watching her now. Anne felt her chest tightening even more.

Just get out, she told herself. Get away from here. Go back to your car and drive to the police station. The police will notify the vicar. Just get out.

She was about to step back towards the main doors when she saw the blood on the floor near the font.

Droplets of it gleamed dully. There was more on one of the stone pillars close by. She guessed it was cat blood. There had been so much of it that had dripped on the stonework beneath the poor creature. But, she reasoned, how had there come to be splatters of it inside the church as well? She moved towards the font, careful not to step in the spilled blood. Her footsteps echoed inside the cold building. The stained-glass face of Christ and half a dozen saints watched her impassively as she advanced.

Anne felt light-headed and wondered if her blood pressure had risen higher than it should. She had her tablets in her pocket. She wondered for a second if she should just sit still in one of the pews and wait until help arrived. The vicar would be here soon anyway. It might be more sensible to wait for him. Let him discover why there were droplets of blood inside the church too. However, Anne disregarded her own advice and continued to advance towards the font, her eyes now fixed on the red streaks that had run down the stonework of the receptacle.

The marble figure of Christ that hung on the large crucifix overlooking the altar also peered indifferently down upon her as she approached the font. If it had seen what happened inside the church then it was keeping the information to itself. The white lips were motionless, the eyes expressionless. Anne looked up briefly at the figure and shook her head in what was almost an apologetic gesture that He had been forced to witness such an outrage.

She glanced once more at the blood on and around the font then she stepped nearer and looked into the holy water itself.

It took Anne only a second to realise that there were several large lumps of excrement lying at the bottom of the receptacle.

Even if she'd bothered to peer a little longer at the thick brown lump, she probably wouldn't have realised that the reeking faecal matter was human.

As it was, Anne turned and ran as fast as she could, her head spinning, her lips moving in a silent litany. Then, as she was halfway up the aisle, she finally gave voice to the scream she'd been holding in from the time she entered the church.

Christ and all the saints looked on silently.

10

North London

Mason made his way back down the corridor slowly and carefully but with very little discomfort. The muscles in his legs and lower back ached but, he told himself, that was due to more than a week of inactivity and confinement to bed as much as it was to any residual damage caused by his beating. He'd come to look forward to his trips to the lavatory. No longer reliant on a bedpan or a commode to relieve himself, for the last two days he'd been making his own way to and from the toilet. He'd even managed a short stroll to the hospital canteen. Relishing freedom from the confines of his room he'd sat and drunk two cups of tea before returning. Now he pushed the door of his room open, ready to return to his bed and the second-hand battered paperback he'd purchased from the hospital shop for ten pence.

He didn't recognise the suited figure standing beside his bed as he walked in.

The man turned to face him and Mason saw that he was in his early forties, perhaps a year or two older than the teacher himself. The newcomer reached inside his jacket and pulled out a thin leather wallet that he flipped open for Mason to inspect. The teacher glanced at the photo within, then at the face of his visitor as if to ensure that the likeness matched that of the man now standing before him.

'Detective Sergeant Ray Weaver,' the older man announced, pushing the ID wallet back inside his jacket. 'The nurse said it was all right to talk to you, Mr Mason, I hope this is a convenient time.'

Mason nodded and clambered back between the sheets.

'It's not like I was going anywhere,' he added.

The detective reached for one of the plastic chairs and seated himself beside Mason's bed.

'How do you feel?' Weaver enquired.

'Better than I did when they brought me in,' Mason informed him.

'You know why I'm here, Mr Mason, so I won't waste your time. The quicker we can take a statement from you, the quicker we can initiate proceedings against the youths who attacked you.'

Mason looked impassively at the detective.

'Has anyone been arrested yet?' he wanted to know.

'Not yet,' Weaver told him. 'We need you to positively ID them before we can continue with the investigation. We need you to name names.'

'I'm pretty sure who it was.'

'Who were they, Mr Mason?'

'Well, I couldn't see their faces clearly but I'm pretty sure I know who it was.'

'We need you to be sure, Mr Mason.'

'There were five of them, two or three were wearing hoods.'

'The whole case is reliant on your evidence. On you identifying them.'

'I'm pretty sure I know who they were.'

'That's not good enough, Mr Mason.'

'And what if I don't identify them?'

'Then we haven't got a case.'

'Five of the kids I teach beat me almost to death and you're telling me there's nothing you can do about it?'

'You have to see it from our point of view, Mr Mason,' the detective told him. 'If there's not enough evidence in the first place then the CPS will just dismiss it.'

'I want those little bastards arrested,' Mason interrupted.

'Then give us some names.'

Mason sighed.

'I can't be sure,' he muttered.

'Then we can't help you,' Weaver explained.

'They're animals. If they get away with this they could do it to someone else.'

'I realise that and that's why we need you to identify them.'

'How many times do I have to tell you? They were covered up. Hiding their faces. I didn't see them clearly.'

Weaver regarded him silently for a moment then sucked in a deep breath. He fished inside his wallet for a small rectangular piece of card that he pushed towards Mason, holding it before him until the teacher took it.

'That's got my number on,' the detective explained. 'If you remember anything give me a call.'

'So that's it?' Mason said with an air of finality. 'Just like that? Finished?'

Weaver hesitated a moment then got to his feet.

'Like I said, call me if you remember anything,' the policeman said, pausing at the door.

'Thanks for your time,' Mason added, caustically.

Weaver hesitated for a second then pushed the door open and stepped through.

41

Mason glanced at the card, holding it before him between his thumb and forefinger then he drew in a deep breath and closed his fist around it. He dropped it onto his bedside table.

Callum Wade

From his vantage point at the top of the hill, Callum Wade could see the lights of Walston below him. Hundreds of yellow and white pinpricks set against the darker panoply of the surrounding hills.

Callum sipped from his can of cider and took a deep breath, savouring the scent of wet grass and rain-sodden trees. He loved this spot and had done since he was a child, since his parents had first brought him here when he was four. Even though that event was now thirteen years in his past Callum could still remember it vividly. Sitting on a thick grey blanket on the hillside with his mum and dad and his older sister, eating the picnic that his mum had made, playing games on the hillside in the summer sunshine. Most of all, he remembered rolling down the hill through the tall, uncut grass and the butter-cups, the smells in his nostrils and a feeling of absolute contentment.

This place always made him think of his childhood and this evening was no exception. He walked along the crest of the ridge, finishing what was left in his can but sticking the empty into one of the back pockets of his jeans. He had no intention of leaving it here, no desire to litter the countryside that he had always been brought up to respect so much. He thought how much he would miss Walston when he left and particularly how much he would miss this hillside and the smells that he associated so strongly with such times of happiness in his life.

He had lost his virginity here too. Given up that last vestige of innocence just three weeks ago to a girl he'd known since he was six. Callum had never been a great one for girls. He got on well with them and he certainly would have liked to have sampled the pleasures of sex before but, he decided, the wait had been worth it. Even if the girl had been drunk. She'd told him the following day that she didn't think they should become too involved. Not with him preparing to leave but they could go out for a drink now and again and she said that sex would be fine as long as her boyfriend didn't find out. Well, it was only for a few weeks, wasn't it? Callum was only too happy to agree. He was going to see her later (her boyfriend was working nights) and the thought of what they would do made him smile. He'd been thinking about her all day.

Callum wasn't frightened of leaving Walston or his home. He wasn't afraid of where he might be sent once his training was over. He knew that the time would come for him to do his tour in some Godforsaken part of the world and that when that time came there would be a chance he might not return. His mum had cried when he'd told her he'd joined the army. His dad had cried too but with pride. Callum had been a little overwhelmed. He'd never seen his dad cry before. It had almost started him off too. His sister would definitely cry when he told her, he thought, smiling. They'd worry about him while he was away, but that was only natural.

Ahead of him was the stone bridge that spanned the train tracks leading in and out of Walston. The station itself was about a mile away, just about visible from the centre of the bridge. Callum walked to the centre of the structure and leaned on the parapet, looking down at the tracks, realising that one of the express trains from London would be passing beneath him in the next minute or so. He smiled to himself. He'd only been to London three times in his life and now he was getting ready to embark on a career that would take him around the world.

He heard the rumble of the approaching train and saw a couple of magpies that had been standing on the metal rail take flight. The rumbling grew louder and Callum could actually see the dark outline of the train approaching now. It would be doing seventy by the time it reached the bridge.

Callum swung himself up onto the parapet of the bridge and stood there, swaying slightly as he looked down at the tracks and the fast approaching train.

He actually saw the driver's face for a split second, the man's eyes stretched wide in horror and realisation.

Callum Wade stepped off the parapet and dropped like a stone towards the onrushing engine.

11

Walston, Buckinghamshire

The farm was five miles from the centre of the town. A twenty-minute drive if the narrow roads weren't too busy. Just over sixty acres that supported a small dairy herd, sheep, pigs and just enough arable crops to survive. And, if Andy Preece was honest with himself, that was all he was doing. He survived. He made just enough money to run the farm. Just enough to support his family. His wife worked too. She had little choice. The money that the farm made was barely adequate for their needs. They needed a more stable, regular wage coming in as well.

Andy sold some of his produce to local restaurants and hotels. Even some of his animals, but the farm wasn't big enough to attract attention from the supermarket chains. He simply couldn't produce anything in sufficient quantity to ensure a contract with one of the top retailers. That was where the money was in farming. In mass-produced crops or battery-farmed animals.

He'd thought about battery farming, he'd thought about specialising in one specific crop (asparagus, his wife had suggested) but none of the suggestions had been viable. He wanted to be comfortable. Not rich. Not rolling in it. He just wanted to be able to run the farm and make a profit without working eighteen hours a day and worrying constantly whether or not there was going to be enough money to pay the electricity, gas and water bills and keep the kids in clothes. Andy hated it when they asked him for anything new. He hated it when they asked if they could have a holiday this year. He'd been promising them one for the past four years but he knew deep down that his promise was an empty one. He would never make enough money to give them the holiday they wanted. Not even a week in some grotty caravan on the coast somewhere. That hurt him deeply.

The farm was a millstone around his neck and, in the past few months, the prospect of selling it had become even more enticing. But there was something stopping him. Something stronger than the desire to feel secure. Something more powerful than the need to support his family with more than just a pittance. He knew he could retrain for another trade. At thirty-nine, he had been brought up on the farm and it was all he knew but there were opportunities out there if someone was willing to take them and Andy Preece had never been frightened of hard work or the thought of a new start.

What held him back was his pride. The farm had been run by his father and by his grandfather, handed down through the generations like a jewel that is slowly losing its lustre. Andy felt that, if he sold the farm, he would be betraying the memory of his father and grandfather. They had sweated and toiled to make the place what it was so that it could be passed on to him. His father had taught him that it was a man's duty to provide for his family and those sentiments, engrained from childhood, were difficult to eradicate. As Andy climbed into the

47

Land Rover he looked at himself in the rear-view mirror but found that he couldn't hold his own gaze. The eyes that had looked back at him had looked lifeless. There was no fire. No ambition. Only tired resignation. Even if his mind wouldn't accept that his days on the farm were finished, his eyes already betrayed that realisation.

'Come on, Sam,' he called, slapping the passenger seat.

A black and white collie bounded across the farm yard and leapt up onto the seat. The animal looked around expectantly at Andy as he reached over and closed the door behind it. He ran a hand affectionately over its sleek head then twisted the key in the ignition and pressed down on the accelerator. The engine purred into life and Andy drove across the yard towards the dirt track that led into the small range of hills about half a mile away. The sun was rising behind those hills, spilling a cold white light across the land. Birds were already singing in the trees. Nocturnal predators were returning to their lairs. The night had retreated again.

The collie sat upright on the passenger seat, ears pricked up as it gazed out at the countryside.

'What are you thinking?' Andy asked, glancing at the dog. 'That I should sell up? You'd be just as happy living in the town, wouldn't you?'

The dog turned its head when it heard his voice.

Andy ruffled its fur with one hand.

'You don't care, do you?' he murmured. 'Why should you? It's not your problem. I wish to Christ it wasn't mine.'

He guided the Land Rover around a bend in the track, flanked on one side by a barbed-wire fence and on the other by a high hedge. The fence posts were missing or broken in several places and Andy shook his head wearily.

'Better get that fixed too,' he murmured.

The dog started to bark.

'All right, calm down,' Andy said, lowering the sun visor in the Land Rover as the early morning sunshine momentarily blinded him. 'I'm not asking you to help.'

Still the dog barked, rising from its seated position on the passenger seat now.

'Sit down, Sam,' Andy snapped, pushing the dog's hindquarters back towards the seat.

The collie barked even more loudly, its head pointed straight ahead, its ears sticking straight up. It resisted Andy's attempts to calm it, the sound of its barking filling the vehicle, ringing in the farmer's ears.

'Sam,' he shouted, slowing the Land Rover down to negotiate a gently flowing stream that snaked across his land.

The dog's barking now subsided into deep guttural growls. Still it was gazing ahead, as if it could see something that Andy couldn't.

'What the hell is wrong with you?' he muttered.

The growls were punctuated by subdued yaps now and, as Andy glanced again at his dog, he saw that its hackles had risen. It had also slunk backwards, as if trying to push itself through the seat. Its lips were drawn back from its teeth as it continued to growl, head still pointing directly ahead.

Andy brought the Land Rover to a halt, swung himself out of the vehicle then walked around to the passenger side and flung the door open.

'Out,' he snapped, clapping his hands.

The dog wouldn't move. It remained on the passenger seat, growling.

12

North London

Peter Mason paid the taxi driver and stepped back from the road as the vehicle pulled away.

He fumbled in the pocket of his jacket and pulled out his keys, wondering why his hands were shaking slightly. He'd been fine leaving the hospital, fine inside the confines of the cab with the smell of his own freshly laundered clothes strong in his nostrils.

Mason stood motionless on the pavement for a second longer, allowing a youth in his late teens to speed past on a skateboard. He weaved in and out of pedestrians, finally disappearing around a corner out of sight. Mason sucked in a deep breath and clutched his keys more tightly. So tightly in fact that the metal dug into his palm. The jolt of pain seemed to shock him from his trance and he advanced towards the wood and bevelled-glass door ahead.

There were cracks in the glass. It looked as if someone had struck it with a stone. It needed repairing. As he pushed his key into the door, Mason wondered if he should alert the landlord.

Why bother? You won't be living here for much longer.

A lorry passed by noisily outside, the sound reverberating both inside the small hallway and also inside his head. Someone on the pavement shouted. There was a loud laugh. Mason closed the front door hurriedly, wanting to shut the noise out.

It was much cooler in the hallway and he stood there motionless for a moment. There were mail boxes mounted on the wall just inside the door, each one bearing a name and Mason unlocked his and pulled out several letters and a padded bag. He scanned the envelopes disinterestedly. Circulars. Bills.

He headed towards the staircase on his left. It took him up to the first of three floors. There were two flats on each level and a basement dwelling too. All were occupied. All the residents paid the same exorbitant amount of rent as Mason. On the first of each month it was extracted from his bank account, tugged like a tooth from recalcitrant gums.

Well, that won't be your problem soon, will it? The only things you've got to think about now are finding another job and getting out of London.

He reached the door of flat number three and selected another key, pausing a second before letting himself in.

It felt cool inside the flat. Even in the summer it always felt a few degrees below the outside temperature. The sun never shone directly through the windows of the flat, mainly because of the taller buildings that flanked it. Mason dropped the mail onto a table beside the phone.

He switched on his laptop as he passed. It sprang into life. The screensaver was a tropical beach and Mason glanced at it dumbly for a second, wishing he was there, stretched out on the golden sand with the sun beating down upon him and the waves rushing softly to the shore. Christ, that must feel good. What he wouldn't give

51

to be there. To be anywhere other than here. He continued on into the kitchen and filled the kettle. The milk in the fridge was off. He stood gazing accusingly at the carton, wondering whether or not he should pop out to the shop at the end of the road and get some fresh.

Fuck it.

He'd drink it without just for now. He put two big spoonfuls of sugar into his mug with the tea bag and waited for the kettle to boil. Back in the sitting room he checked his e-mails.

Nothing of interest there either, he thought, deleting the messages once he'd read them.

I've been away for two weeks and nothing has happened. Nothing.

He wandered back into the kitchen and made his tea. He found a couple of broken Rich Tea in his biscuit barrel on the worktop. They'd do for now. Carrying them in one hand and the mug in the other he returned to the sitting room and sat down at the laptop once again, gazing at the screen blankly.

He knew what he had to do. He had to start some-where. Mason sipped at his tea, wincing when he burned his tongue.

You should have got that milk.

No. Too much to do.

13

Walston, Buckinghamshire

Andy Preece looked angrily at the collie. The dog was still on the passenger seat of the Land Rover, its head pointing forward, its lips drawn back to show its teeth as it growled.

'Sam, for Christ's sake,' Andy snapped. 'Get out.' He clapped his hands. Even banged on the side of the vehicle in an attempt to persuade the animal. The sound reverberated across the stillness, the only sound now the low rumbling growl of the dog. As Andy watched, it slunk lower onto the seat, the growls degenerating into whimpers.

'What the hell is wrong with you?' Andy said, quietly.

The dog looked at him for a second then jumped down from the Land Rover. It stood beside the door and Andy could see that it was quivering. It continued to gaze ahead. Andy turned to look in the same direction but he could see nothing. The field to his right was hidden by the same high hedge that had flanked him for most of the drive. To his left, visible over a low stone wall, was another field but ahead of him he could see only a copse of trees and, beyond it, a gentle slope that led up to a low ridge.

The dog was gazing in the direction of the copse, barking every now and then, the sound alternated with either the whimpering or the growling that Andy had heard earlier. He opened the back of the Land Rover and reached in, pulling the double-barrelled shotgun from inside. He broke it, checking that it was loaded then he laid the weapon over his forearm and glanced in the direction of the copse once again. It was less than fifty yards away. Andy began walking towards it.

The dog hesitated for a moment then barked loudly and scurried along to join him but, instead of racing ahead, the collie kept close to him, almost bumping into him. Andy glanced down at the dog then ahead of him towards the trees. There was tall grass around the copse but the field that it stood in was bare earth. Andy slowed his pace, not quite sure why he had. The dog's erratic behaviour, as much as he hated to admit it to himself, had unsettled him. What the hell had made it react like that? Was there a fox inside the copse?

He looked down at the animal as if expecting an answer. The dog padded on towards the trees, travelling with its belly close to the ground. He saw its nostrils flare and, as they did, it began to growl again.

'What is it?' he asked, stopping ten yards from the perimeter of knee-high grass.

The dog, now rooted to the spot, continued to growl.

Andy snapped the shotgun closed and hefted it before him. He took another couple of steps towards the trees but the collie didn't follow. It remained where it had stopped, gazing fixedly at the copse but not moving closer.

Andy was less than five yards away now.

The smell began to fill his nostrils and he coughed; it was so vile and cloying.

54

'Jesus,' he gasped, advancing more slowly, as if the stench was palpable and he had trouble pushing his way onwards. The fetid stink reminded him of rotten meat.

That thought had barely passed through his mind when he saw the blood.

It was smeared on the trunks of a number of the trees near him and sprays of it covered the grass before him. Andy could see from the rusty colour of the fluid that it had congealed. Whatever had left its life fluid on the bark and the blades had done so some hours ago.

Andy glanced behind him and saw that the dog was now lying on the ground whimpering softly. It made no attempt to come closer. Andy swallowed hard and stepped into the copse, the shotgun held firmly in his grip. The stench was stronger amongst the trees. It was darker within the confines of the copse too, the branches seemingly knitted together above him to form a canopy that the morning light was having trouble penetrating.

There was more blood too. Lots more of it. Andy held the shotgun more tightly and advanced deeper into the copse.

If this was a fox or badger kill then whatever it was it was big, he mused. A rabbit or even a lamb wouldn't cause a stench as overpowering as this and it certainly wouldn't have left so much blood.

Then he saw the sheep.

It was hanging from the branches of a tree to his right, suspended by its hind legs. Its head had been torn off, its body slit from neck to rump. What remained of its intestines hung from the gaping gash that had practically cut it in two lengthways.

'Jesus Christ,' Andy gasped, taking a step backwards, his eyes still fixed on the butchered carcass. He felt his stomach contract and, for a moment, he thought he was going to be sick but the feeling passed. He sucked in a deep lungful of the rancid air, wanting to be away from this sight. Wanting to be out of the gloomy embrace of the trees.

However, as he prepared to retreat he finally lost his battle and his breakfast came rushing up his throat.

There were other sheep hanging from nearby trees. He counted seven before he finally turned away and vomited until there was nothing left in his stomach.

Desperation

The man ran as best he could in the cramped confines of the tunnel. More than once he thought about dropping the spade so that he could move more easily but he decided that it was best to keep the implement with him.

If the time came he may well need it as a weapon.

As he ran he realised, to his relief, that the tunnel was widening once again and he found extra energy at this discovery.

From behind him, the sounds of movement had become more frequent and also, to his distress, much louder. That would seem to indicate that whoever was now following him was gaining.

Above him, the thick brown matter that he'd seen on the tunnel roof was still there and, as he sucked in each fresh breath, it was tainted with that same purulent stench that he'd recoiled so strongly from when he'd first encountered it. But now the smell seemed the least of his worries. He was breathing heavily, gasping for breath in the tight confines of the underground culvert, his heart hammering against his ribs and sweat beading on his face.

More than once he thought about turning the torch behind him in an effort to see how close his pursuer was but he didn't want to give away any more clues to his whereabouts. It was just possible that whoever was chasing him had careered off down one of the smaller, narrower walkways that led off the main tunnel.

The man's legs were aching, his feet soaking wet and, more than once he almost slipped in the liquescent mud he hurried through. Just ahead there was another puddle and, he noticed, some bricks had fallen from the walls and roof of the culvert. They formed a small obstacle that he would be forced to clamber over. Steadying himself he picked his way onto the pile of crumbled masonry, ducking his head low to prevent his hair scraping the ceiling of the tunnel and becoming coated with the putrid dark slime that covered the stonework there. However, he couldn't help himself and he felt the cold muck dripping on his face and scalp as he climbed.

He instinctively shot up a hand to wipe away the vile secretion and, as he did, he slipped on a lump of fallen brickwork. He stumbled and fell, the spade slipping from his grasp, the torch cracking hard against one wall. The impact was enough to shut it off and blackness flooded the tunnel.

The man hit the ground hard, grunting with pain as he slammed into the wet floor beneath him. He rolled over in the moisture, reaching for the torch, desperate to see its light again, fearful of this almost tangible darkness. He shook the implement violently and it flickered back into life. But the beam it gave off now was sickly yellow, not the powerful glow it had possessed when he'd first entered the underground tunnels. He shook it once more. Flicked it on and then off but still it produced only the same feeble yellow glow that was barely more adequate than a candle would have been. But it was still light and he clung to that. Better the paltry glow of a match than nothing at all in this place.

He picked up the spade and moved on, ignoring the pain in his ankle. He must, he reasoned, have twisted it when he fell. Every time he put weight on it pain shot up his left leg.

58

But there was no time to feel self-pity and certainly no time to rest and inspect the injury.

The sounds from behind him made him all too aware that his pursuer was now very close.

He wondered how much longer he had.

14

North London

Mason woke with a start, sitting bolt upright on the sofa where he'd fallen asleep. He looked anxiously around, as if to reassure himself of where he really was, desperate not to be in the place he'd found himself in his nightmare.

Fists and feet slamming into you.

His mouth was dry and his heart was pounding. He sucked in a couple of deep breaths, his mind finally getting a fix on his surroundings.

'Shit,' he murmured, pressing both hands to his face.

It's all right. There's no one trying to kill you. You're in your flat.

Again he looked around, squeezing his eyes tightly shut for a moment. The same images that had assaulted his subconscious flooded briefly across his mind and he opened his eyes again. Breathing heavily, he got to his feet and wandered through into the kitchen where he spun the tap and filled a glass with water. He drank it quickly, gulping down the clear liquid as if it was life saving.

How long have I been asleep?

He looked at his watch and was surprised to find that it had been almost three hours since he'd dropped off. His head felt as if someone had stuffed it full of cotton wool. He shook it gently as if to clear the fuzziness, then he drank some more water. Walking back into the living room he crossed to the window and looked out, down into the street below.

It was busier than when he'd first arrived. There were some schoolchildren passing on the opposite pavement, young kids. No more than nine or ten, he guessed. A taxi was sitting helplessly behind a large lorry that was having problems negotiating a path through the parked cars on one side of the street. The taxi driver was shouting something at the driver of the lorry, occasionally sounding his hooter as if that simple act would magically remove the articulated obstacle from his path. The passenger in the taxi was leaning forward, presumably asking how much longer they were going to be stuck in the jam. Traffic moving in the other direction had also slowed to a crawl. Mason watched two youths, both about sixteen, standing outside the hairdresser's directly opposite.

One was smoking and Mason looked on as the first offered the second a cigarette while they both glanced through the windows into the salon, their attention taken by a blonde in her twenties who was having extensions attached.

Mason sipped at his water, feeling his heart thump a little faster.

Those bastards are about the same age as the little fuckers who almost killed you.

He drew breath slowly and deeply.

It doesn't mean they're the same. Not all kids that age are like the ones who attacked you.

He watched as the two youths finally made their way along the street and out of sight.

Go on, fuck off.

Mason continued to gaze out into the street for a moment longer, not really seeing the activity before him, only aware of the sounds drifting up to his flat. He finally turned away and returned to the sofa, flopping down disconsolately on it. He gazed at the laptop then read and re-read the letters he'd written that afternoon before falling asleep. Mason would, he told himself, print them off after he'd eaten. The thought of eating made him think that he hadn't much food in the flat. Perhaps he should take a quick walk to the shops and get enough to last him a couple of days. He hesitated, the noises from the street still filtering through the stillness in the flat.

You can't sit in here for the rest of your life, can you?

He got to his feet and walked through into the kitchen again, once more checking in his cupboards and his fridge for a likely meal.

A few minutes down the street to the supermarket. You know what you need. You won't be gone more than an hour. Get some bloody food. And some milk while you're at it.

Mason stood gazing into the empty fridge and found, to his surprise and dismay, that his hands were shaking. The thought of leaving the flat for any length of time had done this, he told himself.

'Come on,' he said aloud, trying to reassure himself. He pushed the fridge door shut and reached for the jacket he'd draped over the back of one of the kitchen chairs. He pulled it on and took a couple of steps towards the hallway.

As he reached for his keys he realised that his hand was quivering so violently now that he could barely keep it under control. He blinked hard, his head suddenly feeling as if it had been inflated. He tried to swallow but his throat was dry.

'Panic attack,' he told himself but that understanding did nothing to alleviate symptoms that were growing rapidly out of control.

Mason swayed uncertainly, convinced he was going to faint.

'Fuck,' he rasped, retreating to the living room, hands flailing before him as if he'd suddenly been struck blind. 'Fuck.'

His breathing was rapid now and he dropped onto the sofa like a stone, a thin sheen of sweat covering his face and the back of his neck. He closed his eyes, the dreadful feeling of light-headedness gradually subsiding. The doctor had warned him about this, he'd even recommended him having a prescription for tranquillisers but Mason had refused. He'd be fine, he'd said.

Right, really great. On top of the fucking world.

He held his hands out before him, seeing if the trembling had stopped.

Mason was still considering this when the phone rang.

15

Walston, Buckinghamshire

Becky Harwood was two days past her twenty-third birthday and hungover like never before.

As she slid into her jeans and sweatshirt she blinked hard, hoping that the action would relieve the pain inside her head. Perhaps it was a tumour, she thought. Her grandfather had died of one. Maybe it had skipped a generation and she was now the recipient of the Harwood curse. Becky smiled to herself and stood up, padding out of her room towards the bathroom. Once inside, she splashed her face with cold water and inspected her reflection in the mirror, groaning when she saw the sallow image that stared back at her. Nothing that a shower and some make-up couldn't salvage, she mused. She would, she decided, take a shower when she returned from the stables, just like she did every morning. That was part of the problem. She did exactly the same thing every single morning and had been repeating the action since she was nine. Her father said that as long as she lived at home she had to contribute and Becky's contribution to the running of the household was to exercise the five horses that her father owned.

When she'd been younger she'd loved it. She and her brother, Josh, had fed, groomed and ridden the horses every single morning. It had been hard work when she'd moved to secondary school, getting up to see to the horses on a school day and then trekking into Walston to learn for the rest of the day. Becky had voiced her objections to her daily routine with a vociferousness that grew more intense the deeper into her teens she got. However, she had persisted with her task. Even when Josh had left home to attend university in Durham she'd continued. Her pleas to her father to hire someone to help her or, better still, take over from her completely, had fallen on deaf ears. But Becky realised that the riding stable was the family's main source of income so she had helped despite her protestations. When she left school her father had promised her a full-time job at the stables. It had seemed a reasonable offer. What she hadn't bargained for was how badly paid she'd be.

Lack of money and lack of excitement was a potent mixture to a girl in her early twenties and, for some time now, Becky had been planning her escape. Even if she only worked in an office, she thought. It had to be more exciting than caring for horses for the rest of her life. And yet something deep inside her that felt uncomfortably like betrayal told her she should stay with her parents and help them with the family business. Nonetheless she still wondered how long family loyalty could be put in the way of personal desire.

She pinned up her blonde hair then cleaned her teeth, listening to the sounds of movement from downstairs. Plates being laid out on the large wooden table, cutlery being placed beside it. The radio was on too. Becky could hear it. Radio Four. It was always Radio fucking Four. Or one of the classical stations. She was beginning to think that her parents listened to that station just to torment her.

Perhaps if she had her own place. She smiled to herself, wondering how the hell she would ever afford to move out. She certainly couldn't rent anywhere on the pittance that her father paid her. She had friends in Walston she could share with, she reasoned. Becky glanced at herself in the mirror once again and her face lit up at the mere thought of flat-sharing. The freedom it would give her. She could get up every morning and not have to listen to Radio fucking Four for a start off.

She hurried down the stairs and into the hall, slipping her feet into her wellington boots and pulling on her coat before stepping outside. There was a cool breeze blowing across the yard and Becky shivered slightly as she closed the front door behind her. It was only a short walk to the nearest of the stables and Becky scurried towards the white-painted door, the fresh air clearing her head a little. Perhaps, she told herself, she'd feel better after breakfast.

She unlocked the stable door, frowning a little as she realised how quiet it was. Normally the horses could hear her and they neighed or whickered excitedly, knowing that there was food and attention coming their way. Becky pulled the door open, wondering why it was so quiet inside the building.

Even as she stepped inside and slapped on the lights there was no sound. The fluorescents in the ceiling sputtered into life and Becky stepped into the stable. She looked towards the first stall expecting to see an elegant bay nose its way into view. There was no sign of the animal nor of its four companions in the stable. Then Becky realised that she was standing in something sticky. Something with a tacky, glue-like consistency that smelled strongly of copper.

She looked down and saw that it was congealed blood.

It covered the floor of the stable. Coated it like a reddish-brown carpet. Becky swallowed hard and moved towards the first of the stalls, wondering if she should wait and fetch her father first. Something was badly wrong here. She looked over the wooden partition and she screamed hysterically, turning on her heel without even checking the other stalls.

Becky ran back towards the house, tears streaming down her face, her stomach churning.

She had to tell her father that the bay was dead. That its eyes had been pierced with something long and pointed before its head had been almost severed. No wonder there was so much blood.

Had she looked in the other stalls she would have seen that the remaining horses were in exactly the same state.

Holly Preston

In all of her seventeen years and ten months on the earth, Holly Preston had never felt tension like this. She had never experienced such stomach-knotting fear as that which now gripped her. Barely able to swallow because her throat seemed constricted, she stood in the bathroom of her parents' house with the pregnancy-testing kit standing on the glass shelf above the sink, the instructions spread out on the top of the toilet lid beside her.

She was late. Her period, something Holly could normally predict with robotic precision, was overdue. Her heart pounded a little faster even at the thought. She inspected her reflection in the mirror of the bathroom cabinet as if the pale-skinned, long-haired image there would be able to reassure her. For a moment she sat on the edge of the bath, running a hand over her slender legs as if that act would distract her from the gravity of the one she was about to perform. Her legs, she told herself, needed shaving. She'd take care of that little chore after she did the test. Not that the state of her legs would really matter if the test turned out to be positive.

If she was honest with herself, Holly hadn't really thought about the full impact upon her life if she was actually pregnant. She didn't want a child, not at her age. She knew that her parents wouldn't approve and she was sure that her boyfriend wouldn't be very happy. She'd thought briefly about the possibility of an abortion but she hadn't got a clue how to go about getting one or where to go. Least of all, she hadn't a clue who would accompany her if such an eventuality came to pass.

She had friends who would come with her but she prayed that she didn't have to ask them.

It had been an accident. She had been unlucky. What were the chances of the condom splitting? Holly was sure there were statistics regarding this subject but, if she was honest, she didn't really care. She didn't give a toss how many condoms in every hundred split while in use. Perhaps she should just have gone on the pill as her boyfriend had insisted in the first place. It would have been easier, he'd told her. And safer, he'd insisted. It would also, she thought, have saved her the agony she was going through now.

Not wanting to consider the possibilities any longer, she flipped up the toilet seat, positioned herself and held the stick from the pregnancy kit beneath her legs. She managed to direct her stream of urine onto it eventually, muttering to herself when she splashed her fingers. Satisfied that she'd followed the instructions accordingly, she flushed the toilet then rinsed her hands and put the stick down, glancing at her watch to check the time. She sat down on the edge of the bath again, staring at the stick, willing the result to be negative.

She could hear her parents talking beneath her. She heard her dad shout something at her younger brother and, despite herself, Holly managed a smile. Then she glanced back in the direction of the urine-splashed stick and the smile faded as quickly as it had come.

She checked her watch again and paced back and forth inside the bathroom. Although paced wasn't really the right word given how small the room was. She took two steps to her right then two steps back again. Hardly pacing but it did the job.

Holly snatched up the stick and inspected it.

Negative.

She swallowed and wanted to smile. Again she checked the instruction sheet that had come with the pregnancy-testing kit.

Negative. It was bloody negative. She wasn't pregnant.

Holly had never felt relief like it. It coursed through her system like some magnificently benign drug. She jumped up, barely able to suppress a shriek of delight. She checked the stick then jumped again. A little jump not just of joy but of sheer unbridled relief.

What if it was wrong, she thought briefly, but the thought was swept away on a wave of euphoria the like of which she'd never experienced before.

She gathered the stick, the instruction sheet and all the other paraphernalia that had come out of the box and stuffed the whole lot into the pocket of her robe. She'd dispose of them later. No one need ever know. As soon as she'd had her bath she'd ring her boyfriend and tell him that there was nothing to worry about. Perhaps now he wouldn't finish with her as he'd threatened to do if she had been pregnant. She might even see if she could meet up with him later that night. His dad was working late. His house was empty. They could have sex to celebrate her not being pregnant. Holly grinned broadly and opened the bathroom cabinet.

She took the razor blades from inside and selected a

new one, turning it over carefully between her fingers, the keen edge gleaming.

Holly caught sight of her reflection once again, a wide smile plastered across her features.

She was still smiling when she drew the blade across her throat, slicing through both carotid arteries and opening her throat like a gaping, blood-filled mouth.

16

North London

As Mason picked up the cordless phone he wiped a hand across his forehead and felt a thin sheen of sweat there. It was across the nape of his neck too. He blew out his cheeks and exhaled, pressing the phone to his ear.

'Hello,' he said, hoarsely.

'Pete?'

For brief seconds he didn't recognise the voice, he merely stood there with the receiver gripped in his hand.

'Hello,' he repeated.

'Pete, it's me. Are you all right?' the voice at the other end of the line said.

'Natalie?'

'I called the hospital. They said you were released this morning. I thought I'd check you'd got home safely. See if there was anything you needed.'

Mason nodded to himself but didn't speak.

'Pete, are you OK?'

'Sorry. I had a bloody panic attack. I've never had one before. It took me by surprise. I . . .' He let the sentence trail off.

'Are you all right now?'

'Yeah, I'm . . . it's going. My head's clearing. I feel better, really. The doctor said they'd give me some tablets if I needed them but I said I didn't want them. I don't want to be hooked on Valium for the rest of my life.'

'It might be an idea just for the time being.'

'No, I don't need any tablets. I'll be fine.'

'You're bound to feel a bit fragile to begin with, Pete.'

'I didn't expect to feel like this.'

'After what happened to you I'm not surprised.'

There was a moment's silence during which Mason thought he should have said something more profound but that moment passed.

'I packed some things this afternoon,' he said, finally. 'Some clothes.'

'You're still determined to move away then?'

'As soon as I can.'

'What about work?'

'I've applied for three teaching jobs. I should hear something in the next few days.'

'I thought you wanted to get out of teaching.'

'I want to get out of London. I *can't* get out of teaching. What the hell else am I going to do? It's not as if I'm qualified to do anything else, is it, Natalie? If I could, I would.'

'What if you don't get offered any of the jobs?'

'I will. I know I will.'

'At least you haven't lost any of your self-confidence by the sound of it.'

'Thanks.'

'Have you spoken to the police about the attack yet?' she continued.

'For what it's worth,' he snapped, 'there won't be a court case. They can't bring a prosecution without positive ID and I can't give them that. The little fuckers are just going to walk.' He explained in more detail while she listened.

'I can't believe it, Pete,' she said almost apologetically when he'd finished.

'Like I said, I just want to get out now, Natalie. This has made me even more determined.'

There was a long pause.

'Do you need any help packing?' she asked.

'Want to make sure I go?'

'If I can help . . .' The words were lost in a crackle of static.

'I appreciate that, Nat. If you want to come over then that would be great. Perhaps we could have something to eat. A final meal before I leave.'

'Does that mean you want me to cook?' she laughed.

Mason wiped his forehead once again and exhaled deeply.

'Come over, Nat,' he asked, quietly. 'I'd like to see you. If you haven't got any other plans, of course. I don't want to intrude.'

Another moment of silence.

'What time?' she asked.

'About eight. And bring a takeaway with you, eh? You choose. Whatever you want. I'll give you the money when you get here.'

'All right. I'll see you later,' she assured him and hung up.

Mason gently replaced the phone in its charger. He glanced at his watch. Two hours before Natalie arrived. He managed a smile. She'd be on time. She always was.

He held one hand before him and was glad to see that he'd stopped shaking. At least for the time being.

Confrontation

The light was fading rapidly.

The battered torch was now supplying just a glimmer of sickly yellow to guide the man through the impenetrably dark tunnel. He knew that it would last only a few more moments and then he would have to hurry on in pitch darkness, unable to see anything, able only to guide himself along by feeling the cold stone walls of the culvert.

And, behind him, whoever was following him was close. He guessed less than twenty yards. Perhaps, he thought, if he managed to reach one of the side tunnels he could hide in there, wait until his pursuer had passed. It was all he could think of. His only other choice was to run as fast as he could on his already aching legs, on one ankle he knew he had twisted badly and possibly even broken. Either way he knew he had very little chance of escaping this underground labyrinth alive.

The thought sent a cold shiver the full length of his spine and when he tried to swallow he found that his throat was too dry. He shook the torch again, trying to bully it into supplying him with more light but it was useless. He could only see a few feet ahead now.

He splashed through another deep puddle and stumbled again, almost lost his footing but somehow remained upright.

Behind him, his pursuer didn't seem to be having any difficulty with the slippery ground or with the impenetrable darkness. With each passing second the sounds from behind him grew louder. The other figure down there with him drew nearer.

The man gripped the spade more tightly. Perhaps, he thought, he would have a chance to use it. To swing it as hard as he could in the confines of the tunnel. One last chance to save himself.

The torch went out again.

'No, no,' he gasped under his breath and he shook it once more. It flared briefly, the brilliance of the beam restored for fleeting seconds before the cloying sickly yellow of the dying bulb returned. He hurried on, hands scraping against the bare walls so hard in places that he lost the skin from his knuckles. The pain from his ankle grew worse. His lungs felt as if they were on fire.

He tripped and fell once again, landing hard on his hands. He rolled over, trying to get to his feet, the last light that the torch had to offer now fading in the blackness like a candle in a high wind.

'God help me,' he panted, close to tears now.

Behind him, his pursuer was within fifteen feet.

The man raised the torch and aimed the dying beam in that direction. As he did, the feeble beam illuminated the other presence in the culvert.

The man began to scream. Roars of frustration, pain and terror filled the subterranean tunnel. Any thoughts he had of fighting back were gone.

There would be no point. Not now. Not in view of what faced him.

'Oh God, no,' he shrieked.

His screams reverberated off the walls and ceiling of the tunnel.

Finally, the torch went out for good.

The screaming man couldn't see the one who stood over him any more.

And perhaps that was just as well.

17

Walston, Buckinghamshire

From the road, the cottage was almost hidden by trees. It was accessible only by a narrow dirt driveway and an even narrower path bordered on both sides by a lawn that was in need of a good trim. Weeds had begun to poke up through the cracks in the path.

The building itself was in relatively good condition. The stonework had been well maintained, the roof re-tiled only two years earlier and a new front door fitted less than a month ago. The wooden porch needed a coat of creosote and the windows of the dwelling could have done with some fresh paint around their frames but little else would have caught the eye of a visitor.

There was a one-car garage to the side of the cottage. The door was padlocked and held even more firmly shut by a rusty chain.

There was a small garden to the front of the property, a larger one to the rear. In this bigger back garden, laid mostly to lawn but with some untended flowerbeds too, there was also a small wooden shed and a greenhouse. Several of the panes were broken and had been replaced with pieces of thick Cellophane secured with gaffer tape. There were four tables inside the transparent structure but they supported only empty flower pots. When the wind blew strongly the panes rattled in their frames and the door of the greenhouse moved gently back and forth on rusted hinges, sometimes banging against the frame so hard that the glass threatened to shatter.

The rear garden was enclosed by high privet hedges on two sides and a drystone wall on the other. Standing at the bottom of the garden, any visitor would have been able to look over the wall towards the town of Walston itself, less than a mile away by car.

Inside the cottage, the same view was available from the window of the main bedroom. From the study window, also to the rear of the structure, the garden was visible. The study had been added, almost as an after-thought, in the 1930s but had been maintained well and appeared a natural extension of the main building. It was a small annexe that held a large wooden desk and some bookshelves. There was an antique-looking television aerial propped on the tiled roof.

The study led off from the small hallway and the living room. This was a much larger room from which the stairs rose at the far end, the bottom step close to the door of the kitchen. Upstairs, two bedrooms, a bathroom and a large attic, accessible via a pull-down ladder, completed the complement of rooms.

The cellar ran beneath the entire extent of the house. There was a trapdoor opening in the kitchen that could be pulled up and, beneath it, a set of bare stone steps led down into the subterranean gloom below. This black-ness was dissipated by a single unshaded bulb that hung in the centre of the ceiling, accessed by a switch close to the cellar entrance but, even when the light was on, there were shadows it wouldn't penetrate.

Areas of darkness and hidden corners that hid their secrets from prying eyes.

18

North London

'But Pete, this is crazy. You don't even know if you're going to get any of the jobs you've applied for and, even if you do, you've got to find somewhere to live.' Natalie Mason shook her head and shrugged then let out a long sigh. 'I don't think you've thought this through at all.'

Mason sipped from his glass and looked at her evenly. The smell of their Chinese food was still heavy in the air, the plates still on the small kitchen table.

'Don't worry about me,' Mason told her, lifting his wine glass to his lips. 'I'll find a job.'

'I don't doubt that you will but I just don't think you'll get one as easily and as quickly as you think. It could be weeks before you hear from some of these schools. Even longer before you even get an interview and then you've got to get the job.'

Mason held up a hand to silence her.

'Well, all I can do is wait, isn't it?' he exclaimed.

'And what do you do while you wait? You've got to have money coming in. You can't just sit around.'

Mason shrugged.

'I'll find something to do,' he insisted. 'Something's always turned up in the past.'

'You've been lucky, Pete. Your luck might have run out.'

'Thanks for the vote of confidence.'

'You know what I mean. There are plenty of other teachers out there looking for work. Why not go back to the school where you were teaching?'

He cut her short.

'So your suggestion is that I return to the place where the little fuckers who almost killed me still go? Let them laugh at me every fucking day because they've got away with almost killing me? Cheers, Natalie.'

She exhaled wearily and opened her mouth to speak again but he cut in.

'I can't do it, Nat,' he breathed. 'I just can't.'

She shook her head.

'And what about you?' he asked. 'What does the future hold for you?'

'Does it matter? You're not going to be around to see me, are you? Not if your grand plan works.'

Mason wasn't slow to catch the scorn in her tone.

'Do you blame me for wanting to get away from here after what happened?' he challenged. 'I want to get out of London, put this whole fucking episode behind me and start again and all you can suggest is that I stay as I was before.'

'It's a big step, Pete. I hope you're ready for it.'

'Nearly getting killed was a pretty big step too.'

She nodded and sipped some more wine.

For long moments they sat in silence, gazing across the table at each other then Natalie looked around at the dirty plates and the empty cartons of food.

'I'd better help you tidy up. I can't come round here, eat and drink and then just go home, can I?' she intoned.

'Leave it. I'll do it in the morning. It'll give me something to do while I wait for my job applications to be answered, won't it?'

'I'll finish this then I'd better go,' she told him, sipping more from the glass.

'Stay for a while. I'll make coffee.' He got to his feet then turned and looked around at her. 'Unless you've got somewhere to get to in a hurry. Someone to see.'

'Like who?'

'Another bloke?'

'You know I haven't got anyone to see, Pete.'

Mason filled the kettle with water then spooned some coffee into two mugs he retrieved from the wooden mug tree on the worktop.

'There must have been other blokes since we split up,' he mused. 'I mean, you're a good-looking woman, Nat.'

'And you're still full of shit.'

'I'm trying to pay you a compliment,' he grinned. 'So, come on, tell me. Have there been other blokes?'

'Do you want the gory details?'

'Why not?'

'All right, there've been three. Two one-night stands and one big mistake that passed for a relationship and finished about seven months ago. What about you? There must have been other women. You had a roving eye even when we were married.'

'I resent that accusation,' he smiled.

'It's true.'

'I never cheated on you, Nat.'

'I didn't say you did. I just said you had a roving eye.'

Mason shrugged then poured hot water onto the instant coffee, stirring slowly.

'There's been no one else,' he sighed. 'If I couldn't make love to you after Chloe died what makes you think

I could do it with anyone else? I wasn't interested in you. I wasn't interested in anyone.'

He carried the cups to the table and stood close to Natalie who looked up at him.

'Sorry I've got no milk. Shall we sit in the living room?' he offered. 'It's more comfortable.'

She hesitated a moment then got to her feet and followed him through into the other room. Mason seated himself on one end of the sofa and watched as Natalie took her place at the other end.

'I won't bite,' he told her. 'Not unless you want me to.'

She held his gaze then reached for her coffee and took a sip.

'What's this all about, Pete?' Natalie asked, wearily. 'All the small talk? The bullshit? This?' She waved a hand back and forth in the air, designed to encompass both of them. 'Why now?'

'We're only talking, Nat. Where's the problem?'

'We're talking now, Pete. When we were married we never did. Not about what mattered anyway.'

'If you mean about Chloe.'

'Yes, I do,' she interrupted. 'And about us. How our sex life died too. I know it was only natural after a loss like that but we needed that closeness, Pete. We needed each other and you never came near me. Not for two years after she died. Do you wonder that we split up? You weren't there for me when I needed you most. In every sense.'

'So a decent fuck would have kept you happy?' he said, venomously. 'That would have saved our marriage?'

'But you accepted that distance between us so easily. It was as if you gave up. Just like you gave up on Chloe.'

'I loved her more than I thought it was possible to love anyone,' Mason said through clenched teeth. 'Don't

84

ever say I gave up on her because I didn't. There was nothing I could do. Nothing *we* could do. I wasn't going to sit around and watch her die.'

'But you let me, didn't you?'

'I couldn't come to the hospital. I didn't want to see her hooked up to those fucking tubes, her life draining away a bit more every day.'

'Neither did I, Pete but I still did it. I went for Chloe's sake. You stayed away for *your* sake, you selfish bastard.'

'Perhaps I did,' he snapped. 'I couldn't face her. I couldn't deal with the questions. With *her* questions. She asked me once if she was going to die. What was I supposed to do? Lie to her? Tell her that everything was going to be fine when I knew it wasn't going to be?' He shook his head.

'But you expected me to be there for her. You knew I'd have to answer her questions.'

Mason lowered his gaze.

'And that was when you lost respect for me?' he murmured. 'That was the beginning of us splitting up, wasn't it?'

'That and your drinking. You were happier with a bottle in your hand than you were with me.'

'It was the only way I could cope, Natalie.'

'By downing a bottle of vodka a night. Very helpful, Pete.'

'It helped me,' he snarled. 'I didn't know how else to cope with what was happening to our daughter or to us. And I'm sorry. Don't you think that a day goes by I don't think about her and want her back? Want the three of us together again? But that's not going to happen, is it? That was in the past. Everything's changed and it's not going to get any better.'

'And that's why you're running away.'

Mason didn't answer.

'Don't you think it's a bit late to be making a fresh start, Pete?' she continued.

'There's only one way to find out, isn't there?'

He reached for his coffee and sipped it. When he looked at Natalie again he saw something behind her eyes. A look that he recognised from another time. A look of disdain that bordered on contempt.

'I'd better go,' she said, quietly.

When she got to her feet he didn't try to stop her.

19

Walston, Buckinghamshire

Amy Coulson shuddered at the touch of warm female flesh on either side of her. In the gloom of the room every feeling and sensation seemed heightened. The intoxicating scent of perfume, freshly washed hair and the perspiration that came from such intense and pleasurable physical exertion filled her nostrils as surely as if it was a narcotic.

She closed her eyes as she felt gentle feminine hands brushing over her skin. Warm breath washed over both her ears as the two figures with her on the bed moved closer, kissing and nibbling at the sensitive appendages. They moved in perfect unison, as if they belonged to one single entity.

Amy felt hands on her breasts, one pushing urgently beneath her white vest top and enveloping the plump globe. Slender fingers squeezed her erect nipples and she arched her back as the feelings already running through her body intensified.

Around the large bed she sensed rather than saw the other figures moving closer, anxious to watch the spectacle before them and this only increased her excitement.

Amy turned first one way then the other and, both times, she was met by slippery, tender lips that she kissed enthusiastically. Female lips that pressed against her own before pushing soft tongues into her mouth and against the hard white edges of her teeth.

She knew that the girls on either side of her were barely a year older than she was. Seventeen or eighteen but no more.

As were the other figures gathered around the bed. The figures that watched so intently in virtual silence, keen to be closer to what lay before them, revelling in it. Drinking it in. But Amy didn't care about that. All that concerned her were the electric jolts of pleasure coursing through her body, each one growing more intense.

She felt wonderfully light-headed. As if she was floating. She knew that the drink she'd consumed and the drugs she'd taken were helping to create this feeling but more than anything, it was the undiluted physical pleasure she felt that was the most intoxicating part of the cocktail. She let out a long, low sigh of desire and fixed her own mouth to the one on her left, kissing intently as she felt two hands now roving wantonly over her breasts and stomach.

One of the hands then slid lower, towards the top of her tiny panties, gliding over the soft material to probe at her mound and the heat between her legs. She kissed more deeply, her eyes tightly shut as she felt more lips on her neck and she turned to repay this latest delight. Amy felt another hot and eager mouth only a fraction from her face and she pushed her tongue out to greet it. She felt it enveloped by this new and welcoming cavern and she kissed its owner as passionately as she'd kissed the first. She felt her own tongue engulfed by the lips and mouth of the girl to her left and she responded fiercely as the searching hands to her right continued to slide across her stomach and up beneath her top, again toying with her stiff nipples, drawing them out until they felt as if they would burst with the pleasure and expertise of the touch.

All around the bed the watching figures drew closer.

Amy broke the kiss momentarily but only to gasp her pleasure. She returned to it seconds later, a thin silver thread of saliva clinging to her bottom lip and dangling from it like filament. As she drew her head back once again one of the probing tongues licked the saliva away. Amy arched her back as she felt the questing hands pulling agitatedly at her top, trying to free her sensitive breasts from beneath the material.

Smiling, Amy sat up momentarily, pulling the top off herself and throwing it to one side. She lay back down, welcoming the attention now lavished upon her swollen and exposed nipples. One soft, expert mouth worked on each of the hardened buds, tongues flicking gently back and forth while hands continued to stroke across her panties and also up and down the inside of her thighs. They left gleaming trails of saliva in their wake, one of them licking lower to the sensitive area at the top of her thighs then down the inside of the slender leg until they reached her calf. Amy bent her leg as she felt it being gently lifted and then she gasped again as she felt the hot mouth close over her little toe. She smiled as the tongue pushed between her toes then its owner sucked each of the digits in turn, finishing with her big toe.

Amy murmured something unintelligible. The expression of a feeling of such ecstasy that it had no recognisable exhortation. And while the mouth continued to trace outlines up and down the sole and arch of her foot, stopping occasionally to return to her toes, the girl on the other side of her also sank lower, her own probing tongue flicking up towards the already slick gusset of Amy's panties. The questing tongue flicked across the material briefly then poked beneath it to taste Amy's wet and swollen cleft. Again she let out a groan of pleasure and lifted her bottom to allow her panties to be pulled off. Naked, she lay on her back, legs wide, her mouth open slightly, her tongue resting on her bottom lip.

The two tongues met between her legs in an explosion of pleasure and Amy couldn't contain herself any longer. The feelings were building up inside her more intensely than she'd ever felt before in her life. Like water smashing against a crumbling dam. She had no way to hold these feelings back and she had no wish to. As one tongue lapped frenziedly at her throbbing clitoris, the other probed deeply into her soaking depths, tracing the outline of her vaginal lips lovingly and expertly.

Amy felt fingers being pushed between her slick and puffy lips as the motion of the two tongues increased.

There was a grunt of pleasure from somewhere in the darkness but it didn't come from Amy. Not this time.

The figures around the bed moved nearer but Amy didn't care. Her pleasure was reaching heights she'd never experienced before. She pressed her head into the pillow, arched her back and prepared to surrender to the feelings roaring through her quivering body. She felt the first unmistakable and unstoppable waves of her climax begin to jolt her body.

Someone close to the bed muttered something but Amy didn't hear what it was. Even if she had it wouldn't have mattered to her. Nothing did for now.

She didn't even mind the cameras pointed at her.

20

North London

'No, this isn't open to negotiation. I'm not coming back.'

Mason held the phone against his ear and stood gazing out of the sitting-room window as he spoke. Below him, the late afternoon traffic was clogged in the street, the pavement busy with people. Mason watched indifferently, puffing slowly on the cigarette he'd lit before making the call.

'I know as headmaster you're responsible for your staff but were you really expecting me back at the school after what's happened?' he continued.

The voice at the other end of the line was hesitant but finally said something almost apologetically.

'I can't believe you expected me back,' Mason declared. 'Not in a month, six months or a year.'

The voice on the other end was silent for a moment.

'You won't have any trouble finding someone to take my place,' Mason said. 'Perhaps it'll be someone who'll remember to mind their own business. Let the little bastards get on with things and not interfere.'

The caller enquired about the police investigation.

'I don't know what's happening,' Mason said, curtly.

'Without enough evidence they'll walk. That's our fucking justice system for you.'

There was a moment of awkward silence then the voice asked what he was going to do next.

'I'll carry on teaching,' Mason explained. 'But not here. Not in London. I'm sick of this bloody place. I think I was before the attack. It was as if it took that to make up my mind for me.'

At the other end more words were spoken.

'I know, I know,' Mason retorted. 'I'm sure everyone will be sorry to hear the news.' He rolled his eyes. 'They were all so sorry none of them bothered coming to see me in hospital.' He sucked on his cigarette and blew out a long stream of smoke that dissipated slowly in the air.

The voice apologised again and told him that no one had visited because of his situation.

'I didn't expect anyone to come while I was in a coma,' Mason snapped. 'It would have been pointless, wouldn't it?' He took another drag on his cigarette.

More perfunctory words from the other end of the line.

'No, I'm not on medication. They offered me tranquillisers but that's about it,' Mason explained. 'Valium.'

Another comment.

'I know, your wife was on them for about four years, wasn't she?' he continued. 'They say the bloody things are more addictive than heroin. There's no way I want that.'

At the other end of the phone, the caller assured Mason that he could count on good references for a new job when the time came.

'Thank you,' Mason said. 'With any luck someone will be in touch with you pretty soon.'

Another question.

'I don't care where I have to move to,' Mason went on. 'The further the better as far as I'm concerned.'

The voice asked what his wife thought.

Mason was quiet for a moment, watching the plumes of smoke curling upwards into the air.

'It's not really her problem any more, is it?' he stated, flatly.

The caller apologised for forgetting that Mason was separated.

'I forget myself sometimes,' he offered. He finished his cigarette and stubbed it out in the ashtray on the windowsill, standing there to gaze out once more into the street below.

The caller wished him good luck in his search for a new job.

Mason nodded to himself.

The voice assured him that if he changed his mind then his position was still open.

'Not in a million years,' Mason said, flatly.

21

Walston, Buckinghamshire

Amy Coulson sat upright on the bed, her naked body tingling. She gently kissed the blonde girl in front of her on the lips, her own fingers now gliding down her companion's taut stomach towards the downy triangle of hair between her slender legs.

The blonde girl drew in a sharp breath and cupped Amy's face with her hands, returning the kiss fiercely. As Amy enjoyed the sensations she felt the other girl move behind her. The second girl, her shoulder-length dark-brown hair brushing Amy's back, slid both hands onto Amy's breasts, massaging them gently, pulling tenderly but insistently at the erect nipples. Amy turned to look at the girl long enough to kiss her too.

The brunette responded by squeezing Amy's breasts more tightly before allowing her fingers to slide between Amy's legs where they found her slippery cleft and throbbing clitoris easily. Amy moaned under her breath as she felt two of the probing digits slip inside her.

The blonde girl began kissing Amy's neck, licking below her jaw line and down to the hollow of her throat then back again, occasionally leaving slick trails of saliva on the skin. Amy closed her eyes and surrendered herself to the attentions of the two girls, the unmistakable feelings of orgasm growing swiftly between her legs as the two fingers became three now pushing and rubbing more intently and insistently.

The blonde girl adjusted her position so that her face was level with Amy's breasts then she ducked forward slowly and began lapping at each erect nipple in turn.

Amy pushed her chest forward slightly, eager to present the swollen buds to the blonde who curled her tongue expertly around each one, leaving them glistening with saliva.

The brunette whispered something in Amy's ear, her tongue flicking the lobe when she'd finished and Amy nodded eagerly. The other two girls watched as she manoeuvred herself onto all fours, her pert buttocks poking into the air.

There were several appreciative grunts from around the bed, the other figures having moved so close they were virtually within touching distance of the three girls before them.

Amy arched her back as she felt the brunette licking along her spine down towards her buttocks. At the same time, the blonde girl swung herself around so that her head was beneath Amy's slick vaginal lips. Simultaneously, as if it was part of a well-rehearsed routine, the blonde and the brunette began to use their tongues on her. One on her sensitive clitoris, the other on her puckered anus.

'Oh, fuck,' Amy hissed, gripping the sheet with both hands as fresh waves of pleasure cascaded over her. Her head was spinning again and she wondered if it was possible to pass out from sheer ecstasy. Another few moments of such incredible treatment and she was sure she would find out. She stiffened as the feelings grew in intensity. The tongue that had been circling her anus now pushed inside it, stimulating nerves that were as yet untouched. At the same time, her clitoris was bathed in moisture as the blonde girl flailed tirelessly at it, sliding two fingers into her vagina as far as the second knuckle. Amy prepared for her next climax.

'All right, that's enough.'

The voice that lanced through the gloom was unmistakably male.

'No, not now,' Amy panted, in frustration, looking around in the direction from which it had come. 'Don't stop now.'

The two girls sat up on either side of the bed. Amy turned to look at the watching figures, lowering her buttocks as she did.

'No, stay like that,' the male voice told her, sharply.

'If you say so,' Amy giggled. 'Like it this way, do you?'

'How do you like it?' the voice breathed and Amy felt the bed move as its owner climbed on behind her.

'I like it every way,' Amy told him, breathlessly. 'But they were doing fine.'

'Hold her down,' the young man snapped.

'You don't have to hold me,' Amy assured him, pushing her naked bottom towards him. 'Come on.'

She felt his penis push against her slippery vaginal lips, felt something warm dripping onto her anus and realised that the blonde girl was drooling her mucus onto the tight ring. Using two fingers, she began to massage Amy's sphincter.

'So that's what you want?' Amy breathed. 'Go on then.' She looked back over her shoulder. 'But stop if it hurts,' she added, a note of caution in her voice.

Someone laughed.

Amy laughed too but there was no humour or joy in

her exhalation. However, as she felt the blonde's fingers push gently inside her anus, she relaxed once again, allowing the sensations to envelop her.

'Stop if it hurts,' another male voice, this time with an American accent echoed. 'Yeah, right.'

There was more laughter.

Robbie Parker

Robbie Parker didn't want his dad to die.

However, no matter how many times people reassured him that everything was going to be all right, when Robbie heard words like cancer and malignant he couldn't believe. Even at the age of seventeen, Robbie had heard the words enough times to know that they carried an awful and unedifying weight.

He dared not believe that his father was going to recover from the bowel cancer he had, despite the fact that his operation was going ahead the following morning. What if he convinced himself that his dad was going to be fine and then everything went wrong and he died? He wasn't a young man after all, he was well into his fifties.

Robbie took another cigarette from the packet he held and lit it, puffing away for a moment, watching the smoke curl slowly up into the still night sky. From his position on the top of the multi-storey car park in the centre of Walston, Robbie could see the pub where his dad drank most nights. It was called the Four Emblems. It was more like a club than a pub. The same old faces met up there almost every night and many lunchtimes as well. Robbie had been in there with his dad a few times and sat sipping lemonade and watching his dad playing dominoes.

All that, Robbie told himself, would be over soon. If his dad died.

His parents had been separated for the last three years. Robbie lived with his mum and two sisters in a house on one side of town while his dad had a small, one-bedroom flat. This made it a little uncomfortable when Robbie stayed with his dad at selected weekends but he slept on the sofa and gladly gave up his bed for Robbie.

His sisters never saw their father. They preferred not to. Or rather Robbie's mum preferred them not to. He still wasn't sure why. He wasn't one hundred per cent certain why his parents had even split up. All he knew for sure was that his dad was ill and, as far as Robbie was concerned, he might not be getting better.

He took another drag on his cigarette and turned as he heard movement behind him.

Someone was returning to their car. A tall man in a suit who glanced warily in Robbie's direction as he pushed his laptop onto the back seat, pulled off his jacket and then slid behind the steering wheel. Robbie could see his chubby face through the windscreen as he drove past.

Robbie wondered if he was going home to his family. He wondered why that man couldn't have cancer instead of his dad. Taking a last drag from his cigarette he tossed the butt over the parapet and watched the car as it made the descent from the top storey of the car park down to the street below. Robbie could see it pulling out into the road and moving away.

Most of the shops in the town centre were shut now and the offices had emptied hours earlier. Robbie could smell the pleasing aroma of baked bread rising from the back of the Cottage Loaf and he could hear the periodic crashing and clanging as the bakers inside prepared the rolls, loaves, sausage rolls and cakes that would be on sale the following day. The centre of Walston seemed deserted on this particular night. Robbie wondered about getting a bus out to the hospital to visit his dad but then remembered how furious his mother had been the last time he'd undertaken such a selfless act without consulting her first. Miserable bitch. Robbie was sure she didn't care if his dad died or not.

He decided to have one more cigarette before walking home. Better make sure that his mum couldn't smell it on him. That was something else she hated. She said his dad had got cancer because he smoked but Robbie didn't want to believe that. Besides, people got lung cancer from smoking, he told himself, not bowel cancer. The cigarettes were the only escape he had apart from the internet porn.

For hours every night he would trawl websites, masturbating endlessly over the images that flickered before him. It helped him to forget about his dad. It gave him the only pleasure he got in life. For two or three hours he escaped from his own thoughts.

He lit himself another cigarette and took a drag. The fresh air would remove any traces of his secret habit, he told himself. It would take him a good half hour to walk home from here. Then he'd go straight up to his room, keep away from his mum until the next day. He had two new websites to check out. One of them was just lesbian sex, the other dealt exclusively with threesomes. Robbie couldn't wait. He had the beginnings of an erection merely thinking about it.

Robbie looked over the parapet down at the deserted town centre. Then, almost wearily, he lifted himself up onto the concrete barrier, standing with his legs splayed, balancing effortlessly on the narrow ledge.

He stepped forward into empty air.

Two seconds later, his body hit the concrete fifty feet below.

22

North London

The attack came upon him suddenly and Mason wasn't ready for it.

One minute he was standing in the aisle of the supermarket leaning on the trolley and peering intently at the shelves of pasta, the next, he thought he was going to faint.

It was as if someone had suddenly pumped his head full of compressed air. His heart began pounding hard against his ribs, as if he'd just finished a long and gruelling race. He felt a sheen of sweat on his face and the palms of his hands. His legs began to shake. Mason found that he was breathing quickly through his mouth, his tongue dry and chalky.

'What the fuck,' he murmured to himself, gripping the handle of the shopping trolley more tightly for fear that he might collapse.

A woman in her forties looked accusingly at him as he uttered the words then she hurried past him, pausing at the end of the aisle to look back in his direction, perhaps afraid that he might be following her. In his current state, Mason couldn't have even described the woman let alone registered the expression on her face.

As far as he was concerned, his head was still inflating. Perhaps, he thought, it actually was. Growing in size, filling with air until the climax of this episode would come when his skull exploded. He tried to swallow but his mouth and throat were too dry. He blinked hard and attempted to control his breathing but still he took deep, almost racking breaths.

That's why your head's inflating. You're breathing too hard. Ha ha fucking ha . . .

'Stop,' Mason said under his breath as if voicing his concern would end the panic attack. It had no such effect. He stumbled forward a couple of steps, wondering perhaps if he started moving whether or not the feeling would pass.

He could barely lift his foot. It was like trying to raise a dead weight. He looked down, his vision swimming for terrifying seconds. His foot hadn't left the floor. Mason felt as if he was rooted to the spot, magnetised to this piece of supermarket floor.

Go on. Fucking move. Walk. Get out of here. Leave the fucking trolley and move.

He daren't take his hands off the trolley, fearing it was the only thing keeping him upright. Again he tried to slow his breathing and again it was useless. His chest was beginning to hurt, to tighten.

Perhaps you're having a heart attack. Or a stroke. That's it. That's why it feels as if your head's inflating. One of the arteries in there is going to blow. You're going to die. Right here and now in the middle of the fucking pasta.

Mason closed his eyes tightly, simultaneously taking one hand off the trolley long enough to dig his nails hard into his palm. The brief moment of discomfort jolted him and he used the nail of his index finger to gouge into the flesh of his thumb. The pain was more pronounced this time.

Mason was vaguely aware of two young women passing him, both of them manoeuvring pushchairs. He heard them say something as they passed and one of them ducked past him to pick up a packet of pasta from the shelf nearby. The girl holding the pasta looked at him.

'Are you all right?' she enquired.

Mason looked at her, aware of how pale he must look. He felt as if all the blood had been sucked from his face. He could feel more beads of perspiration on his forehead now.

'Do you want me to get help?' the girl persisted.

Mason opened his mouth to say something. He wanted to ask her if she could fetch a member of staff. Perhaps if he sat down for a moment, away from the glare of the banks of fluorescents above him, he would feel better. Perhaps his head would stop expanding.

Ask her if your head looks like a balloon. Ask her if she can hear your heart beating because the way it's banging she must be able to hear it. The whole fucking shop must be able to hear it. Go on. Ask her.

No words emerged from Mason's mouth. He merely felt his lips flickering uselessly but no sound came forth. He managed to shake his head, his only response to the girl's enquiries. It felt to him as if his head was on a spring and that it would never stop moving. It would just keep on going back and forth for the rest of the day and the foreseeable future, like some out of control toy in the hands of a persistent child.

Chicken head. Chicken head.

'I'm OK.'

When he spoke the words, they sounded as if someone

104

else had said them. They seemed to be coming from somewhere behind him.

OK. You don't fucking look it or sound it.

'Thanks,' he persisted, his words slightly slurred. 'Yeah, I'm all right.'

Perhaps you have had a stroke.

The young woman looked at him for a moment longer then she and her friend moved slowly away from him, both of them turning to look back at him. One of the kids in the pushchairs turned and waved good-naturedly at him.

Mason clung onto the handle of the shopping trolley, relieved that his heart wasn't hammering so fast and so hard in his chest now. He was even more delighted that his head seemed to be deflating. He wiped a hand across his face and felt the sweat on his flesh.

'Jesus Christ,' he murmured, sucking in a slower and deeper breath.

He stood there for a moment then left the trolley and walked as quickly as he could out of the supermarket.

23

Walston, Buckinghamshire

Amy Coulson moved slowly up the stairs, muttering irritably under her breath when the stairs creaked beneath her. She didn't want to wake her parents. They'd be angry that she'd stayed out so late as it was and the last thing she wanted right now was a confrontation before she went to bed.

She'd got the taxi to drop her on the corner of the street and she'd walked the fifty yards to her house along the darkened thoroughfare, glancing at her watch every now and then as if to remind herself of how late she actually was. However, her progress had been slower than usual because of her discomfort too. Even now, as she reached the landing and turned right towards the bathroom, she winced at the burning sensation between her buttocks.

She moved as hastily as she could into the bathroom and turned on the shower, stripping off her clothes quickly. She tested the temperature of the water with one hand then stepped beneath the cleansing jets. Amy closed her eyes and allowed the water to splash her face. She remained like that for a moment then opened her eyes and reached for the soap, washing her body but paying particular attention to her buttocks and vagina.

Amy soaped that most sensitive area, wincing slightly as she ran her fingers over her anus.

She'd never been penetrated there before and it had been painful to begin with. On more than one occasion she had thought about asking them to stop but the feelings had passed and she had allowed them to continue. By the time the third of them had pushed his thick erection into her sphincter she had become accustomed to the sensation and, by the time the fifth boy poured his thick seed into her anus, she was almost enjoying the feeling. All helped by the constantly stroking and probing hands of the two girls who had been in the room as well. Amy hadn't been too happy about the way they'd treated her once they'd finished, snapping at her to get out. Even the two girls had merely dressed and left the room. When she'd asked the oldest of the boys when she could see him again he'd merely laughed and pushed her away but she knew he'd call. If he didn't she'd see him in the town.

She hadn't even cared that they'd taken photos with their expensive digital cameras or that they'd recorded the entire scenario on camcorder. It had been fun and, as much as she was a little sore now, Amy couldn't deny that she'd enjoyed herself for much of the night. Especially the touch of the two girls. She wondered to herself if she would ever have contemplated having sex with another girl if she'd been sober but the hesitation vanished as she remembered her experience. The soft caresses of their fingers and tongues and the series of orgasms they'd brought her to. How she wished she'd been able to do the same to them. Perhaps next time, she mused, switching off the shower. She stepped out, drying herself with the large white towel that was draped over the radiator. She inspected her body in the mirror as she wiped moisture away.

There were several red marks on her hips and buttocks where the boys had gripped her skin a little too tightly as they'd reached their own climaxes, she decided. Amy raised her eyebrows. They'd fade soon enough and no one would see them. Perhaps she'd show them to her best friend when she told her about the events of the evening. Maybe she'd even tell her what happened. Amy decided to leave out the part about the two girls. Perhaps if she just mentioned one of them. The blonde one, Sammi. And maybe it might be better if she only explained that she'd had anal sex with two of the boys, not five. Or perhaps, Amy mused, she should keep the entire escapade to herself.

She stepped from the shower and wrapped the towel around herself. Then she brushed her teeth quickly and headed for her bedroom where she pulled on pyjama bottoms and a white T-shirt before placing her mobile on the bedside table and sliding into bed. She flicked out the bedside lamp.

With any luck she'd hear her alarm at seven the following morning. If not, she reasoned, then her mum would wake her. She always did.

Amy settled herself, a slight smile touching her lips as she remembered the events of that night.

Her phone buzzed, vibrating with each ring. She snatched it up quickly and flipped it open, seeing that she'd received a text. Who, she wondered, was sending her messages at this time of night?

She recognised the name and smiled thinly as she prepared to read the text.

U R A DIRTY SLUT.

Amy frowned and thought about sending a message back. She closed the phone again and was about to settle down for the second time when another message arrived.

CUNT.

It was followed swiftly by a third.

SLAG.

And a forth.

CHEAP CUNT.

By the time the fifth one arrived, she was almost in tears.

24

North London

'I realise it's to be expected considering what I've been through,' Mason said. 'But that doesn't make it any easier to cope with. I thought I was dying.'

As he sat in the kitchen with the phone jammed between his ear and his shoulder, he looked at the letters before him, moving them slowly back and forth as if he was shuffling giant playing cards.

'We've got an appointment at five this afternoon,' the doctor's receptionist told him. 'Can you come along then?'

'Will the doctor give me something?' Mason insisted.

'I can't say that, Mr Mason, you'll have to discuss it with him,' the receptionist went on.

'I'm not coming to the surgery for nothing. I want some bloody tablets to help me. I want to know that he'll give them to me.'

'You could call your consultant at the hospital, I'm sure he'd give you a prescription. Especially if he recommended tranquillisers to begin with.'

Mason sucked in a deep breath.

'I'm sure the doctor here will be able to help you,' the receptionist continued.

'All right, I'll take that five o'clock appointment then,' Mason sighed.

He hung up.

Again he shuffled through the mail he'd picked up. A couple of circulars. Junk mail. Bills. And a white envelope bearing a crest. Mason saw the postmark and opened it excitedly. His heart was thumping hard.

Perhaps it's another panic attack.

He sipped at his tea, wincing when he found it was cold. He tutted irritably and continued to open the white envelope.

The paper was headed and the crest was there again, this time embossed with gold foil. A smile spread across Mason's face and he read aloud.

'Langley Hill, private boarding school,' he said, running one index finger over the bas-relief of the words as if he were blind and reading Braille. 'Dear Mr Mason, further to your letter.' Mason allowed the words to trail away into the air and he continued reading to himself, his eyes flicking swiftly but intently over the words before him. By the time he reached the bottom of the page and the sweeping signature of the headmaster (a certain Mr Nigel Grant), there was a broad smile plastered right across his face.

'We invite you to an interview at the school,' he read again, finally standing up from the table. 'We do hope that you will be able to attend.' Mason punched the air triumphantly. 'You're fucking right I will,' he said. He walked briskly from the kitchen to the bedroom, pulling open his wardrobe, inspecting the clothes that hung within. He ran his hand along the fabrics and nodded. His charcoal-grey suit. That should be perfect for the interview.

The one you wore for Chloe's funeral.

Mason swallowed hard as the recollection hit him like a thunderbolt. He stood motionless before the wardrobe for a moment then slowly removed the suit and raised it before him on the hanger.

Nice suit. You haven't worn it since, have you?

He brushed some fluff from the shoulder and slipped the jacket on, checking the fit.

Why bother? You haven't put on any weight since she died. Perhaps you'll look as smart as you did that day. That day they put your daughter in the ground.

He looked at his reflection in the mirror, angry with himself for allowing the memories to intrude so brutally.

Yes, after all, you're supposed to be happy now, aren't you? The last thing you want is thoughts of your dead daughter fucking up your day.

Mason pulled the jacket off and slid it back onto the hanger then he hooked the curved metal over the handle of the wardrobe and stood there looking at it.

I'm sure Chloe would have approved.

The tears that began to roll down his cheeks came more quickly and more plentifully than he would have thought possible. He sat down on the edge of the bed and sobbed uncontrollably.

25

Walston, Buckinghamshire

Miserable fucking day, thought Amy Coulson.

She lay on her bed gazing blankly at the ceiling, the residue of a headache still gnawing at the base of her skull. She'd taken two or three paracetamol during the day at work but they hadn't relieved the symptoms much. It had been busy in the shop too, no time to sit and take it easy. Amy had worked at the Cottage Loaf bakery in Walston for almost six months since leaving school. She'd left with no qualifications so, her mum and dad had told her, she'd been lucky to get any job at all. It wasn't particularly hard work and the people she served had got to know her and she liked many of them who came in on a regular basis. Especially the guy who worked at the mobile phone shop next door. He came in every day for his sandwich at lunchtime. Always tuna and sweetcorn. And every day he chatted to her. He had this particular day too but, she had noticed at the time, without his customary smile and, even more puzzling to her, he had barely looked at her even when she handed him the sandwich. Just one of those days, she'd thought.

The headache, she assured herself, was due to what

she'd drunk and taken the previous night. She always got a hangover when she mixed her drinks and, the night before, she'd drunk more than usual. Perhaps, she mused, they'd slipped her something. Fuckers. Rich, arrogant fuckers. She sat up slowly and swung her bare feet onto the carpet, taking the two steps to her desk and the laptop perched there. She'd been talking to one of her friends on MSN when she'd been forced to lie down because of the headache and sickness but now they'd both subsided sufficiently, she went back to the computer and prepared to continue her conversation.

WTF DID U DO LAST NITE?

The message came through from another of her friends who had just signed in.

WENT OUT Amy typed in.

U MUST B RAW 2DAY.

Another message. She didn't recognise the sender this time.

WHO R U? she typed.

CHECK OUT YOUTUBE another message told her.

WOT A SLAG trumpeted another message.

U MUST HVE N ARSEHOLE LIKE A CLOWN POCKET another offered.

UR ON YOUTUBE U SLUT.

MEGAROTIC.COM IS GD. U SLAG.

The messages were flooding in now, most of them from names she didn't recognise.

Amy frowned, minimised the communication and typed Megarotic into the search engine, gazing in bewilderment at the screen as the search results came up.

'Adult content,' Amy murmured and clicked on the entry. Two scantily clad blondes appeared holding signs that read share files and enjoy videos. There was a light blue sign announcing enter here. Amy clicked on it.

MEGAROTIC porn appeared before her. Below it there were thumbnails accompanied by descriptions.

'Oh my God,' she murmured.

The second picture in the column was of her own face.

SLUT GETS ASS FUCKED AT ORGY.

Amy could feel herself shaking. She prepared to click on the image, not really sure if she wanted to see it or not. Finally, she did.

SLUT GETS ASS FUCKED AT ORGY she saw displayed over the small screen where it announced buffering video. Amy waited. She heard the voices a millisecond before the image appeared and, instantly, she realised that she was looking at herself on the screen.

'Oh, Jesus,' she gasped. There was a section to the right of the screen marked RELATED VIDEOS. Amy saw her own image in all ten of the thumbnails there too. One of the captions was the same, another read DIRTY SLUT ENJOYS GANGBANG. Another proclaimed WHORE LOVES LESBO PLAY AND THEN ASSFUCK.

On the main screen, she could see herself writhing with pleasure, framed by the two girls she'd been with the previous night but their faces were pixelated out, only hers was visible, slicked with perspiration and contorted in pleasure. But this time, unlike the previous night, she could also see the other figures gathered around the bed. All male. All naked and all sporting very prominent erections. As she watched she could see two of them slowly stroking their stiff members, their muttered words inaudible to her. Like the two girls on the bed with her, their faces were also pixelated and unrecognisable.

Amy felt as if she had been dipped in iced water as she watched the clip. She tried to swallow but her throat was too dry.

As she watched she saw the camera pan down, a little shakily, the full length of her body, from her tousled blonde hair to her breasts that were gleaming with saliva. Then further, towards her neatly trimmed mound that was partially hidden by one of the girls' heads. Finally the user of the camcorder moved the camera all the way down to her feet and back up her shapely legs once again.

When the tape reached the point of the first anal penetration Amy paused it. She stared at the image before her, her veins still feeling as if they were full of iced water but an undeniable warmth now between her legs, as if seeing the incidents of the previous night had aroused her in spite of herself. She flicked the play button once more and watched as the first young lad climaxed, spurting his semen into her anus.

Then she switched it off and sat staring at a blank screen for long seconds. She was about to watch the remainder of the tape when her phone rang.

26

North London

Peter Mason sipped at his coffee and noticed that his wife was watching him over the rim of her cup.

'I must have seen more of you since we split up than I did when we were living together,' Natalie told him.

Mason smiled.

'It seems like that,' he agreed. 'But then again, I've had a lot to tell you just recently.'

He put down his cup and held her gaze for a moment longer.

'I really do appreciate this, Nat,' Mason told her. 'The way you've been there for me. The way you've listened. I know I had no right to expect it.'

'Like you say, who else were you going to tell?' She took another sip from her cup then put it down. 'This school in Buckinghamshire, Langley Hill,' she began. 'How much do you know about it?'

'It's one of the top private schools in the country. A slightly better class of pupil than I've been used to.'

'You always said kids were kids, it didn't matter where they came from.'

117

'I think it helps if they don't come from sink estates,' Mason said, flatly.

'What happened to your youthful socialist zeal, Pete? The "everyone is equal and entitled to an education" rant you were so fond of when I first met you.'

'It's easy to lose your idealism when you've been beaten almost to death by the kind of people you used to spend your life defending.' He reached for his cigarettes and lit one. 'Besides, idealism is for the young. When you get to my age ideals are a bit like old photos. You have them but you don't like showing them off.'

'Can you adapt to the way they teach at this private school?' Natalie offered almost apologetically. 'It is going to be a complete change and you know you're not very fond of change.'

'The school must think so or they wouldn't have offered me an interview, would they? Moving from public to private sector teaching isn't a problem unless you allow it to be. Like you say, kids are kids.'

'Even rich kids?' Natalie mused.

'I'll have to see, won't I?'

'What time do you leave in the morning?' she enquired.

'I'll leave early,' he informed her. 'Make sure I don't get stuck in traffic. I shouldn't have any trouble finding the place. They sent a map and, apparently, it's almost impossible to get lost.' He shrugged. 'Let's hope they're right. They said I could have lunch with them after the interview. Have a look around the school.'

'And what if you don't like what you see?'

'If they offer me the job I'm taking it, Nat. No matter what.'

'Ring me and let me know how it goes.'

He nodded and took another puff on his cigarette.

'What's the nearest town to the school?' Natalie wanted to know.

'A little place called Walston,' Mason informed her. 'Some sleepy little market town I'd imagine. A picture postcard place.' He smiled. 'I can't wait.'

27

Walston, Buckinghamshire

Amy Coulson sat at the desk in her bedroom, her eyes fixed on the screen of the laptop.

The MSN dialogue boxes seemed to fill the screen.

WOT A SLUT

SLAG

UR A DIRTY BITCH

And a dozen others that she could see just by sitting where she was. If she read lower then there were dozens more messages of a similar ilk, all emblazoned in accusatory letters. The fact that some were accompanied by smiley faces didn't really make her feel any better.

WAIT TIL UR MUM N DAD FIND OUT

Of all the messages, that was the one that burned with the most painful clarity. Amy gazed at it again and sniffed. She wanted to cry but felt that there were no more tears inside her. She'd been weeping almost uncontrollably for the last four hours, her desperate sobs occasionally interrupted by bouts of furious anger.

She'd tried to phone Andrew Latham several times (the first occasion being after she'd discovered the recording of herself on the first of the four sites that he'd posted it on) but to no avail. Latham wasn't answering. She'd had a text from him. It was still plastered across her mobile now.

SILLY GIRL

She picked up the mobile and flung it away angrily. It slammed into the wall close to her bed, several hairline cracks spreading across the display screen.

She would have rung the others too but she didn't have their numbers. Only Latham's. She'd spoken to the two girls before but only to discover their names. Sammi Bell and Jo Campbell. The blonde and the brunette. Simple as that. Nothing else. She didn't really care either. As far as she was concerned they were to blame as well. Perhaps they had known what Latham was going to do when he'd invited her to the party. Maybe they had been as willing to share in her humiliation as he was.

Except he wasn't sharing in it, was he? He had engineered and overseen her humiliation. His anonymity was still intact. His and the two girls and the other four who had been present the previous night. No one knew their names or identities. Amy was the only one recognisable in the video, God help her.

She wondered why Latham had done this to her. She had never harmed him, never caused him any pain. Did he hold her in so much contempt that this kind of public humiliation was second nature? Was that why he had posted the video on so many different websites?

LIVESEX
MEGAROTIC
PORNHUB
XVIDEOS
PIMPBUS

He had put links to all of them on his Facebook page,

the bastard. Anyone clicking on the networking site would have instantly been able to find the other sites and, to her distress, many obviously already had.

She looked at the site names, all minimised at the bottom of her screen. When she clicked on each one an image of her surrounded by her tormentors appeared. In the first she was on all fours with a figure behind her, his penis deep inside her anus. Amy clicked on the site and closed it. In the second she was still on all fours but this time there was thick white semen oozing from her backside. She closed that site too. The third image showed her with a penis in her mouth, her eyes closed in ecstasy, her tongue poised on the bulbous head of the erection. The fourth was of her lying on her back while two of the boys masturbated close to her face. Amy closed those two as well.

Again she sniffed but, once more, no tears came. Amy sat back on her chair, her eyes still fixed on the screen.

WAIT TIL UR MUM N DAD FIND OUT

She swallowed hard as she read the message once again.

WAIT TIL UR MUM N DAD FIND OUT

At last, more tears did come, trickling slowly down cheeks that were already damp with moisture.

What would they say? What would they do? A tiny voice inside her mind told her that they need never find out but a louder and more dominant one insisted that it was only a matter of time before her humiliation was discovered.

And then what?

They won't throw you out. They won't judge you.

But then Amy knew that her own humiliation would pale into insignificance compared with the shame they would feel. Her dad would probably shout at her, tell her she was stupid to be fooled the way she was but, in time, he would forgive her. Her mum would also be angry but, in time, they would both accept what had happened. Wouldn't they?

But even if they did forgive, they would still be ashamed. They wouldn't tell her that but she would feel it in every angry glance, hear it in every heated word.

And Amy knew she couldn't carry a burden like that.

She got to her feet and padded across to her bedroom door. She was alone in the house. Her dad was on night shift, her mum wouldn't be home for another hour or so, longer if there were any unexpected admissions to the local A and E where she worked as a sister. Amy knew that she wouldn't be disturbed.

Barefoot, like a penitent trudging towards longed-for salvation, she made her way down the stairs and headed towards the back door. From there, she moved towards her dad's shed.

All she needed was inside.

28

North London

Mason couldn't sleep. Despite the two Valium he'd taken an hour before retiring, he still couldn't drift off into the oblivion he wanted so much. He tried to tell himself that it was the excitement that was hampering his rest. The adrenalin coursing through his veins at the thought of his interview the following day. He knew what success in that interview would mean. Not just a prestigious job in one of the top private boarding schools in the country but the chance to begin a new life. A fresh beginning away from the city he had lived in all his life but had come to hate so passionately.

Only in the last few hours, alone and in the silence of the night, had he begun to contemplate what failure would cost him. If he didn't get this job then what else was there? Search endlessly for other positions in the capital? Move to another part of the country and just hope that something turned up? Because things just didn't *turn up*, did they? Not in real life. Not in *his* life anyway. Why, he wondered, couldn't things just run smoothly?

Why had he been attacked and almost killed?

Why had his daughter died of viral meningitis?

He sat up in bed and shook his head, as if that action would dispel those thoughts. He gazed into the gloom of the bedroom, one eye on the dormant TV set perched on a cabinet on the far side of the room. Unable to sleep, he jabbed the appropriate button on the remote and images appeared on the screen. He flicked agitatedly from channel to channel. News. A history programme complete with sign language for the deaf. A documentary about motorway safety and baseball. Fucking baseball.

Mason sighed wearily and swung himself out of bed. He wandered through into the kitchen and filled the kettle, propping himself against one of the worktops as he waited for it to boil. He screwed a cigarette between his lips and reached for his lighter. He flicked it and found he was out of fuel.

'Shit,' he grunted and took the cigarette out of his mouth for a moment before deciding to light it from the flaring blue flame of the gas hob. He sucked hard on the cigarette then blew out a stream of smoke, watching it unfurl in the air like an opening flag.

He wondered if it was too late to ring Natalie. Too late to burden her with his doubts and anxieties.

She's probably asleep.

He checked the clock on the oven.

It's not her business any more. It hasn't been since you walked out on her. Despite the fact that you've seen more of her since you left hospital than you have since Chloe died.

He wondered if he would miss her once he got the job at Langley Hill.

(If he got the job at Langley Hill.)

And decided that he would.

And if you don't get the job? What then? Do you crawl

125

back to her? Hope that she'll have you? Hope that she'll forget what a selfish, gutless fucker you were after Chloe's death?

The kettle boiled and Mason poured the hot liquid onto a tea bag, stirred it around a little then dumped the bag in the sink. He carried the mug into the sitting room and crossed to the window, gazing out into the street below.

He wondered why neither of them had ever found anyone else after they'd split up. Natalie was still a very attractive woman and yet she'd managed to avoid any emotional entanglements and he himself had never even been close to stumbling into another relationship. Had he done the wrong thing by leaving? Should they still be together?

Yes. And Chloe should still be alive.

Mason sipped slowly at his tea and, once more, tried to force the image of his daughter from his thoughts.

Coward. Can't even face her in your mind. Just like you couldn't when she was dying. When she needed you.

He turned away from the window and sat on his sofa, gazing blankly into the air. From the bedroom he could still hear the TV set, the words drifting languidly to him much like the smoke from his cigarette that was forming, shroud-like, around his head.

A single tear rolled unannounced from his eye and trickled down his cheek. Mason didn't even bother to wipe it away.

29

Walston, Buckinghamshire

Margaret Coulson dug wearily in the pocket of her coat and pulled out her front door key. Even as she pushed it into the lock she shook her head irritably. The walk from the bus stop to her house normally took less than ten minutes. The entire journey from the hospital only took thirty minutes but not tonight. It had taken her more than an hour and a half to get from work to her home. First she'd been delayed at the hospital because of a car accident, the two victims having been brought in only minutes before she was due to leave. Fortunately neither of them were hurt too badly, Margaret mused. The worst injury was to the driver who'd suffered a fracture of his left wrist and some deep cuts to his face. The passenger had suffered only minor cuts to her face and neck but was in shock. No one else had been involved.

Despite the relative simplicity of the injuries, the delay in the arrival of a doctor to attend to them had ensured that Margaret was already late by the time she got on the bus to begin her homeward journey. When the bus then succumbed to a flat tyre five minutes after leaving the stop, she realised that it was just one of those nights.

Just one of those nights. Margaret turned the key in the lock and wished that she could be as philosophical about the delay. She was already tired. She hadn't been sleeping very well during the last two or three nights and a friend of hers at work had given her a couple of sleeping pills to ease the discomfort. She had been hoping to try them out a lot sooner. She was on the same shift for the next week and, in many ways, she preferred the late hours. Except on this particular night. When she was on early shift she was at least home with her husband during the day and she saw more of her daughter too. Perhaps, she thought, trying to salvage something from what had been a lousy night, she and Amy could even have lunch together some time this week.

It was a thought that brought a tired but welcome smile to her face as she stepped into her hallway, careful to close the door quietly behind herself for fear of waking her daughter.

She needn't have worried about that.

In the darkness of the small hallway, Margaret Coulson didn't immediately see what awaited her. Only as her eyes became accustomed to the gloom and then, as she reached out with one hand for the light switch, did she realise its nature.

The body of Amy Coulson was hanging from a length of rope, suspended in the middle of the hallway, secured to one of the landing balustrades above.

It didn't take Margaret's training as a nurse to tell her immediately that Amy was dead. In the harsh glow of the hall light she could see the milky whiteness of her daughter's cold skin. She knew that the teenager would be cold even before she touched her. As it was, Margaret stood transfixed for several moments before finally extending one shaking hand and touching Amy's left foot.

Cold as ice.

She must have been dead for a couple of hours at least. Her body was hanging almost completely motionless too, disturbed only by Margaret's gentle touch. Any movement that had occurred after the initial drop to the end of the rope had long since subsided.

Margaret looked up at Amy's face and saw that the eyes were closed. The lips were parted slightly and she could see the tip of a swollen and blackened tongue protruding through them. There wasn't a mark on the body otherwise apart from the vivid red discoloration of the skin where the rope had bitten so deep into the soft flesh of the throat. Whether she had broken her neck in the fall or slowly strangled, Margaret neither knew nor cared. Amy was unblemished. She hung there like a porcelain doll, suspended by some vengeful child.

Margaret was surprised at her own reaction. Shocked by the sight she moved slowly, almost robotically, around the hanging body, still gazing up at it. Numbed by what she saw. Unable, it seemed, to scream or shout. Helpless.

She managed to swallow hard as she turned towards the phone which she picked up and pressed lightly to her ear. That done she jabbed three nines and waited to be connected to the emergency services. They would be here within minutes, Margaret knew.

She also knew with stomach-knotting certainty that there was no need for them to hurry.

30

Walston, Buckinghamshire

Mason tried to settle himself on the wooden bench once again but finally stood up, anxious to stretch his legs once more.

The drive from London had taken him less than ninety minutes but the need to stretch his legs hadn't been caused by the drive. He just couldn't sit still. His heart was thumping a little more quickly than normal, despite the fact that he'd been sitting in this outer office for more than ten minutes. It was, he told himself, the adrenalin coursing through his veins now, and which had been since he first hauled himself out of bed that morning, that was causing his discomfort. He knew that beyond the thick oak door across the outer office lay the room of the Headmaster of Langley Hill private boarding school. The man who would effectively decide his future. Of course, Mason only knew that the headmaster was in that room because he'd been told so by the smartly dressed woman in her late forties who sat behind the desk opposite him. She had her dark-brown hair in a bob and Mason could see a few strands of grey against the darker background. Her make-up was carefully applied, except for her lipstick which looked as if it had been put on with a paint roller.

She had informed him that she was the headmaster's assistant. She had made the appointment he was keeping this morning. Mason glanced in her direction once more and when she looked up from her keypad she met his gaze.

Mason smiled at her and paced slowly back and forth, his eyes flicking over the large notice board behind him.

'Can I get you another cup of coffee, Mr Mason?' she asked.

'No thanks,' he said. 'Too much caffeine.'

'I'm sure Mr Grant won't be much longer.'

'Like I said, I was early. There's no hurry.'

She nodded politely and returned to her work. Mason felt as if he was intruding inside her work space, distracting her from the myriad duties that she, as the headmaster's assistant, had. He wanted to leave the room, walk the stone corridors of the school. In fact, he just wanted to walk until he was called in to see the headmaster. Mason hated sitting around. He hated waiting. He'd never been a patient man.

'Do you live at the school?' he finally asked, immediately feeling guilty for interrupting her.

'No,' she told him, smiling politely. 'I live in the town like most of the staff.'

Mason nodded.

'Have you worked here long?' he continued.

'Almost twelve years,' she informed him, her long fingers resting tentatively on eight keypads. She was waiting, Mason thought, not daring to resume her work in case he asked her another question.

He nodded, looked at his watch and checked it against the large clock suspended on the wall behind the woman.

'I'm just going to nip to the loo,' he said, deciding that he'd just given her more information than she either needed or desired.

The woman nodded, this time without looking at him.

'You know where it is, don't you?' she said, her eyes still fixed on her computer screen.

'Down the corridor on the right,' he said and slipped out of the outer office.

Despite the morning sunshine that was flooding through the windows on one side of the corridor, it was still quite cool within the stone walkway. Mason crossed to the nearest window, his footsteps echoing on the polished slabs beneath him. He peered through the glass, looking out over the grounds of Langley Hill. They stretched away as far as the eye could see. There were several sets of rugby posts in view and, in the far distance, Mason could see what appeared to be a hockey match going on.

He stood there for a moment longer then turned and walked slowly down the corridor in the direction of the lavatories, amazed at how quiet it was within the school. Granted, he didn't know how close the nearest class-rooms were but, even if they were on the floor above, Mason had expected to hear some raised voices. Some indication that several hundred pupils were being educated at this hugely expensive seat of learning.

Just because it isn't what you're used to. No screaming and swearing every few seconds. Perhaps money buys silence as well as privilege.

He reached the toilets and entered, once more struck by the silence. Mason stood at one of the urinals, marvelling at the fact they weren't defaced by all manner of graffiti.

Something else you're not used to.

132

He relieved himself and washed his hands in one of the large porcelain basins nearby. He studied his reflection in the mirror above.

Tie not too tight. Freshly shaved that morning. Suit looks good.

They couldn't reject him on his appearance alone, he mused, drying his hands on the roller-towel. He stood there for a moment, sucking in a deep breath that was only faintly tinged with the odour of disinfectant then, composing himself once more, he set off back up the corridor towards the outer office.

He almost collided with the two girls as he emerged from the toilet.

'Sorry, girls,' he said as one of them stepped back to avoid the collision.

One was blonde, the other dark haired. Both were no more than seventeen, their uniforms immaculate. They were both carrying leather satchels laden down with books.

They nodded and lowered their heads almost deferentially, as if the barely avoided collision had been their fault and not his.

Mason hurried back towards the office.

Sammi Bell and Jo Campbell turned and watched him for a second before continuing on their way.

31

When Mason glanced at the grandfather clock that stood to the right of Nigel Grant's desk, even he was surprised to see that almost two hours had elapsed since he'd first entered the headmaster's office.

He'd been aware of the loud, rhythmic ticking of the clock throughout the interview but not the passage of time marked by that unbroken sound. Mason told himself that the length of the interview had been a good thing. He had enjoyed a reasonable rapport with Grant who was a personable enough man in his late fifties, dressed in a dark-grey suit, a pair of thick glasses perched on the bridge of his aquiline nose. His hair was thick, combed back quite severely, relatively free of grey but flecked with dandruff that also dotted his shoulders and collar in one or two places.

Mason did his best not to look at the offending flakes. At least not when Grant was looking at him.

'Did you know anything about the school before applying for the job, Mr Mason?' Grant asked, still running his alert green eyes over the CV that Mason had presented him with upon entering his office.

'By reputation, naturally,' Mason said. 'That was one of the things that attracted me to the position.'

'That's very kind of you to say. We try our best.'

Grant sat back in his chair and folded his hands on his belly, rubbing the tips of his thumbs together gently as he regarded Mason across the large antique desk.

'If you get the job,' Grant began, 'the environment that you find yourself in will be very, very different to what you've been used to.'

'I appreciate that, Mr Grant,' Mason told him. 'But as I told you earlier, as far as I'm concerned, children are children. Even if their parents are all multi-millionaires.'

'I'm not sure what proportion of our pupils' parents fall into that category, Mr Mason, but I'm sure not every child here is from such a financially privileged background. Some of them are from what we would somewhat scathingly refer to as working-class homes. Their parents care about their education though and they're prepared to sacrifice other things to ensure their children receive the best possible education.' Grant continued tapping his thumbs together as he spoke. 'But you're right, a very large percentage of the pupils at Langley Hill do come from rich backgrounds. And that, unfortunately, brings its own problems both for them and for us.'

'What kind of problems?'

'Some of them are spoiled. There's no other word, I'm afraid. They come from privilege and some have no idea how to cope with that. Their inability to cope sometimes manifests itself in their attitude. They can be difficult.'

'Like all kids,' Mason said, smiling.

Grant nodded slowly.

'If you mean some of them are arrogant, I can cope with that,' Mason assured him.

135

'Arrogant is perhaps the wrong word, Mr Mason,' the headmaster said, now tapping his thumbs against his shirt. 'But certainly some of the older pupils can be trying *because* of their backgrounds more than anything. Wealth can be a burden as well as a blessing. Certainly it brings its share of problems when you're sixteen or seventeen years old.'

'I'll have to take your word for that.'

Grant nodded.

'Well, some of the children here are from exceptionally privileged backgrounds,' the headmaster continued. 'At least four are the sons of ambassadors. Two are the offspring of Arab princes and the progeny of various assorted celebrities are too numerous to mention. Your head isn't turned by fame, is it, Mr Mason? I ask because some of my staff, in the past, have found that a problem.'

'I think everyone is equal, no matter how much money they have in the bank. And as for this situation, we're teaching the kids, not the parents so I don't foresee a problem.'

The headmaster nodded once more, a slight smile on his lips.

'Excellent,' he said, quietly.

'Do you live here?' Mason enquired.

'My wife and I have quarters within the school. One of the perks of the job. Nine other staff members are also resident here. The remainder live in Walston itself. It's a purely arbitrary selection process I'm afraid. Some positions come with residential quarters, it's as simple as that. The English department and the history department have always had quarters inside the school. It's something of a school tradition and has been for more than a hundred and fifty years. I'm not sure who initiated it. No doubt one of my predecessors with a predilection for those subjects found it prudent to offer a little more than just money to anyone teaching those particular subjects. Don't ask me why. Your own position comes with additional residential quarters.'

Mason raised his eyebrows expectantly.

'A small cottage in the grounds of the school,' Grant explained.

'Really,' Mason intoned, genuine interest in his voice.

'It's nothing very grand, Mr Mason, but it's very welcoming.'

'Would it be possible to see it?'

'If you'd care for a tour of the school,' Grant said, getting to his feet. 'I'm sure we could take a small detour to the cottage.'

They both headed for the office door.

32

'The school was built on the site of an old monastery that was demolished during the Reformation.'

Nigel Grant walked briskly, his tone as enthusiastic as his gait. The hand gestures he made were also animated as he warmed to his subject.

'During Roman times, there was a Druid settlement here. The area round about has always been a prosperous one. The school itself wasn't built until 1798,' he continued. 'Originally it was just intended to be a school for the local children, those who lived in and around Walston. It wasn't until the 1850s that the whole place was extended and became a private school. It might interest you to know that it's built on two ley lines. The confluence of two ley lines is supposed to signify fertility, rebirth and passion.'

'I'll bear that in mind,' Mason grinned. 'It sounds as if this area has quite a history.'

'It's colourful.' Grant smiled and continued speaking as they walked.

Mason listened appreciatively, his gaze flicking over the buildings that comprised Langley Hill. The entire imposing edifice that made up the main building was shaped like an enormous letter X. The centre of the cross housed a gigantic hall, a small chapel and, on the first floor, the quarters of the teaching staff. The extended branches of the shape were the home of classrooms, three gymnasiums (all possessing the most modern equipment) and, on the first floor, the pupils' living areas. A number of the rooms contained two single beds and were shared by pupils but Mason noted that the majority were singles.

'Nine thousand pounds a term buys a certain amount of privacy,' Grant informed him as they wandered along one of the corridors on the first floor.

'How many of your staff have come from the maintained sector?' Mason wanted to know.

'Of the thirty-six full-time staff employed here, none. You'd be the first.'

'What about you? Have you always taught in private schools?'

'Yes, both myself and my wife.'

'What does your wife teach?'

'She used to teach French,' Grant said, his tone softening. He sucked in a weary breath as if suddenly tiring of the conversation. 'Since her illness she can't.' He allowed the sentence to trail off.

'I'm sorry. Is it serious?'

'She suffered a stroke six months ago. It all but paralysed her on her left side and she lost most of her sight.'

'I'm very sorry,' Mason repeated, quietly. 'Can nothing be done for her?'

'The doctors say no and I'm not about to question them.'
Mason nodded.

'I think the feeling of helplessness is unbearable,' he said. 'Seeing someone you love suffer but not being able to do anything about it.'

139

'Have you had experience with that kind of thing?'

'My daughter died of meningitis when she was five.'

'That's awful. I'm sorry.'

Mason nodded, surprised at how easily and quickly he had found himself willing to discuss the matter with a total stranger.

'That's one of the reasons I want to get out of London, to get away from my old life,' he continued. 'The memories are too painful. My wife says I'm running away.' He grinned humourlessly. 'We've been separated for four years.'

'Yes, I noticed in your application that you were single. They say that many couples who lose a child split up. I suppose it's just an unfortunate by-product of the suffering.'

'Either that or you realise the only thing holding your marriage together was your child.'

Grant eyed Mason evenly for a moment then walked on along the corridor towards a set of wide stone steps that led down towards the main hall of the school. There were a number of smaller children passing through the hall, all decked out in their distinctive uniforms. They were being led by a blonde-haired woman in her mid-thirties who nodded amiably in the direction of the headmaster as she approached with her wards in tow.

'Good morning, Headmaster,' she said.

'Good morning, Mr Grant,' the children echoed, standing perfectly still behind the woman teacher.

'Kate, this is Mr Mason,' Grant announced. 'He's here about the position in the history department. Mr Mason, this is Kate Wheeler.'

Mason nodded in her direction, hoping that he was not making it obvious that he was transfixed by her. She was, he decided, little short of stunning. He wanted to

140

take a more appraising look at her, to allow his gaze to glide slowly over her shapely legs and slim buttocks. He wanted to take more time admiring her perfectly chiselled features and her wide brown eyes.

'Good luck,' said the woman and Mason was sure that he could detect the hint of an accent in her soft tone. Irish, he thought.

'Do I need it?' he smiled.

She returned the gesture, holding his gaze for a moment longer than he expected. He noticed her eyes flicker briefly towards his left hand.

Checking for a wedding ring? Don't kid yourself.

'It's good to meet you, Miss Wheeler,' Mason said as she prepared to lead her children away. 'Hopefully we'll meet again.'

She raised her eyebrows and smiled once more before heading out of the hall with the children.

'Geography and games,' Grant announced. 'Miss Wheeler, I mean. A number of the staff here are responsible for more than one subject.'

Mason nodded, surprised with himself at how much of an impact she had made upon him.

'Shall we continue?' the headmaster offered. They walked on.

33

'I'll be perfectly honest with you, Mr Mason,' Grant said as they left the confines of the main building and headed outside. 'It's unusual for a school like Langley Hill to even interview a teacher who's worked exclusively in the maintained sector, as you have. Normally our staff are drawn from other private schools. The other applicants who I've interviewed have all been from the private sector.'

'What made you change your mind and offer me an interview?' Mason enquired, slowing his pace to match that of his companion.

'I'm trying to find a way of saying this without sounding either condescending, patronising or just downright insulting,' Grant smiled.

'Don't worry about that, I'm very thick-skinned.'

The headmaster sucked in a deep breath, as if the words he was about to speak carried some intolerable gravitas.

'It was felt that the school should broaden its scope,' he began. 'Embrace alternative teaching strategies and skills as well as those we already have here. Most of the staff here and at other private schools were themselves

Oxford or Cambridge graduates. Your own degree, while no less worthy, was achieved elsewhere. Your path through the industry has been different. Your views and opinions are likely to be different and that's never a bad thing.'

'You wanted to see what it would be like slumming it?' Mason grinned.

Grant laughed good-naturedly.

'Certainly not,' he said. 'I have nothing but respect for anyone who works in the maintained sector. I would imagine it brings pressures and problems that are completely different from anything myself and my colleagues have encountered. I won't beat around the bush. There are situations that you must have dealt with in your time that neither myself nor my staff have ever been confronted with. I think that kind of experience would be useful, even in this somewhat rarefied environment. Your adaptability is an admirable quality, Mr Mason, and one that I feel would be welcomed at Langley Hill. Both by pupils and by the other staff.'

'That's very kind of you to say but, as I said before, kids are kids. I'm sure the pupils here can be a handful sometimes.'

'They require a firm hand occasionally but it isn't always easy negotiating with children from such privileged backgrounds and who are used to having everything they want at the drop of a hat. Some struggle with the requirements of the school both intellectually and socially. Paying such high fees for the education of your child doesn't guarantee they'll flourish in a school like Langley Hill. You offer them a different perspective with your background.'

'What about my predecessor? What was his background?'

'Mr Usher was recruited from another private school.'

'Why did he leave? If you don't mind me asking.'

Grant could only shrug.

'He had his reasons,' he announced, curtly. 'It's just that those reasons weren't extensively discussed. Certainly not with me.'

Mason wasn't slow to catch the newly found iciness in the headmaster's tone and, when he looked at the other man, he saw that his face was now set in hard lines.

'Did he leave for a better job?' Mason wanted to know.

'No,' Grant said, flatly. 'As I said, I'm sure he had his reasons but he didn't discuss them with me. I'd appreciate it if you didn't speak about Mr Usher with any other members of staff. As far as everyone here is concerned, the matter is closed.'

Mason thought about pursuing the conversation but felt it might be better to just leave the subject alone now.

Grant strode on ahead of him towards a slightly over-grown hedge just off the main driveway. As Mason hurried to keep up with him, he saw that the headmaster was standing next to a wrought-iron gate set into the hedge. Beyond it was a path that led to the front door of a small cottage.

'Should you accept the job, Mr Mason,' Grant announced, 'this would be your quarters.'

'It's beautiful,' Mason said, genuinely delighted by the look of the small property.

'Would you like to look inside?' Grant held the gate open and ushered Mason forward.

'With all due respect,' Mason said, quietly, 'I think that might be tempting fate. I can't see the point in looking at my proposed living quarters if I don't even know that I've got the job or not.'

'I see your point,' Grant agreed, nodding. 'Would you like the offer in writing or will a verbal proposition suffice for the time being?'

Mason smiled, hoping that he hadn't misinterpreted either Grant's words or his tone.

'The job is yours if you want it, Mr Mason,' the headmaster announced. 'As per the terms we spoke of in my office. I knew within thirty minutes you were the man for the position and our conversation since has only served to reinforce that view.' He extended a hand that Mason shook warmly. 'When would you be able to start?'

34

For the first time in months, Mason felt elated. He could think of no other word to describe the air of ebullience that had enveloped him. As he drove away from the school, glancing at the majestic buildings in his rear-view mirror, he felt his heart beating faster. A combination of anticipation and delight that he hadn't experienced for far too long. He felt as if he had been pumped full of adrenalin. His blood seemed to be on fire and it was a wonderful feeling.

When he felt he was close enough to the road, far enough away from the school, he shouted loudly. Triumphantly. If it had been safe to take both hands off the wheel he would have punched the air. He caught a glimpse of his own reflection in the mirror and saw that there was a wide smile plastered across it. As soon as he got back to London he would ring Natalie and tell her his news. Tell her that he'd got the job. That he'd be leaving London. Leaving for ever.

He wondered about driving into Walston itself, having a look at the town that was going to be his new home.

The word sounded a little hollow at first.

Home.

He thought about the cottage. The tour that Grant had taken him on had been brief. Just enough to show him that the dwelling was welcoming and, to his relief, needed very little in the way of renovation. The bedrooms needed a new coat of paint but that could wait until he was settled in. Settled into his new home.

The word now had a slightly more impressive ring as he ran it through his mind.

He turned the car onto the road and followed the signs to the motorway. With any luck, he'd be back in the capital before five.

'He's perfect.'

Nigel Grant stood gazing out of his study window, watching the driveway down which Mason's car had disappeared moments earlier.

'Just the kind of man we need,' the headmaster continued.

'How can you be sure?' another voice from inside the room asked.

'Trust me, he's what we're looking for,' Grant insisted.

'That's what we thought about Usher,' a third voice added. 'And look what happened with him.'

Grant was silent for a moment, still looking raptly out of his window, his hands clasped behind his back.

'How many others applied for the job?' the first voice wanted to know.

'None of the others were suitable,' Grant said, hurriedly. 'Everything about Mason is what we were looking for.'

'You'd better be right,' added a last voice.

Only then did Grant turn, apprehensively, to look at the owner of that voice.

35

North London

Natalie Mason lifted her coffee mug in salute and managed a smile.

'Congratulations,' she intoned.

'It should be something stronger than coffee,' Mason said, nodding at her. 'This is the best bit of news I've had for Christ knows how long.'

'Better than hearing you weren't going to be brain damaged by your beating?' Natalie offered.

Mason raised his eyebrows quizzically.

'All right, *one* of the best bits of news I've heard for a while,' he conceded. 'Thanks for meeting me like this, Nat,' he continued. 'But I wanted to tell someone about the job.'

'And I was the only one?'

He nodded.

'We've probably seen more of each other since you came out of hospital than we have in the past two years,' Natalie reminded him. 'I don't think we came out for coffee like this when we were married.'

'Circumstances change things.'

'Some things, Pete. Like the man said, seasons change, times change but people don't.'

Mason regarded her across the table for a moment.

'This is a new start for me, Nat,' he said, quietly.

'For you, Pete.'

'Come with me.'

She looked surprised for a moment then a slight smile spread across her lips once again.

'I don't think that would be wise,' Natalie murmured.

'But things are going to change, I know that. Things between us can be the same again,' he insisted, reaching towards one of her hands.

Natalie felt his fingertips sliding gently over her skin and, when she looked into his eyes, she saw that he was looking at her almost imploringly.

'We can start again,' he told her.

She drained what was left in her mug, put the receptacle down and drew one index fingernail slowly around the rim.

'Once you've left London there's no sense in you keeping in touch with me,' she told him. 'If this is going to be a fresh start for you then you need to make that move completely, Pete.'

He was still touching her hand softly.

'And this is what you want? You're sure?' she asked.

Mason sat forward, excited even by conversation about his new position.

'Nat, it's perfect,' he told her. 'Even down to the cottage in the school grounds. I won't have to scramble around looking for somewhere to live. I won't have to worry about shit like that. I'll be able to concentrate on the job and nothing else.' He looked around him, his eyes flickering to the large plate-glass windows at the front of the café. 'And I'll never have to see this fucking city again.'

'What about Chloe?'

Mason looked puzzled.

'I know that visiting her grave was never high on your list of priorities, Pete.'

Mason raised a hand to interrupt her.

'It doesn't matter how many times I visit the grave, Natalie,' he said, flatly. 'It's not going to bring her back, is it? Once a year. Once a month or once a week. What's the difference? It doesn't mean I think about her any less.'

'Well, once you start this fantastic new job perhaps you won't even have the time to think about her,' Natalie said, acidly.

Mason met her gaze and held it.

'Don't do this,' he murmured.

'Don't do what? Don't spoil your big day? Don't ruin your new start?' Natalie got to her feet. 'Don't worry, Pete. I wouldn't dream of it.'

He stood up and shot out a hand to prevent her leaving. He gripped her arm and pulled her close to him, pushing his face towards hers, his lips brushing her cheek.

'What are you doing?' she rasped.

'I want you,' he hissed. 'Now.'

'Get off me,' she insisted.

His fingertips clutched at the material of her coat but slipped off.

'Natalie,' he said as she turned away from him. 'Not like this.'

She looked back at him once then marched briskly towards the door. The couple on the next table looked at Mason who shot them an angry glance. They continued to gaze at him.

'What are you looking at?' he snapped and they both looked away, returning their attention to their drinks.

Mason hesitated a moment. He thought briefly about pursuing Natalie but instead he just sat down again, staring into the depths of his coffee mug.

It was another ten minutes before he left.

36

Walston, Buckinghamshire

Nigel Grant was breathing heavily by the time he got back to the car.

He wasn't, he insisted to himself, exhausted but just a little short of breath. After all, he had been running and, for a man of his age, he thought he'd covered the ground with admirable speed.

The wooden box he was carrying hadn't helped. Sure enough it was only about a foot square but it was difficult to run as quickly while carrying something and the box had slipped from under his arm a couple of times as he'd made his way across the darkened field.

He had run for a number of reasons. Obviously he wanted no one to see him. Despite the fact that he was in quite heavily wooded surroundings, Grant still feared some prying eye. He had also run because it was getting chilly and he was feeling the cold. But, most of all, he was anxious to be back inside the car and away from this place.

Grant had parked, he guessed, just over half a mile from his destination. Half a mile of slopes and inclines that would have sapped the strength of a man half his age. The ground was slippery too which made his passage more laborious and slowed his pace. He hadn't run all the way back to the car but the last few hundred yards had been downhill and, perhaps lulled into a false sense of security by the slope, he had increased his pace over the last stretch, his eyes on the dark outline of the car as he'd drawn closer. When he'd reached the bottom of the slope he'd paused, sucking in deep lungfuls of air, touching his chest with one hand to feel his rapidly beating heart. For a split second he wondered if he was going to have a heart attack but the pain passed as quickly as it had come and Grant hauled himself carefully over the wooden fence that formed the perimeter of the field.

He almost slipped as he climbed, careful not to drop the wooden box. Once over, he paused again, checking in both directions before walking slowly back to his waiting car.

At any time of the day it would have been unlikely that much traffic would have been passing along the stretch of country road where he was parked but, at this hour, it was virtually certain that the thoroughfare would be deserted. Even so, Grant peered cautiously to his left and right before advancing towards his car. A thin mist was hanging over the hills like fallen cloud, stirred occasionally by the breeze that had sprung up in the past few minutes. The branches of some nearby trees rattled noisily as he walked beneath them and Grant shivered slightly, holding the box more tightly now as he reached the car. After coming all this way he wasn't about to drop his prize.

He opened the driver's side and slid behind the wheel. The box he handed to his passenger.

'I got it,' he said, quietly, starting the engine.

His passenger didn't speak. Her only retort was a sound

like the wind puffing from ruptured lungs. A sibilant hiss that seemed to fill the car as surely as the stench coming from the box that she now held on her lap.

Grant guided the car out onto the road, driving slowly for about a hundred yards, allowing his eyes to become accustomed to the brightness of the headlights after the pitch black of the fields where he'd been for the past thirty or more minutes.

His passenger hissed some more sounds and Grant nodded, his face set in hard lines.

'It's what they asked for,' he replied, his eyes fixed on the road.

The passenger gurgled something else and reached out to touch Grant's hand. He felt cold fingertips on the back of his hand. It was like being touched by a corpse. The fingernails were long and brittle and they scraped uncomfortably against his flesh but he glanced at his passenger briefly and smiled with as much warmth as he could muster.

'You hold it until we get home,' he said, softly, then returned his concentration to the road ahead. A car was approaching on the other side of the road and he winced as the blazing white headlights dazzled him momentarily.

Beside him, his wife held on to the box as best she could with only one working arm. The paralysed one hung uselessly at her left side. When she tried to speak the words came out as little more than breaths of rancid air but Grant could understand her. He looked at her once more and smiled, reaching out with one hand to wipe away some saliva that was dripping down her chin.

She clung more urgently to the box, ignoring the stench that rose from it.

37

North London

Mason looked at the sealed boxes of clothes and belongings piled in his sitting room and nodded in satisfaction.

There it is. Your life in boxes. Ready to go. Ready to start again.

What didn't fit in the removal van he'd take with him in the car along with the more personal items that he didn't want some hulking great Pickfords employee smashing as they shoved them into the van. He lit up a cigarette and wandered across to the window, gazing down into the street below. There were a few people moving about down there, cars still motoring up and down the thoroughfare. He stood there listening to the noise, thinking how much he was looking forward to the peace and quiet of the countryside.

He wouldn't miss the city at all, he told himself. What was there to miss? The hustle and bustle. The noise. The aggravation.

Fuck that. Who needed it?

He drew gently on his cigarette then blew out a stream of smoke.

You'll miss Natalie, won't you?

Mason ran a hand through his hair and finished his cigarette, stubbing it out in the ashtray on the windowsill. He glanced at his watch and retreated to his bedroom, tired by his evening of packing. He lay on the bed and stared at the ceiling, his thoughts on the following morning. On his life from then on. A new life. A fresh start. His back and arms were aching from the packing.

He fell asleep more quickly than he could have imagined.

When Mason woke with a start in the small hours, he was panting loudly as he sat up.

If he'd been woken by a bad dream then he couldn't remember the details of it. Any residual thoughts and images had faded as soon as he'd sat upright. The only thing he knew for sure was that Chloe had featured somewhere in his nocturnal imaginings. As he thought of his daughter, her image pushed its way, almost unwanted, into his mind. He could see her in her school uniform but that image was replaced all too rapidly by one of her lying in her hospital bed. Mason exhaled almost painfully, trying to force the image from his mind but it clung on defiantly.

'Come on, come on,' he muttered to himself as if this mental rebuke would somehow precipitate the departure of the image. It worked to a certain degree and he tried to think about the following day. The move. The new school. The new position.

He swung his legs off the bed, irritated when he realised that he was still dressed. He pulled his clothes off quickly and slid beneath the duvet, hoping that sleep would come to him as fast this time as it had when he'd first lain down.

An hour later he was still hoping.

38

Walston, Buckinghamshire

Kate Wheeler stood outside the door of the room for what seemed like an eternity before knocking. She listened for sounds of movement from inside but heard nothing. Finally, unable to stand there motionless any longer she tapped lightly and walked straight in.

Her father was sitting on the bed on the far side of the room, rocking gently backwards and forwards.

Kate sucked in a deep breath and forced a smile on her face as she closed the door behind her.

'Hello, Dad,' she said, softly, crossing to where he sat. She put out a hand towards him, touched his cheek gently then kissed him on the top of the head.

Leonard Wheeler didn't look up but he did raise one hand as if to ward off her attention.

Kate sighed under her breath and reached for the chair close to the bed. She sat down opposite him, aware that his gaze was directed not at her but at something behind her. Something beyond her, that she couldn't see, that only her father was aware of.

'The nurses said you've had quite a good day,' she told him, warily.

'Where's Jessie?' he asked, suddenly turning to look directly at her.

Kate reached out and touched his hand gently.

'Mum's not coming,' she told him, wearily. 'She's been dead for five years.'

'You bloody fool.' His words came sharply and suddenly and he spoke them with such venom that Kate moved back an inch or two.

'Dad, please.'

He moved across the mattress until his back was wedged against the wall of the room. Again he was looking past her when he spoke, his words seemingly addressed to someone who only he could see.

'I want to know where Jessie is. Why hasn't she brought that cardigan I asked her for?'

'You asked me for a cardigan, Dad. I brought it for you last week when I came,' Kate told him, exasperatedly.

'Get Jessie,' he snapped. 'She knows what I'm talking about.'

'Jesus Christ,' Kate said, her patience snapping. 'No one knows what you're talking about any more, Dad.'

The expression of anger on his face changed immediately to one of bewilderment and he gazed at her with something in his eyes that looked like fear. He pressed himself closer to the wall, cowering away from her as if he thought she might strike him.

'Oh, Dad,' Kate breathed. She could feel the tears welling up but fought them back. She didn't want him to see her cry. She knew he didn't know who the hell she was and certainly wouldn't know why she was weeping but, all the same, she didn't want him to see her lose control. She coughed and cleared her throat, again reaching out with one hand to touch his arm.

159

This time he didn't withdraw but he watched her probing fingers as they gently brushed against his forearm.

'Kate,' he whispered.

A huge smile spread across her face and, this time, she did allow the tears to flow. They rolled down both her cheeks as she sat on the bed beside him, gripping his hand.

'Dad,' she said, urgently. 'Yes, it's me. It's Kate.'

He looked at her and returned the smile and she saw the pain in his eyes too. Pain but something else too. There was the all too fleeting flicker of recognition.

He opened his mouth to speak again but then that flicker was gone, as were the seconds of blissful serenity. Like some demonically possessed being, his face contorted into a visage of anger once more.

'Get away from me,' he snapped, dragging his hand and his arm away from her. 'Whoever you are.'

She stood up, more tears flowing. She looked helplessly at him as he pulled away from her again. God, how she hated the disease and what it had done to him. It had taken from him his thought processes and his personality. Everything she had always loved so much about him and, in their place, it had left a shell. The empty husk of the man she had called father for all of her thirty-four years. Perhaps he was still in there somewhere, locked away like priceless treasure, encased in a recognisable but alien frame. If he was still in there somewhere then Kate had no idea how to reach him and these weekly visits were becoming more and more difficult for her. Sometimes he was quiet but, most of the time, he was like this. She felt hatred inside herself and she knew it was for the disease. Not for this man she had loved so unreservedly for so many years. He had been deteriorating gradually for the past six or seven months.

Withering like an unwatered plant. A little more of him lost to her each time she saw him.

'I've got to go, Dad,' she said, apologetically, moving towards the door of the room. 'I'll see you next time.'

She wanted to hold him and to have him hold her in his strong arms. She wanted the man back who she had lost but she knew that could never be. The medication he was given did something for him but she knew that it would never make him the man he was before the disease struck. The realisation made her weep a little more.

Leonard Wheeler sat still on his bed and watched her impassively.

'I love you, Dad,' she told him.

He didn't reply, he merely turned away from her and stared at a crack in the wall beside him.

Outside the room, Kate turned and walked hastily out of the building, wiping her tears away with a tissue she pulled from her jacket pocket. She walked to her car and slid behind the steering wheel, wiping her cheeks. For what seemed like an eternity she remained immobile, waiting, it seemed, for the tears to stop. When they finally did she reached, not for her car keys, but for her mobile phone. Sniffing wearily, she hit the digits she wanted and waited.

Chloe

The early evening sky was the colour of bruised flesh as Mason approached the grave of his daughter.

A chill wind that had built up gradually during the afternoon whipped across the necropolis and caused Mason to shiver slightly as he stepped off the gravel path onto the wet grass. He pulled up the collar of his jacket and walked on, the small bunch of purple irises clutched in his gloved hand.

The cemetery was deserted and Mason felt as if he was the last person on earth as he stepped briskly between marble and stone tombstones and crosses, heading for his destination. Birds perched in the branches of nearby trees seemed to look down upon the cemetery and its occupants with predatory rather than protective eyes. Mason heard some large crows calling noisily before two took to the wing and rose into the chilly air, silhouetted against the ever-darkening sky.

He slowed his pace as he approached the black marble tombstone he sought.

He tried to swallow but found that his throat was dry. Mason exhaled deeply and stepped closer to the stone.

162

Wiping one hand over the cold marble he read the inscription.

CHLOE MARIE MASON
LOVED SO VERY MUCH
AN ANGEL LOANED BY GOD NOW RETURNED

Mason knelt by the headstone using his hands to wipe away some bird droppings that had splashed the top of the monument. He muttered irritably to himself and pulled a tissue from his pocket, continuing his task.

There was a fresh bouquet of flowers on the small plinth at the front of the stone, placed there by Natalie he assumed. He gently put the irises beside the other bouquet then stood up, his hands clasped before him.

He wanted to say something. Wanted to tell her what he felt. Wanted to say how much he missed her and how much he loved her but, no matter how hard he tried to force the words out, nothing would come.

Mason felt the tears welling up within him and he made no attempt to stifle them.

Warm rivulets began to run down his cheeks and he sniffed as he continued to stand there, still hoping that the words he wanted to say would pour forth as easily as his tears.

He even opened his mouth but he could say nothing.

What would you say to her if she was standing in front of you now?

Mason closed his eyes for a second, trying to force the image of his daughter into his mind, attempting to visualise her standing before him but the apparition was brief and faint.

He opened his eyes again.

Again he tried to speak but, once more, only silence escaped his barely parted lips.

Say what you'd say to her if she was with you now.

He sucked in a deep breath.

'I'm sorry,' he murmured, his voice cracking.

And that was it. That was all of it.

Fresh tears ran down his cheeks but he made no attempt to wipe them away. One dripped onto the black marble itself.

'I'm sorry,' he breathed again, his body racked by sobs. He was shaking uncontrollably. He reached out and gently touched the top of the headstone, feeling the coldness even through his glove. It was like touching black ice.

Mason turned and walked hurriedly away.

In the trees, one of the remaining crows uttered an almost derisory squawk then flew away into the darkening sky.

39

Walston, Buckinghamshire

Mason watched as the last of the packing boxes was set down in the sitting room of the cottage. He dug in his pocket and pulled out a five-pound note, shoving it into the large and slightly sweaty hand of the largest of the three removal men who had accompanied him from London.

'Get yourselves a drink,' Mason instructed.

The man looked at the note with an expression of bemusement but still thanked him before stuffing it into his pocket. He then walked to the front door, closing it loudly behind him.

Silence descended once again and Mason exhaled gratefully, wandering back into the sitting room where he sat down on the nearest of the boxes and gazed around at the interior of the room. It was larger than he'd remembered, even with the furniture in it that his predecessor had left behind.

Why leave a slightly battered three-piece leather suite and bookshelves full of books behind, Mason wondered?

Perhaps he was in a hurry to get out. Why not leave things behind? You did.

Mason got to his feet and crossed to the bookshelves, running an appraising eye over the titles there. Mostly well-read paperbacks. A few textbooks and reference works. Other than that, nothing out of the ordinary.

What are you looking for? Some clue to what your predecessor was like? Do you think he might give something of his character away with the books he read?

Mason reached for a battered paperback copy of *The Godfather* and pulled it from its position between *Campaigns of Napoleon* and *In Cold Blood*. He flicked through the tome briefly then pushed the paperback back onto the shelf.

Something large and dusty touched the back of his hand.

'Shit,' Mason hissed, pulling back in shock.

He glanced down at the floor and at what had fallen onto his flesh.

The spider was about the size of his thumbnail but its legs made it seem much larger.

It had been dead so long it was practically mummified, surrounded by a cocoon of dust as thick as any web it had woven in its own life. Mason shook his head, annoyed with himself for being so jumpy and for having been so startled by the appearance of the deceased arachnid. God alone knew how many more were dotted around the house, he thought. Before everything was unpacked it might be an idea to give the cottage a good clean.

He wandered through into the kitchen and glanced around.

The worktops and the sink, despite having a few small cracks, were clean enough.

Mason reached across to the windowsill over the sink and ran his finger along it.

More cleaning to do.

166

40

Like most small towns Walston boasted a covered shopping centre. A central area that attracted businesses both small and large. A place where independent concerns sat, however uneasily, next to the instantly recognisable names of chain stores and supermarkets that already dominated shopping centres everywhere.

Coffee shops, clothing outlets and electrical retailers vied for attention and custom, drawing the citizens of Walston into this central hub as surely as honey draws wasps. There was a market, almost a last throwback to the days when the town's economy existed solely on its local produce, but that was also covered. The stalls were operated and manned exactly as they had been for hundreds of years but now they traded beneath a canopy of concrete and glass. Older residents of the town could still remember the outdoor market, just as some could still recall the days when the town had a thriving cattle market and herds of pigs, sheep and cows were driven through Walston's streets by farmers. To the younger residents of the town, those memories smacked more of misty-eyed nostalgia. They were happy with their Starbucks, River Island and Currys. Content with their Costa coffee, Top Shop and Tesco. They didn't long for the old days or the old ways. They liked what they had now.

Andrew Latham sat on one of the metal benches and watched impassively as a woman in her eighties trundled past pulling her shopping trolley. He gave appraising glance to the woman who caught his eye momentarily and tried to increase her pace. She didn't like the look of Latham and his companions. She knew they were from Langley Hill, she'd seen them in the town before, dressed in their distinctive uniforms. With it being the weekend, they were attired in casual clothes. Jeans, trainers, T-shirts, tracksuits. All designer wear. All expensive. It was always that little group together, the woman mused. Always led by Latham, the oldest of them. He was tall and his skin was swarthy. His curly hair was jet black and hung as far as his shoulders. His eyes were heavy lidded but blazing when he turned the full measure of his stare on anyone.

The woman didn't care that the group attended an expensive private school, she wasn't interested that their parents were millionaires and celebrities. She had a mistrust and a disdain for all teenagers and it didn't matter whether or not they were the offspring of the rich or the guttersnipes who attended the local comprehensives. They were trouble as far as she was concerned, all of them.

Latham tired of gazing at the woman and, instead, turned to face the girl who sat to his right.

Sammi Bell ran a hand through her shoulder-length blonde hair and noticed that Latham was looking at her or, more particularly, her slim legs, encased as they were in skin-tight grey denim. She was unworried by his stare and met it with a coquettish smile.

'Something on your mind?' she asked.

'This fucking place,' Latham muttered. 'The people who live here are peasants.'

Sammi laughed and reached down to fasten the laces of one trainer.

'You're such a snob, Andrew,' she told him.

'I'm not a snob,' Latham continued. 'I'm just stating a fact. Look at them.' He gestured around him with one hand, a movement designed to encompass everyone within the shopping centre. 'They have no idea how to dress.'

'That's because they haven't got any money,' Precious Moore offered. She was a tall, ungainly girl with a lisp and front teeth that looked too big for her mouth. 'They've got no class.'

'You're a fine one to talk about class,' Latham reminded her. 'Your father's a pop star. What would you know about class?'

'And your mother was a slut,' Jude Hennessey added, his American accent cutting through the hubbub of conversation.

Latham laughed and slapped palms with the American.

'My mum was a TV presenter,' Precious said, irritably.

'Who slept with everyone she interviewed,' Latham reminded her.

'A slut,' Hennessey chided.

'At least I've still got a mum,' Precious countered, glaring at Hennessey. 'At least my mum didn't run off with someone else.'

'She didn't have to. She just fucked them,' the American

snapped. 'And my mother didn't run off. She died.' Hennessey scratched at his prominent jaw line with one index finger.

'Death or divorce, it amounts to the same thing,' Latham interjected. 'I should know, my dad's on his third marriage and the other two still have to be paid every month.'

'My dad says that all men should have a turnstile at the bedroom door because one way or the other, you always pay to get in.'

Latham and Hennessey laughed and looked at the speaker of the words. He was a short, heavily built youth with thin features and a pair of silver-framed glasses perched on his hooked nose. Felix Mackenzie pushed the spectacles back with one index finger and nodded to himself, happy with his contribution.

'Where is your dad now, Felix?' another member of the group asked. Jo Campbell was the youngest of the gathering. Willowy and with features so delicate it seemed that her face might crack like expensive china were it touched too hard. She crossed her slender legs and brushed some fluff from the right knee of her jeans.

'He works in New York,' Mackenzie replied.

'New York's a great place,' Hennessey offered. 'Better than this shit hole.'

'If you don't like our country then fuck off home,' Latham snapped. 'Fucking Yank.'

Hennessey looked at his companion and saw that the older boy's face was set in hard lines. But, even as he watched, Latham began to smile. Hennessey grinned too.

'You can't buy class, no matter how much money you've got,' Sammi offered.

170

Latham raised his eyebrows quizzically then looked at his watch.

'Come on,' he said, getting to his feet. 'It's almost time. Let's get this over with.'

The others followed dutifully.

41

Mason dumped the contents of the dustpan and brush into the bin and pushed open the back door for some fresh air.

His unpacking was more or less complete and a more thorough cleaning of the cottage, he told himself, could wait until the following day. He filled a glass with water then wandered out into the back garden, inspecting the lawn, wondering if he might cut the grass too as part of his moving-in ritual. It was as high as his ankles and hadn't been cut for well over a month as far as he could tell. The same was true of the privet hedge. It was untidy rather than overgrown. Neglected rather than forgotten. Mason wandered to the bottom of the garden and stood beside the stone wall, gazing out over the hills and the countryside in the direction of Walston itself.

'Better than looking out onto a London street,' he murmured, taking a sip of his water.

Chloe would have loved this garden and this view, wouldn't she?

He took another swallow of his water.

Only she'll never see them, will she?

Mason swallowed hard and tried to drive her image from his mind. He turned and looked at the cottage from the rear, happy with the dwelling and excited by the prospect of teaching at Langley Hill. He walked back towards the cottage, taking a slight diversion to inspect the disused greenhouse. He was peering at the piled-up wooden crates inside it when he was aware of movement behind him.

'Settling in?'

Mason turned to see Nigel Grant standing in the garden.

'I was out for a walk and thought I'd see how your move was going,' the older man continued. 'Hope you don't mind?'

Despite it being the weekend, Grant was still wearing a suit and tie and Mason thought that the headmaster looked as if he was on his way to a wedding reception rather than taking a walk in the school grounds. Mason, standing before him in a pair of grubby jeans and a worn sweatshirt, felt suddenly scruffy. He wiped his right hand on his jeans and extended it towards the newcomer.

Grant shook it happily.

'I wasn't sure whether or not to disturb you,' the headmaster announced.

'I thought you'd come to help me carry a few boxes,' Mason grinned.

'Not my *forte* I'm afraid. Is it too early to ask if the move's going well?'

'I'll be sorted by tonight. It helps that my predecessor left so much furniture behind. He obviously didn't want it.'

Grant ignored the comment and wandered down the garden towards the stone wall. Mason followed and the two men both gazed out over the countryside.

173

'My wife used to love country walks,' Grant said, quietly. 'Just ambling about in the fields, enjoying the views and the fresh air. We used to take picnics into the woods near here.' He was silent for a moment. 'I still take her out in the car, drive around but it's pointless, to be honest.'

'There's no hope of recovery?'

Grant shook his head.

'I just feel that it's so unfair,' the headmaster intoned. 'At the risk of sounding self-pitying. She was only fifty-two. Perhaps not in the prime of life but still too young to be struck down the way she was.' He looked at Mason. 'But then you'd know better than I what it's like to suffer with the loss of someone close.'

Mason nodded.

'Do you have any religious beliefs, Mr Mason?' Grant wanted to know. 'I believe that those who do can sometimes rationalise events such as illness or death when it strikes at someone close to them. I wondered if that was how you coped with your daughter's death. If you don't mind me asking.'

'I don't think I did ever cope with it,' Mason admitted. 'And, as for religious beliefs.' He shrugged.

'I tend to subscribe to the notion that God is a sadist but probably doesn't even know it,' said Grant. 'I don't know who said that but I'm sure it was someone infinitely more qualified to talk about suffering than myself.'

'So you don't believe in God?' Mason asked.

'When I look at my wife now, it's a little difficult. The concept of a God of love is somewhat lost on me these days. We still uphold the ritual of the morning assembly at the school, naturally, but I find it all a little tiresome.'

Grant turned and headed back towards the cottage. Mason kept pace with him and ushered the headmaster through the back door before him.

174

'Has anyone been inside the cottage since Mr Usher left?' Mason enquired, closing the back door behind them.

'Why do you ask?' Grant wanted to know.

'I just wondered. I didn't know if any of the kids . . .'

'No one has broken in here, if that's what you mean. They wouldn't do that.'

'How long ago did Usher leave? The cottage is in pretty good condition. It can't have been long ago. What was it, about a month?'

'Longer. Why?'

'I was just curious.'

'About what? I told you that Mr Usher wasn't a favoured topic of conversation around here.'

Mason held up his hands in supplication.

'He left some of his things behind,' he told Grant.

'What kind of things?' the headmaster snapped.

'Books, mainly.'

'Any other personal items?'

Mason shook his head.

'If he has I haven't found them yet,' he said.

'He obviously didn't want the books,' Grant insisted.

Mason saw that the headmaster's cheeks were flushed by now, his lips clamped tightly together.

'I'll let you get on,' he said, flatly, heading for the front door.

Mason hurried after him.

'Thanks for looking in,' he said as Grant strode towards the gate that led out onto the main driveway. The head-master didn't look back. Mason closed the front door once again and decided to continue with his cleaning and unpacking. However, he promised himself, first he was going to have some lunch.

An inspection of the cellar could wait until later.

42

Kate Wheeler saw them enter the Cottage Loaf bakery and she took a hasty swallow of her tea. Her mouth was a little dry and she didn't want to appear tongue-tied when she spoke to them. She didn't want them to see that she was a little nervous.

Andrew Latham led the way to the table where she sat and the others pulled chairs with them so that they could gather around her at the polished wood table where she sat with her tea and the remains of a sandwich. A waitress ambled over to them, order pad at the ready.

'We don't want anything,' Latham said, without looking at her.

'Any drinks?' the waitress ventured.

'Go away,' Felix Mackenzie instructed, flicking his hand towards her dismissively. 'He's told you. We don't want anything.'

'I know you,' the waitress said. 'You've been in here before. You're from Langley Hill, aren't you? You were friends with Amy. Amy Coulson. She used to work here.'

'We're not friends with anyone in this fucking place,'

Latham sneered, still not deigning to grace her with his glance.

'You heard what happened to her?' the waitress went on.

'We're not interested,' Precious Moore informed her.

The waitress hesitated for a moment then turned irritably from them.

'No, actually, wait a minute,' Latham called, still not looking at her. 'We'll have six teas. And don't be too long.'

Precious Moore giggled.

Jude Hennessey smiled.

The waitress regarded him balefully then scribbled the order on her pad and retreated.

'Hello, Miss Wheeler,' Latham said, quietly, pulling his chair closer to the table and edging nearer to Kate. 'Sorry if we're a bit late. Things to do, you know.'

'Do you want another cup of tea, Miss Wheeler?' Sammi Bell asked, noticing that the teacher was slowly turning an empty cup between her palms. 'We'll buy it for you.'

'In case you can't afford it,' added Jude Hennessey.

The others laughed.

'I don't want anything,' Kate Wheeler told them.

'You want *something* or you wouldn't have asked us to meet you here today,' Latham reminded her. 'How's Daddy?' There was a sneering derision in his tone and it was reflected in his eyes when she looked at him. 'Any improvement?'

Kate shook her head.

'Well,' Latham chided. 'If you want to help him, you know what you've got to do.'

Kate looked away from his piercing gaze, glancing instead at the bottom of her cup.

'How much do you know about this new guy?' Latham continued. 'Mason. The history teacher.'

'I've only met him once,' Kate said, softly, aware that the stares of Latham and his companions were trained on her like searchlights. 'He's moving into the cottage today.'

'Perhaps you should go and say hello,' Latham told her, getting to his feet. The others around the table followed his example. Then, led by Latham, they all filed towards the door of the café, halting only when the waitress struggled towards the table with their tea-cups perched precariously on a large wooden tray.

'What about your drinks?' she asked.

'You have them,' Latham grunted, dismissively. He pulled a ten-pound note from his pocket and flicked it in the direction of the waitress. 'And keep the change.'

Precious Moore giggled. Jude Hennessey grinned.

They left watched by Kate and the other occupants of the café.

The waitress set the tray down on Kate's table and retrieved the ten-pound note from the floor.

'Arrogant bastards,' she snapped. 'Who do they think they are?'

Kate didn't answer.

Sarah Tindall

She'd expected to be nervous.

Sarah Tindall had only passed her driving test two weeks earlier, two months after her eighteenth birthday, but she had shown confidence beyond her years behind the wheel and her brother had allowed her to borrow his car with far less protest than she'd expected.

Now, returning from her latest outing, guiding the car along one of the main roads into Walston, she adjusted the volume on the car stereo until the bass shook the vehicle.

Her brother had rung her twice to find out where she was. How long she was going to be and if she'd damaged the car. He'd asked lots of other questions too but she'd merely laughed at his exaggerated concern, promising finally to put a few pounds' worth of fuel in the tank before she returned it. He worried too much. For a man of twenty-two, Sarah felt that he should lighten up a bit, take life a little less seriously. But, for all his worrying, she appreciated his concern. Since the death of their father a year earlier, her brother had taken on the role of man of the house.

Like Sarah, he still lived at home with their mother,

even more reluctant to move out now because of the devastating effect their father's passing had had on their mother. Sarah had spoken to him on a number of occasions about what the future might hold. She had also told him that he would one day have to put his own needs ahead of those of their mother but he had merely nodded sagely and told her he couldn't yet leave their mother alone. Not with Sarah about to embark on a university course in Durham.

She was due to leave Walston in less than three weeks and the prospect filled her with excitement. Not because she wanted to get away from home because she'd always loved how close her family had been but because she saw the move to university as the next chapter in her life. The beginning of her career in medicine. Perhaps, she told herself, she would return to Walston to practise once she'd qualified as a doctor then she could be surrounded by her family once more. However, in the meantime, the years of study she faced were years she relished. She was looking forward to the freedom that university life would give her. Sarah was looking forward to increasing her number of sexual partners. She'd had just two boyfriends in the last four years and she was anxious for more. Being at university, away from the strictures of her home life and the restraints imposed by living in such a closed community, she was excited at the prospect of sleeping with many more men and, she thought, smiling, women too if she felt like it. Away from home she wouldn't be judged and her every move wouldn't be watched the way it was in a small town like Walston. She wanted to indulge, that was the best word she could think of to describe her yearning for more sexual experience. And, once she got to university, she intended to indulge fully.

Sarah slowed down a little as she attempted to change the CD in the car, glancing into the glovebox where her brother kept his discs. She finally selected one and put it into the player, adjusting the volume again as she drove.

A lorry passed her going in the other direction, barely able to squeeze past on the narrow country road. Sarah swerved slightly, fearing for a second that she was going to scrape her brother's car against the juggernaut as it passed. She gripped the wheel tightly as the car bumped into the mud at the side of the tarmac, wet earth spraying upwards as the wheels churned through it. Perhaps, she thought with a smile, she should run the vehicle through a car wash before she got home. Her brother wouldn't be happy if his pride and joy was filthy when she returned it. There was a petrol station on the road she was now driving along, she remembered, and she was sure they had a car wash there. Two birds with one stone, Sarah thought, smiling.

She guided the car around a corner, slowing down slightly to negotiate the bend. There were trees and hedges on either side of the road here and the tarmac bent and twisted sharply to the right and left for the next three hundred yards. She eased off the accelerator, aware that there was another car approaching her from behind. She could see the headlights in her rear-view mirror as the vehicle drew nearer.

Sarah shook her head, irritated at the stupidity of the other driver. He was less than ten feet from her back bumper and seemed intent on getting past despite the hazardous nature of the road. A motorbike swept past in the other direction, the rider swaying precariously as he took the bend.

Still the car behind her stayed close and Sarah now realised with disbelief that he was going to try and overtake her. She thought for a moment about speeding up, making him wait but then she relented and pulled slightly to one side, allowing the other vehicle more room. He shot past like a bullet, brake lights flaring as he struggled to negotiate a bend just ahead.

Sarah cursed him under her breath and drove on, astounded at the other driver's impetuosity.

The road was now straightening out once again and she pressed her foot down a little harder on the accelerator. There was a high brick wall about two hundred yards ahead marking the entrance to one of the local farms.

Sarah pressed down harder on the gas, the car speeding up. She turned up the volume on the car stereo, sound filling the vehicle as it increased in speed. She was humming along to the music, tapping her fingers on the steering wheel as she drove.

She floored the accelerator.

The car was doing seventy when it hit the brick wall.

43

Walston, Buckinghamshire

Mason carefully descended the stone steps into the cellar, the single unshaded bulb that hung from the roof of the subterranean chamber lighting his way.

He was pleasantly surprised that the cellar didn't smell damp. It wasn't thick with the webs of long-dead spiders and there wasn't a layer of dust on the floor so thick that it covered his feet. As he stood three steps from the bottom and surveyed the large expanse of underground room, he was relieved to see that it had been well maintained. The possibilities for storage were endless but, Mason thought, there was ample scope for turning this below-ground area into something more inviting.

You've got a study and living room and two bedrooms as well, how much living space do you need? You're on your own. It's not as if you need to turn it into a playroom for Chloe, is it?

He forced the thought from his mind and descended the last three steps to the floor of the cellar.

To his right and left, the shadows were deep but not so impenetrable that he couldn't see what looked like wall-mounted shelves. Mason crossed to those closest and noticed that there were several canisters of propane gas there. He also saw a camping stove and some metal tent pegs. Perhaps his predecessor had been a fan of the great outdoors, he mused. Beneath the shelves, there were some old, discarded wellington boots and some empty cardboard boxes, one having housed a portable TV. There were a couple of paint tins and a roller, the white paint having long ago dried up and set. Mason saw more empty cardboard boxes and some battered wooden stepladders propped in one corner.

He walked around the cellar, moving his gaze over all the detritus of his predecessor's life. There were more shelves but this time piled up on the floor with their brackets, waiting to be mounted. Maybe Usher had been a bit of a handyman when he wasn't teaching, Mason thought, trying to picture what kind of man had possessed not just his job but his new home before he had.

Why so curious? He probably wouldn't give a damn what kind of person had taken over his position. Why so inquisitive about him?

Mason found another large cardboard box, the lid open. He peered inside and found several jigsaw puzzles. He smiled to himself. Perhaps Usher had also enjoyed the more sedentary diversions offered by such a pastime as much as he'd evidently embraced the vagaries of camping. Mason pulled one of the puzzles free. It was of a Victorian-looking doll. A strange subject for a man to choose, thought Mason. He saw a price marked on the jigsaw box. Two shillings. Perhaps this and the other puzzles hadn't been bought by Usher at all. Maybe they'd been shifted down to the cellar from the cottage above to prevent clutter. Maybe that was what had been done with the camping gear too. Mason reminded himself that he was still no nearer to discovering anything about the man who had lived and taught here before him.

184

He moved to the rear of the cellar and found a large noticeboard with a year planner on it. More likely, he assumed, to belong to Usher. There was an empty fish tank next to it. Then more boxes. Cardboard and wood. These were stacked as high as the ceiling. Wedged one on top of the other like bricks with seemingly no room to pull them free or open them. Many, he noticed, were also sealed with thick tape.

What the hell was in those?

An empty and discarded freezer, the lid open and gaping to reveal some dead moths and spiders at the bottom. Beside it there was a broken hoover. Everywhere in the cellar, the signs were of items that had passed their usefulness. The whole subterranean chamber was filled with the residue of past and unfathomable lives.

He passed the stacked-up plastic garden chairs, pausing a moment when he found another cardboard box, this one piled high with magazines.

The unshaded bulb that lit the cellar flickered and Mason glanced up at it, wondering how long it had been there or, more to the point, how much longer it was going to last. Then he turned his attention back to the magazines.

He pulled the first three out of the box. There was a copy of GQ and two music magazines. Mason assumed, glancing at the dates on them, that they had been bought by Usher. He pulled at the pile nearest to him and saw that the magazines were actually in order by month of publication. He smiled, realising that his predecessor had obviously been something of a hoarder. Mason dug deeper among the neatly stacked magazines, wondering if their subject matter might give him his elusive clue that he sought to Usher's character.

You're doing it again. What's the big deal about what he was like? What difference does it make?

Mason chuckled to himself as he pulled a copy of *Penthouse* from the pile. Still smiling, he flipped it open, inspecting the array of girls within. There were more copies of that magazine and some less sophisticated examples of the genre closer to the bottom of the first box. Mason glanced at the covers then stuffed them almost guiltily back into the cardboard containers where they'd been stored.

The next open box had some jump leads in the bottom and some hardback books.

It was the last box, the one pushed right against the wall, that Mason seemed most interested in. There were several unmarked video cassettes inside.

Porn?

He smiled to himself again then noticed that there were also some smaller cassettes like the kind that would be used in a camcorder. They were scattered on top of some carefully folded shirts and trousers. Mason lifted some clear and noticed that there were sheets of paper jammed down the side of the clothes. He pulled some of it free.

There was writing on it.

Mason, for some unaccountable reason, felt his heart pumping a little faster. Was he, he wondered, about to find out something significant about his predecessor? Was he going to uncover some deep dark secret about the man who lived here before him? He opened a folded sheet up and scanned the words there.

It was a shopping list.

Mason laughed out loud, the sound reverberating within the cellar.

Really earth-shattering. An amazing discovery. Now you know that Usher liked beefburgers, cornflakes and Lucozade as well as being fond of porn, popular music and fashion. That's a major breakthrough.

186

Mason tossed the sheet back into the box, shaking his head in the process.

He was about to close the box and leave the cellar when there was a dull pop from behind him.

The light went out.

'Shit,' Mason muttered, pretty sure that he hadn't got any spare bulbs in the house. He headed for the steps that led up into the kitchen, grunting when he collided with one of the cardboard boxes in the now Stygian gloom. The box toppled over, spilling its contents across the floor in front of him but, in the blackness he now found himself in, Mason had no idea what he'd accidentally upended. He dropped to his knees and realised that it was more paper.

He decided to check it out after he'd replaced the bulb.

Mason actually had his foot on the bottom step when he heard the sound of tentative footsteps from above him and, in that split second, he realised that there was someone else in the house.

44

Mason paused on the steps for a moment, wanting to ensure that the noise he'd heard was actually the creaking of the floor above him. In the darkness of the cellar, sounds seemed to be amplified and, when he heard the same noise seconds later, he was sure.

He moved as quickly as he could up the stone steps, careful not to crack his head on the ceiling as he drew nearer the hatch that led into the kitchen beyond.

Mason pushed open the flap and stepped out.

Kate Wheeler screamed.

'Jesus Christ,' she panted, stepping back, one hand to her chest.

'Not quite,' Mason grinned.

'You scared me,' she told him.

'I can see that. You scared me too. I heard someone up here and thought I'd got burglars.'

'Sorry. I came to say hello. Welcome to the school. Hope you're settling in. All that. The front door was open so I walked in. Sorry.'

'The front door was open?' Mason repeated, frowning. 'I thought I shut that after Grant left.'

'It's shut now. I closed it behind me. Perhaps the hinges need adjusting,' Kate smiled. 'Did you say the headmaster had been here too?'

'Part of his duties I suppose, welcoming a new member of staff.'

Mason looked at her, once again struck by her good looks. He swallowed hard, surprised at himself for feeling so instantly and intoxicatingly attracted to her. They were feelings he had thought dormant for so long, to have them return with such vehemence now unsettled him slightly.

'Geography and games, right?' he stated. 'That's what you teach.'

She nodded.

'For almost seven years now,' she told him.

'The headmaster told me,' Mason admitted.

'And you're a history teacher?'

'Somebody's got to be.'

'At least you get this place with the position. That's a perk.'

'What about you? Where do you live? At the school or in the town?'

'I've got a flat in Walston. Nothing very grand.'

'Where are you from originally? Which part of Ireland?'

'Dublin. My family moved here when I was fifteen.'

'Are they still here now?'

'My mum died five years ago.'

'I'm sorry. What about your dad?'

Kate swallowed hard.

'He isn't well,' she began. 'He has Alzheimer's. He's in a home in Walston.'

'Sorry I asked,' Mason sighed as the kettle boiled.

'It's not your fault,' she told him.

'How bad is it?'

'He's been getting steadily worse for the last six or seven months. I see him as often as I can. But there's nothing I can do to help him. That's what makes it worse. I just feel so helpless.'

Mason nodded and poured boiling water into a mug, dropping a tea bag into it.

'I know what you mean,' he offered. 'I was the same when my daughter died. I couldn't sit there beside her bed just watching her die. I know it sounds terrible but I got to the stage where I couldn't even go to the hospital. We knew she wasn't going to get better. I didn't want to see her like that. I still hate myself for it.'

'You shouldn't.'

He shrugged, pushed the mug of tea towards her then retrieved a bottle of milk and the bag of sugar from the worktop and placed them on the table nearby.

'Sorry,' he said. 'I haven't unpacked the milk jug or sugar bowl yet.'

Kate smiled and helped herself to both.

'Are you married?' she enquired. 'If you don't mind me asking?'

'Not at all,' he smiled. 'We're separated. The business with my daughter was just too much. I think my wife blamed me, resented me or was just plain bloody angry with me for not doing more.' He sighed. 'It broke us up.' He took a sip of his tea.

An uneasy silence descended, eventually broken by Mason.

'Shall we change the subject?' he offered. 'You obviously didn't come here this afternoon to watch me wallow in self-pity, did you?'

Kate managed a smile.

'Tell me all about the school,' Mason went on. 'Which teachers to steer clear of. Which kids I should watch out for. Who gets pissed at staff parties. Which parents I shouldn't ask for their autographs. That kind of stuff.'

Kate chuckled.

'What's the headmaster like?' Mason enquired. 'He seems like a decent enough guy.'

'He is.'

'And the kids?'

She regarded him evenly over the rim of her mug as she sipped her tea.

'Watch out for Andrew Latham,' she said, quietly.

Mason shrugged.

'One of the older boys,' she continued. 'He's in one of your classes on Monday.'

'Have you been checking up on me?'

'I just thought you should know about Latham. Forewarned is forearmed as they say.'

'What exactly should I watch out for?'

'Him and his little group. There's usually five of them with him. Always the same ones. Two girls, Jo Campbell and Sammi Bell. They're beautiful. Stunning. And they know it. Watch yourself with them.'

'Jail bait? Flirt with the men teachers, do they? That kind of thing. I've seen it before, Kate.'

'Not like this, you haven't,' she snapped. 'These kids are different.'

'Trust me, they can't be any worse than the ones in the school where I used to teach.'

Kate sucked in a deep breath and sipped at her tea again.

'Jude Hennessey and Felix Mackenzie are a part of that group too,' she continued. 'There's an American girl called Skye Cuthbert who's friendly with them as well but she's been off for a week or so, I think one of her parents is ill but she's normally part of their group.

191

Precious Moore is always hanging around with them but I think they just tolerate her, she isn't like them. She's not as strong.'

Mason frowned, surprised at the look of concern on Kate's face.

'Thanks for the warning,' he murmured. 'I'll keep my wits about me. But you know what kids are like. Always pushing. Trying to find barriers. Especially with a new teacher.'

'Just be careful,' she added, without looking at him.

'You make them sound like monsters,' Mason smiled.

Kate didn't answer.

'What about my predecessor?' he enquired. 'How did he get on with them? The headmaster didn't seem very keen on discussing him.'

Kate shot him a wary glance.

'What do you know about Simon Usher?' she snapped.

'Very little,' he admitted. 'I was hoping you might be able to tell me something.'

45

'What do you want to know about him?'

Kate held Mason's gaze as she spoke.

'I'm just curious,' Mason told her. 'The headmaster looks as if he's going to have a heart attack every time the guy's name is mentioned. What the hell happened? Why did he leave? That's all I want to know. What's the big deal?'

'No one knows why he left. He'd been ill for a week or two, missed some of his classes too. Then he just never turned up one morning. When people came to check on him he'd gone. Packed up all his stuff and just left. No note. No explanation why and no details of where he'd gone.'

'How well did you know him?'

'Just staff-room conversations, the odd drink after work sometimes but that was it.'

'What kind of guy was he?'

'I told you, I didn't know him that well.'

'Which teachers *did* he get on well with?'

'Why, are you going to grill them about him?'

'I wasn't aware I was grilling you, Kate. Just asking some questions.'

She nodded and sucked in a deep breath.

'Sorry,' she murmured. 'You're right.' She looked at Mason. 'There were rumours about him. That he was involved with one of the students here.'

'In what way?'

'How do you think? Simon Usher had a roving eye and some of the older girls here made it quite obvious that they were available if he was interested. Maybe he was interested.'

'He slept with one of the students?'

'Like I said, it was just rumours. No one knows anything for sure, just like no one knows why he left here or where he went. I told you, these surroundings create even more of a closed society. Every little thing gets blown up out of proportion. People get bored. When they're bored they gossip.'

'So you think it was just gossip about Usher and one of the pupils?'

'I haven't really thought about it but it's possible that something happened. He was a young guy. Good looking. I can understand how some of his girl pupils would have fancied him. Whether they fancied him enough to sleep with him I couldn't say.'

'That would explain why the headmaster's not falling over himself to talk about Usher. It wouldn't look good for the school, would it? A teacher sleeping with his pupils.'

'Like I said, it's just rumours. No one knows anything for sure. Why does it matter so much to you?'

'I've got his job. I'm living in the house where he used to live. I'll be teaching the pupils he taught. I told you, I'm curious. I suppose I should be grateful to him, for whatever reason he left. If he hadn't, I wouldn't have the job or this house.'

'Why did you leave London?'

'I had my reasons.'

'Now who's being mysterious?'

Mason smiled.

'There was an incident,' he confessed. 'I was attacked by some of the kids at the school where I taught.'

'Jesus,' Kate murmured. 'No wonder you wanted to get away.'

'It was a very different school from this one.'

She finished her tea and got to her feet, crossing to the sink where she spun the tap and rinsed the receptacle.

'I'm going to leave you in peace,' Kate announced, wiping her hands. 'Let you carry on with your unpacking.'

'Thanks for the visit,' he said, getting to his feet. 'Listen, would it be against school rules for me to buy you dinner one day next week?'

Kate smiled, her cheeks colouring slightly.

'That's very kind of you but maybe you'd better settle in a little first.'

'Is that a no?'

'It's a "wait a week or so and then ask again". That's all.'

Mason smiled.

'If you want to come back again tomorrow, I could do with some help unpacking.'

'I might just do that,' she assured him as she walked with him to the front door.

Mason watched her as she climbed into her car, waving happily as she pulled away, then he closed the door gently behind her.

Kate Wheeler was more than two hundred yards from the cottage when she brought the car to a halt. She left the engine idling as she reached for her mobile phone, jabbing the digits she needed. She was breathing heavily by the time her call was answered and, she noticed, her hand was shaking slightly.

46

It was wrong.

That was the only phrase that kept going through Frank Coulson's mind as he stood looking down at his daughter's grave. This entire scenario was wrong. His daughter shouldn't be dead. He and his wife shouldn't be standing looking at her resting place. No parent should have to bury their child. It wasn't right. It wasn't the way things were supposed to be.

Especially not for his beautiful seventeen-year-old Amy. She was supposed to have had all her life ahead of her. It wasn't meant to have finished at the end of a length of rope taken from his shed and certainly not ended by her own hand.

Frank Coulson tried to fight back more tears. He had to be strong for his wife. Margaret had crumbled since she'd found Amy's body. Frank couldn't think of another word to describe her emotional and physical descent during the last few days. Normally a strong woman, she had barely been able to function since Amy's suicide. Frank had made all the arrangements (he'd even had to help her dress that morning before they'd left their house).

Not that he was complaining. Organising his daughter's funeral had at least given him something to do. It had occupied his mind since the terrible discovery. Only at night, when they were alone, did he have to confront the thoughts and realisation that he would never hold his beautiful girl in his arms again. Never hear her voice. Never see her married or ever see her present him with the grandchild he and Margaret had so desperately craved. There was none of that to come for Frank and Margaret Coulson. Only the crushing knowledge that their only child was dead and that, as far as they were both concerned, life held very little in store for them that was worth waiting for.

She had been the pinnacle of their world and now she was gone. Frank gripped his wife more tightly to him, feeling her shaking as she stood there beside him. She had barely stopped crying since discovering Amy's body. Her grief had been so complete, so all-enveloping that, for the first day or two, Frank had feared she might follow Amy and take her own life. The doctor had been of course and he'd prescribed some tablets for her but Margaret Coulson had barely looked at the bottle when Frank had returned with it from the chemist. He had sat with her, urging her to take the small white tablets as he watched her dumbly sip at the water he'd given her. Watching as it dribbled down her chin. Frank had wiped it away patiently and stared into her blank eyes looking for some fragment of the woman who had been there before their daughter had died. She looked sedated. She moved around like a zombie and she hadn't spoken more than twenty words since Amy's death.

A tiny, angry part of Frank wanted to follow his wife to that place she now inhabited. A very small piece of him resented her for having been able to shut out the rest of the world. A fragment of his consciousness envied her the state of near stupor she was in. At least she didn't have to face reality. She didn't have to accept that Amy was gone. He wanted that feeling too. That anaesthetised state that provided protection from the overwhelming pain of accepting that his daughter had hanged herself. Anything to allow him respite from the suffering he felt so acutely but was reluctant to show except in moments of solitude.

They couldn't both crumble, could they? The two of them couldn't just give up. One of them had to be strong and support the other. Frank was the one, whether he liked it or not.

He had listened to the words of condolence spoken by the other mourners before and after the service but they had barely registered. Just as the handshakes of commiseration and the kisses of sympathy had done little to drag him from his torpor. The vicar had said something to him about coming to church, about spiritual comfort but Frank had felt only anger towards this man of God. The servant of the God who had taken his only child. Frank wanted no part of what he offered. He wanted his daughter back and no one was going to provide him with that. Not man nor God.

Now, with no one else around, the enormity of their situation seemed to register fully. During the service, Frank had felt as if someone had wrapped him in plastic. Every sound had been muffled, every word distant, every movement slowed. But now, with just the two of them staring down at Amy's grave, Frank began to feel the true magnitude of his pain.

The wind had been mercifully gentle during the service that morning but now, as Frank and his wife stood motionless beside the grave of their daughter, it began to build in pace and ferocity. Frank could feel the first spots of rain in the air too. The Cellophane that encased the bouquets of flowers stacked by the grave rattled noisily as the wind stirred it. One single rose petal came free and was buffeted across the cemetery by the breeze that then promptly died as soon as it had sprung up. Frank, supporting his quietly sobbing wife, moved towards the array of bouquets and wreaths, noticing that the card on one was coming loose. It was on a small bunch of white carnations and it was handwritten.

He looked at it, frowning a little as he read it.

THANKS FOR THE MEMORIES. HA HA.

What the hell was this?

He didn't recognise the name on it. He couldn't think who had sent this floral tribute with such a bizarre message attached. He studied the name once again.

ANDREW LATHAM

47

Mason pushed the light bulb into place and stepped down from the wooden steps.

'Turn it on,' he called from the cellar.

Up in the kitchen, Kate Wheeler flicked the appropriate switch and the new bulb glowed brightly.

'That's it,' Mason called back.

He replaced the steps and glanced around him at the papers that had spilled from the box he'd dropped the previous day, still scattered across the floor of the cellar. He bent down and began picking them up, hearing Kate's footfalls on the steps as she descended to join him.

'My God,' she laughed, glancing around her. 'Is this all stuff that Simon Usher left behind?' She saw the boxes towards the rear of the cellar piled floor to ceiling and shook her head in bewilderment.

'I don't know if all of it's his. Some must have belonged to the person who lived here before him. If it is all his then he was one hell of a hoarder.' Mason indicated the boxes full of magazines.

Kate crossed to one and dug inside. She pulled out

one of the girlie magazines and held it up, a smile on her face.

'There's loads of them in there,' Mason told her, kneeling down to pick up some of the spilled papers.

As he lifted the typed, printed and handwritten sheaf of paper he noticed that there were also photographs among the spilled contents of the box he'd knocked over. He held a Polaroid between his fingers, inspecting the image there. It was a man in his thirties. Dark haired and unshaven, dressed in a pair of jeans and a shirt. He wore a pair of metal-rimmed glasses. His face was expressionless.

'Is this Simon Usher?' Mason asked, holding the photo up.

Kate joined him and looked at the Polaroid.

'That's him,' she acknowledged.

'I wonder who took it?' Mason mused, picking up more of the spilled pictures. He shuffled slowly through them, noticing that they all seemed to be of Usher and, more perplexingly, that the man was not smiling in any of them. He wore the same nondescript expression in every one. They were taken from a dozen different angles, as if the taker wanted to capture his features from every available side. Kate edged nearer to him, also looking down at the pictures, surveying each one as he revealed it.

There were thirty-four photos of Simon Usher standing unsmilingly before the camera.

'Doesn't look too happy, does he?' Mason observed. He nodded in the direction of the box that he'd knocked over earlier. 'See if there are any more in there, Kate.'

Kate crawled on all fours over to the box and peered inside.

'My God,' she breathed. 'There're hundreds in here.'

'Let's have a look,' Mason murmured.

She lifted the box and brought it to where Mason was sitting on the cold stone floor.

'Can't we do this upstairs?' she asked, pointing towards the ceiling. 'Where's it's a bit warmer.'

Mason nodded and got to his feet, taking the box from her. He led the way up the stone steps to the kitchen and then through into the sitting room. They both sat down on the sofa, the box of photos in front of them. Mason dug out a handful and began sifting slowly through them.

'What exactly are we looking for?' Kate wanted to know, also grabbing a handful of pictures.

'I'm not really sure,' Mason admitted. 'Maybe some clue about what kind of guy he was. There might be some answers among these pictures.'

Kate raised her eyebrows questioningly and began flicking through the pile of photos she held.

'I told you,' she said, quietly, eyes fixed on the succession of images before her. 'Usher was a normal kind of guy. Nothing out of the ordinary.'

Mason finished looking at the first batch of pictures (a little dismayed that they showed nothing other than views of the school and its grounds) and reached for more.

'Are you looking forward to your first day teaching again?' Kate enquired, slowly shuffling the pictures she held before her, similarly unimpressed by some shots of the local countryside.

Mason nodded, still transfixed by the Polaroids he was working his way through.

Tiring of the task, Kate placed another batch of pictures on the sofa and got to her feet.

'Maybe a cup of tea would help,' she offered. 'Shall I make one while you carry on with your detective work?'

Mason nodded and Kate wandered off into the kitchen.

More shots of the school grounds. Pictures of Walston. Some more pictures of the surrounding countryside. Mason sucked in a weary breath and reached for more pictures from the bottom of the box. He turned over the first few and found some of the cottage. In one of them, Usher was standing outside the front door, still wearing the emotionless expression he'd sported in the pictures Mason had first looked at. In another he was standing with his arms folded at the bottom of the garden with a panoramic view of the countryside leading down to Walston behind him. Mason noted that the sky behind his predecessor was purple, deep red slashes of cloud across it like cuts on bruised flesh. The picture, he reasoned, must have been taken just before nightfall. There were several more like that, all showing Usher standing with folded arms with his back to the garden wall but with the sky growing progressively darker. Mason frowned, not even sure why this succession of snaps should nag at him.

'Jesus,' he murmured as he uncovered the next picture.

It was a dead dog. He frowned as he surveyed the image then looked at the next. Another shot of the same dead dog.

Its throat had been cut so savagely that its head had almost been severed, that much was clear from the picture. So too was the fact that it had been disembowelled. Cut open from chest to genitals, its intestines spilling out from the riven carcass like bloodied party streamers.

There was something familiar in the background of the picture, something that drew Mason's eye from the vile image of the eviscerated dog. The carcass was lying close to a stone wall and, as he looked more closely, he could see that it was the wall at the bottom of the cottage

204

garden. From the amount of blood that could be seen on the ground around the dead dog it appeared that the unfortunate creature had been killed and mutilated in the cottage garden.

The next shot confirmed this.

Clear for all to see as he stood over the butchered dog, his arms folded and his face expressionless, was the figure of Simon Usher.

48

Frank Coulson paused for what seemed like an eternity before reaching out to touch the door handle to his daughter's room.

He swallowed hard and turned it, stepping inside, closing it behind him as he slapped on the light.

He'd been dreading this moment but he knew that he could put it off no longer. The last time he'd been inside this room his daughter had been sitting at the little desk pushed up against the far wall, seated there tapping at the keys of her laptop. He'd popped in to tell her that her dinner was ready and they'd ended up talking for five or ten minutes about her work that day. It was a small, inconsequential memory, he mused, but now it was all he had left of her.

Coulson gritted his teeth, knowing that what he was about to do was going to take as much strength as he'd ever been forced to summon before. He crossed to her desk and switched on her laptop, seating himself at her desk. Was this, he wondered, where she'd been sitting when she decided to kill herself? He closed his eyes tightly, trying to force that image from his mind. He spoke her name softly under his breath as he opened his eyes and as he did he noticed that her mobile phone was lying on the desk too. He picked it up and flipped it open. There were more than a dozen messages.

Never to be answered now, he thought with a painful stab of realisation.

His right hand was shaking slightly and he clenched his other into a fist, holding it in that position for so long that his nails dug into his palm. He grunted, satisfied that the trembling had subsided.

Coulson wasn't an expert in modern technology, the nuances of such teenage necessities as texting and e-mail were lost on him but he was sufficiently versed in the workings of a computer and a mobile to find what he sought. He flicked the requisite buttons on the mobile and found the entry marked PHONEBOOK.

Once it appeared he reached into his pocket and pulled out the card he'd taken from the small bouquet of carnations at the cemetery earlier that day. He held it before him and, again, considered the name.

ANDREW LATHAM

And the message.

THANKS FOR THE MEMORIES. HA HA.

What the hell was that supposed to mean? Why would anyone leave that kind of message on a grave?

He scrolled through the names entered in the phonebook of his dead daughter's phone. He found Latham's number immediately.

There was a lilac-coloured notepad on the desk and Coulson wrote the number on the top sheet with a blunt pencil he found close by. He would, he promised himself, ring the number later. He wanted to speak to Latham. Find out how well he'd known Amy. See what he had to say for himself. Coulson told himself that he'd make the call after he'd ensured that his wife was safely tucked up in bed. She was downstairs now, sitting helplessly in the living room. If he could only persuade her to take some of the tablets the doctor had given her then perhaps she would sleep. Once he'd seen her safely into bed then he would make the call.

Coulson quickly scrolled through the rest of the names in the phonebook to see if there were any more he recognised.

There weren't. Not even the very last one.

Frank Coulson had no idea who Simon Usher was.

He turned his attention to the laptop.

49

'Two questions,' Mason murmured as Kate Wheeler looked sheepishly at the photo of the slaughtered dog. 'Why did he do it and who the fuck did he ask to take a picture of it?'

Kate didn't speak, she just shook her head slowly, eyes still fixed on the photograph.

'A normal guy,' Mason murmured. 'Nothing out of the ordinary.'

'I wouldn't have said that if I'd seen these, would I?' Kate countered, irritably. She regarded a fifth picture of the dead dog that had been taken from closer range. 'Sick bastard.'

'From what Usher looks like in the pictures, how long ago would you say these were taken?'

Kate took one from him and traced one nail over the outline of Usher's face.

'Weeks,' she offered, returning the picture to him.

Mason looked at the next series of pictures. There were more of Usher standing in the garden, this time without the butchered dog. There was, however, a large patch of dark fluid on the grass at his feet.

'He killed the dog here by the look of it,' Mason muttered. 'Was it his? Did he have a dog?'

Kate shook her head.

'Perhaps I should ring the police,' Mason insisted.

'What for?'

He looked incredulously at her.

'A guy kills a fucking dog in his own back garden then disappears and you don't think there's anything suspicious?' he demanded.

'For a start off we don't know if the two events were linked. I doubt that he left this school and this job because he killed a dog and, even if he did, he hasn't done anything the police would be interested in.'

'The slaughter of a dog. You don't think that would be of any interest to them?'

'Peter, just wait a minute. Look at what you've got here. You find some stuff in your cellar, left behind by a man who taught at this school just before you arrived. A man who has left his job but not given anyone a forwarding address. Among his personal belongings you find some photos. Some very unpleasant I grant you but, even if you put all those things together, what exactly have you got? What is so sinister about that collection of events?'

Mason regarded her evenly for a moment, her words registering.

'He butchered a dog,' he said, quietly. 'I'd call that pretty sinister. And then he got someone to take photos of him standing over it.'

'Weird, yes. Sick, yes. But no more,' she insisted.

'Do you think we should tell the headmaster? Let him know what kind of man Usher was?'

'Why? What good will it do? What will it matter? Usher's gone. He's left. What he did when he was here isn't important.'

210

'It might be to whoever owned that dog.'

'Well, that's something else we'll never know, isn't it? We don't know who the dog belonged to and we've got no way of finding out. What's more, I'm not sure we've got any right to.'

Mason sucked in a deep breath and leafed through several more of the pictures.

'Leave them, Peter,' Kate urged.

'I want to have a look through the rest of them,' he insisted. 'Just a quick look.'

'Well,' she sighed, getting to her feet, 'if it's all the same to you, I won't sit here watching you while you do it. If you find anything else then tell me tomorrow.'

Mason got to his feet, dropping some of the pictures.

'I have to go anyway,' she told him. 'There are a couple of lesson plans I need to go over before the morning.'

He walked her to the front door and opened it for her.

'Thanks for helping me tidy up and unpack and all that,' he smiled.

'My pleasure,' she told him. 'If I were you, I'd forget about whatever Simon Usher used to get up to and concentrate on your own life.'

'Thanks for the advice.'

She leaned forward and kissed him lightly on one cheek. Mason smiled as she turned and hurried away up the path towards her waiting car. As he watched her pull away he reached up with two fingers and gently touched the part of his cheek that she'd kissed. He heard the sound of her car engine receding down the driveway and he closed the front door. Perhaps she was right. He should dump all the photos back into the box where they'd been found and put the whole lot where they belonged, hidden away in the cellar.

211

Mason nodded to himself. Yes, that's what he'd do. Just one more quick look through the pictures and then he would.

As he walked back into the sitting room he switched on the lamp he'd placed beside the television and the room was bathed in a dull yellow glow. He didn't bother to close his curtains.

He may have thought differently had he known he was being watched.

50

Frank Coulson saw the name Andrew Latham listed in the contacts section of Amy's e-mail account. He made a note of the address next to the phone number he'd already scribbled down then he clicked on the portion of the screen marked inbox.

More messages that would also never be answered, Coulson thought, looking at the eighteen messages displayed before him. He recognised many of the names beside the messages. Friends of Amy's, many of whom had been at the funeral earlier that day. He'd been struck by how many friends she'd had, touched by how many had come along to pay their respects.

He moved the cursor to the first message, wondering if he should actually open it. Even though his daughter was dead, this felt like an invasion of her privacy and the thought that she wasn't going to burst into the room screaming at him for meddling with her personal effects only served to hurt him more. He would have given anything in the world to have her burst in now yelling at him, demanding he leave her room. One single tear welled in his left eye and rolled down his cheek.

'I'm sorry, princess,' he whispered under his breath.

He clicked on the first message and opened it. Dated the morning after his daughter had taken her own life it had been sent by a girl called Charlotte Stone. Coulson remembered her. Pretty girl with long dark hair. She worked as a waitress in a café in Walston. She'd been friends with Amy since primary school and she'd been at the funeral that day.

```
Why has he done this to you? I told you
he was a bastard. I think we should have
word with him. They're all the same at
that school . . . Spoiled rich brats.
     Love Charlie.
```

Coulson ran a hand through his hair and opened the next message. Like Charlie's first communication, this one was also dated the day after Amy's death.

```
I looked at what Latham did on those
websites. He is such a fucking bastard.
You have got to stop seeing him. I know
it's none of my business but you can't
let people treat you like that. Especially
not Latham. He is a pig.
     Love Charlie.
```

The third message was junk e-mail. So was the fourth and the fifth was notification that Amy's order of a pair of brand-new skinny jeans had just been despatched. Coulson scrolled down and found another message from Charlotte Stone.

```
I know you've already seen it and I looked
at the videos he posted on Youtube and
that porn one. What a fucking sick
bastard. Call me. I rang earlier and left
a message. We need to talk.
     Love Charlie.
```

He read two more messages from Charlotte Stone, both of them listing names of websites that Amy should look at. He had no idea why.

Now Coulson began to cry, the tears coursing down his cheeks as he sat at his daughter's desk. He made no attempt to wipe them away but merely clicked on the websites mentioned in the e-mail. It didn't take him long to find them.

By the time he'd watched the films with his daughter in, he was sobbing uncontrollably. But, as well as sorrow, Frank Coulson was enveloped by the most intense anger he'd felt for many years.

He glared at the name of Andrew Latham, his teeth gritted furiously together.

51

Andrew Latham took a sip from the can and scanned the screen of his laptop, checking what he'd written.

He nodded approvingly to himself and got to his feet. He took a couple of steps across his room and eased up the volume on his stereo. He looked at the selection of CDs beside the unit, selecting the one he would play next.

It was then that his phone rang.

Latham checked his expensive watch and saw that it was almost eleven fifteen.

The phone continued to vibrate on the desk, set on silent as it usually was.

Latham returned to the desk and picked it up. He didn't recognise the number but flipped it open and accepted the call anyway.

For long moments he didn't speak and it seemed like more of an afterthought when he finally opened his mouth.

'Hello,' he said.

'Is this Andrew Latham?' the voice at the other end of the line asked.

'Who wants to know?' he enquired, not recognising the voice. It was someone much older than himself, that much he knew but otherwise he was oblivious of the identity of the caller.

'My name's Coulson,' the caller told him. 'Frank Coulson. You knew my daughter, Amy.'

'Did I?'

'Don't try to be a smartarse with me, sunshine,' Coulson snapped. 'You know bloody well who she was.'

'I know a lot of people and I'd appreciate it if you didn't swear at me over the phone. I haven't done anything to you.'

'You did plenty to my daughter though, didn't you, you little bastard? You and your rich fucking friends.'

'Now wait a minute, old man, I didn't do a thing to your daughter.'

'I saw the videos. I looked at what you put on the internet. I saw how you humiliated her. All of you.'

'I don't know what you're talking about,' grinned Latham.

'I found your name on her computer and on her phone. I saw the flowers you sent to her funeral. I saw what you wrote on the card.'

'I'd have thought you'd have appreciated the flowers.'

'Why did you have to write a message like that?'

'You saw the videos, I would have thought that was obvious.'

'You little bastard. She killed herself because of what you made her do.'

'I didn't make her do anything. Now would you mind telling me why you're bothering me at this time of night?'

'I wanted you to know that you're not going to get away with what you did. None of you.'

'This is harassment you know. I could have you arrested for this. Now go away.'

'This isn't over, Latham.'

'Am I supposed to be frightened?'

'I couldn't give a fuck who your father is and how much money he's got. Those bloody teachers at that school might treat you and all your little friends like you're something special, but not me. I want to talk to you. I want to know why you hurt my Amy. I'll go to the police if I have to.'

'And tell them what? That your daughter knew me and some of my friends? I'm sure they'll be very impressed.'

'Perhaps I'll speak to that headmaster of yours, tell him what you're like.'

'I think he already knows,' grinned Latham.

'I told you, you won't get away with this.'

'Listen, I appreciate the call but it's late and I'm tired.'

'Fuck you.'

'No, fuck you,' Latham snarled. 'And don't blame me because your daughter was a slut.'

He snapped the phone shut and banged it down onto the desk.

It rang again almost immediately and he smiled to himself as he lifted it up and glanced at the number. Coulson calling again. Latham shook his head and slid the phone into one of the desk drawers, covering it with a sweatshirt so he couldn't hear the buzzing as it vibrated against the wood.

He walked across to his bed and lay on it, gazing out of the window into the night.

The phone rang three more times before he finally drifted off to sleep.

52

Mason was standing behind his desk as he watched them file into the classroom.

Immaculate in their expensive uniforms, some carrying books in bags that cost as much as his monthly wage. They were the oldest pupils at Langley Hill and also the most senior that he'd taught on this first day. The other lessons had gone smoothly enough and Mason had been delighted at how well the lessons had worked out and at how polite the pupils had been. He'd had to raise his voice a couple of times to quieten some of the more excitable among them but, other than that, his first day had been uneventful. Enjoyable even.

Now as he watched the older pupils take up position behind their desks he regarded them evenly, nodding greetings occasionally when one of them smiled at him. He waited until the last one was in position, standing obediently behind their desks then he motioned for them to be seated. They did so with the minimum of noise, settling themselves until every one of them sat looking appraisingly at him.

It was a class of twelve, split evenly between girls and

boys. Mason moved to the front of his desk and perched unceremoniously on it.

'Good afternoon,' he said.

'Good afternoon, sir,' they chorused in almost fault-less unison.

'My name is Peter Mason and, as I'm sure you're aware, I'm new here at Langley Hill so, if I get things wrong occasionally perhaps you'll help me out.' He looked at the class before him. 'If you can tell me your names that would help. Then at least I'll know who I'm shouting at.'

There were several chuckles and Mason smiled to himself.

'Let's start with you,' he said, pointing at a boy seated near to the front of the room.

'George Parry, sir,' the boy told him.

Mason nodded and looked at the girl seated at the next desk. He recognised her striking good looks from somewhere and he was conscious not to gaze too intently at her.

'Samantha Bell, sir,' she told him. 'But I prefer Sammi.'

Again Mason nodded.

'I'll remember that,' he said.

'Precious Moore, sir,' the next girl told him.

'Josephine Campbell, sir,' the girl with the light brown hair informed him.

'Or Jo, perhaps?' Mason offered. This girl too was little short of stunning and, again, as with the blonde, there was something vaguely familiar about her.

You saw her and the blonde the day you came for the inter-view here.

The girl nodded and smiled.

The introductions continued until Mason came to the last figure in the room. Tall, shoulder-length hair and a swarthy complexion.

220

'Andrew Latham, sir,' the boy said, languidly.

Mason nodded again, hoping that his expression had not betrayed him when he heard the name.

So, you're the one I've got to watch out for, are you?

'Right, now that we've introduced ourselves, perhaps we should do some work,' Mason said.

There were a few groans.

'Unless there are any questions before we get started,' he smiled.

'What kind of questions, sir?'

The words came from Felix Mackenzie.

'Anything you want to ask me?' Mason told him. 'Anything you're concerned about. I know it's not always easy for a class when a new teacher takes over.'

'We call them masters here, sir,' Mackenzie told him. 'Not teachers.'

There were some subdued giggles.

'Thanks for putting me straight on that, Felix,' Mason said. 'I'll try to remember it.'

'What did your pupils call you at your last school, sir?' Mackenzie enquired.

'Some called me Peter, some called me Mister Mason,' the teacher informed him. 'What they called me behind my back I'd rather not know.'

More good-mannered laughter.

'Will you be picking up where Mr Usher left off with our work, sir?' Sammi Bell enquired.

'How far had he got? You were studying the rise of Napoleon, weren't you?' Mason continued.

'We'd got as far as his coronation,' Jo Campbell explained.

'Anyone remember the date of that?' Mason asked. 'Without looking at your books.'

'December the 2nd, 1804.'

Mason knew that the answer had come from Latham even without looking up.

'Very good, Andrew,' he said.

Latham looked back impassively at him.

'That date is quite prophetic as far as Napoleon is concerned because one year later he would fight one of his greatest ever battles on the same date. Does anyone know which one?'

'Austerlitz,' Latham said, unhesitatingly.

'Excellent, Andrew,' Mason said. 'Have you been practising so you can impress me?' He smiled.

'Do I need to impress you then, sir?' Latham said, quietly.

'Hopefully you'll all impress me with your ability to learn,' Mason told them. 'Now, shall we get on?'

'You said we could ask you some questions, sir.'

Mason turned in Latham's direction when he heard the words.

'What did you want to ask me, Andrew?' he enquired.

'How did you get this job here at Langley Hill, sir?' Latham wanted to know.

'The headmaster obviously thought I was the best man for the job,' Mason told him.

'Do you think you're the best man for the job, sir?' Latham continued.

'I hope I'm as good as Mr Usher was,' Mason said, smiling.

'What makes you think he was any good, sir? If he was that good he'd still be here, wouldn't he?' Latham said, flatly.

'How did you all get on with Mr Usher?' Mason wanted to know.

No one spoke.

'Did you like him?' the teacher persisted.

'Does it matter, sir?' Latham offered. 'We're here to learn, not to make friends with our masters.'

There was some subdued laughter.

Smartarse little bastard, thought Mason.

'Some of us made friends with him, sir,' said Felix Mackenzie, impassively.

There was more laughter.

'Do you like living in his house, sir?' Precious Moore enquired. 'It must be better than having to live in the town.'

'Walston seems like a nice place,' Mason told her. 'Why don't you like it?'

'The people are common, sir,' Precious Moore told him. 'They've got no style.'

'Or money,' Jude Hennessey echoed.

The others laughed.

'You can't judge people on how much money they've got,' Mason said. 'Just because someone's rich it doesn't make them a better person than someone with nothing.'

'Are you a communist, sir?' Hennessey smirked. 'That's the kind of thing a communist would say.'

'I believe that everyone should have a roof over their heads and a good job. Does that make me a communist?' Mason stated.

'I suppose where you come from everyone is poor, sir,' Felix Mackenzie offered. 'You used to teach in a state school, didn't you?'

'Yes I did and the kids I taught weren't that much different from you guys,' Mason explained. 'Their parents didn't have as much money as your parents but they were still just kids.'

'Do you mean chavs, sir?' Mackenzie added to another chorus of laughter.

'What do you mean by chavs?' Mason challenged.

223

'Council house and violent,' Latham interjected. 'That's what chav means.'

There was more derisory laughter.

'You can't brand everyone who lives in a council house with a tag like that, Andrew,' the teacher said.

'So, do you like Mr Usher's house, sir?' Precious Moore asked again.

'It's a very nice cottage,' Mason told her. 'But it wasn't Mr Usher's. It belongs to the school.'

'He thought it was his,' Latham stated. 'He thought he owned it. He thought he was more important than he really was. Lots of people are like that, aren't they, sir? They think they're something but they're really nothing.'

Mason regarded the boy evenly and Latham held his gaze. The remainder of the class were silent.

'Do you think your wife would have liked it, sir?' Latham asked, a slight grin on his lips. 'If you'd still been together?'

Mason could feel his heart beating a little quicker, the anger building steadily within him.

'I think that's enough questions,' he said, with an air of finality. 'Time we did some work.' He turned his back on the class for a moment and retreated behind his desk where he picked up a piece of chalk and began writing on the blackboard.

'Miss Wheeler liked the cottage, sir,' Latham continued. 'She must have, she spent enough time there.'

53

For a moment, Mason didn't turn around. He heard Latham's words but didn't turn to face the boy, not wanting him to see the look of surprise on his face.

'You know who we mean, don't you, sir?' Latham continued. 'Miss Wheeler. She teaches geography. She's Irish.'

Finally, forcing a slight smile, Mason stepped away from the board and faced the class.

'I know who you mean,' Mason said, quietly. 'You shouldn't be disrespectful about other masters and mistresses, Andrew.'

'I wasn't being disrespectful, sir,' Latham opined. 'I was just telling you something in case you didn't know.'

'Do you know Miss Wheeler, sir?' Mackenzie interjected. 'Have you met her yet? She's very pretty.'

'I know Miss Wheeler,' Mason exclaimed. 'But that's not really any of your business, is it?'

'I thought that masters weren't supposed to fraternise,' Latham laughed.

The other class members laughed as well.

'What makes you think that Miss Wheeler and Mr

Usher were friends?' Mason asked, trying to control his irritation.

'I think they were more than friends, sir,' Sammi Bell offered.

'Even if any of this is true, it's got nothing to do with us, has it?' Mason said, defiantly. 'What masters get up to in their spare time is their own business.'

'I don't think Mr Grant would agree with you, sir,' Mackenzie added. 'He doesn't like that kind of thing.'

'Thanks, Felix, I'll try to remember that,' Mason sighed.

'Do you think Miss Wheeler is nice, sir?' Sammi continued, flicking at her blonde hair. 'I think she is. She takes us for games. She's got a gorgeous body. Sometimes in the changing room she just walks around barefoot in her top and shorts.' She looked directly into Mason's eyes and smiled. 'I don't think she wears anything under her top because when her nipples are hard you can see them clearly under the material. They're really big. They must be so sensitive when she's turned on.'

'Sammi,' snapped Mason. 'That's enough.'

'You sound like a lesbian, Sammi,' Jude Hennessey chided.

'You wish,' Felix Mackenzie added, grinning.

The rest of the class laughed.

'She has got a great body,' Jo Campbell added, glancing derisorily at the American. 'I think so too. I can see why men find her so attractive. Her accent's sexy too. I'd sleep with her and I'm not gay.'

Mason swallowed hard.

'Prove it,' Hennessey leered.

'Let's get back to work,' Mason insisted.

'Do you think her accent's sexy, sir?' Jo wanted to know.

'Right, that's it,' Mason snapped, uncomfortably.

'It's a shame about her father, isn't it, sir?' Latham intoned.

Again Mason shot Latham a penetrating glance but found it returned almost unblinkingly.

'I mean, he's not going to get better now, is he?' the boy continued. 'They can't cure Alzheimer's. And it must be so frustrating for her, having to see him like that. His mind going a little bit more every day.'

'I'm not going to tell you again,' the teacher said, firmly. 'There's work to do. We're not here to discuss other members of staff. Let's get on.' Again he turned his back on the class, the knot of muscles at the side of his jaw pulsing angrily.

Behind him, Latham smiled triumphantly.

54

The staff room at Langley Hill was cavernous. There was no other word to describe it, Mason thought. The ceiling was high and vaulted, the beams exposed like the ribs of some prehistoric monolith. The walls were lined with bookshelves all creaking under the weight of tomes that seemed to date back as far as the origins of the building itself.

There was a large oak table in the centre of the room around which several high-backed seats were arranged. There were armchairs and two old sofas in the rest of the room, some worn and faded, others recently re-upholstered. The air smelled of stale coffee, old books and polished wood.

'Went the day well?'

The voice startled him and he turned to see who'd spoken the words.

There was a portly man standing behind him. He was dressed in a baggy grey suit and a bright-yellow knitted waistcoat that clashed horribly with the pink shirt and striped tie he also sported. He had short black hair and large eyes that reminded Mason of a wounded Labrador.

'Your first day?' the man repeated in his somewhat hushed tones. 'How did it go? Didn't kill any of the little bastards, did you?'

'I didn't know that was allowed,' Mason said, smiling.

'Only if their school fees aren't up to date,' the newcomer told him, extending a pudgy hand by way of welcome. 'Richard Holmes,' the man added. 'English.'

'Peter Mason. History,' he offered, shaking the hand warmly. 'Any little bastards in particular who I might have killed?' Mason enquired.

Holmes chuckled.

'There's several in year seven,' he admitted. 'Vile shrieking brats that they are.'

'I was thinking more of year eleven,' Mason offered. 'Andrew Latham in particular.'

'You'll have to get in the queue if you want to string him up, my friend.'

Holmes sipped at his coffee, winced and nodded in the direction of the staff room door.

'Fancy a walk?' he asked. 'I haven't had a smoke since this morning and if you light up in here then you instantly become more of a health threat than the bubonic plague.' He gestured towards some of the other teachers in the room. 'Most are non-smokers. I'm one of the few who's still happy to wave the flag as a social pariah. I'd give up too but I'm terrified of becoming like them.'

Mason grinned.

'Follow me,' Holmes instructed. 'Our vice has been catered for.'

The two men walked out into the corridor, past several locked classroom doors and out into the late afternoon air, emerging in a high-walled garden that sported several heavy wooden benches and tables.

'Our faults are well hidden here,' he remarked, gesturing

229

to the towering walls around them. 'God forbid any of the little darlings should see we suffer from such common failings. Though I dread to think what some of them get up to in their rooms when backs are turned and the lights are out.'

Mason smiled warmly, already impressed with his new colleague.

Holmes reached into his jacket pocket and retrieved a pack of cigarettes, lighting one up with his disposable lighter. He offered one to Mason who took it gratefully, taking a deep drag on it.

The two men walked across to the nearest wooden bench and sat down.

'There are others who are as addicted as we,' Holmes told him with mock disdain. 'But they try to hide it. Some are ashamed to show their weakness. Unlike me. And, also, apparently, you, o blessed newcomer.'

Mason's grin widened.

'How long have you taught here?' he wanted to know.

'Since dinosaurs ruled the car park,' Holmes breathed. 'A long, long time. I came here from university about thirty-five years ago and I've been here ever since. I'm one of the longest-serving members of staff, so I'm told. The headmaster usually informs people of that fact when introducing me. As if merely surviving for that amount of time in this establishment is worthy of praise.'

'And is it?'

'To some.'

They sat in silence for a moment, comfortable with the solitude around them and with each other's company.

'You mentioned Andrew Latham inside,' Mason said, finally. 'What do you know about him?'

'What do I need to know? He comes from money. His family are rich and Master Latham is never slow to remind people of that fact. But he wouldn't be the only one here like that. He's an irritatingly intelligent little bastard and he knows it. Be careful with him.'

'You're not the first one to warn me about him. Kate Wheeler told me to keep an eye on him and his little group.'

'Ah, the ethereal Miss Wheeler,' Holmes said, smiling wryly. 'Our Gaelic temptress from the Emerald Isle. She's a lovely woman. If I was twenty years younger and she wasn't so choosy I may well be interested myself. Caught your eye, has she? You wouldn't be the first.'

'She is very attractive if that doesn't sound too un-professional, talking about colleagues that way,' Mason admitted. 'And she's been very friendly. She called in over the weekend to help me move in.'

'Of course, you've got the cottage?'

'Do you live at the school?'

'Yes. I reside as a prisoner in this place where I am employed.'

'After thirty-five years, there can't be much that goes on here that you don't know about.'

Holmes shrugged.

'It's hard to avoid some of what happens, my friend,' he said, quietly.

'How well did you know Simon Usher? The guy I replaced. No one seems to want to talk about him.'

Again Holmes shrugged.

'A personable enough young man,' he began.

'Why did he leave?' Mason enquired.

'If I knew I'd tell you. I saw him two days before he left. He told me he wanted to speak to me about something but he wouldn't be specific as far as the subject.'

'I found some of his things in the cellar of the cottage

when I was moving in. There were photos and letters too. Boxes and boxes full of stuff.'

'Such as?'

'You can have a look if you want to. You can walk down to the cottage with me later and I'll show it to you.'

Holmes nodded and got to his feet.

'There you are.'

The voice made both men turn and, as they did, they saw Nigel Grant advancing towards them. The headmaster's smile faded slightly when he saw that Holmes was in the process of stubbing out his cigarette.

'Excuse me, Richard,' Grant said. 'I wanted to speak to our new addition about his first day, gather his impressions and see how he's settling in.'

'Be my guest, Headmaster,' Holmes announced. 'I have work to do anyway.'

'What about that drink?' Mason said, raising his eyebrows as he looked at the retreating English teacher. 'You can come down to the cottage tonight about eight if you want to.'

Holmes nodded.

'Yes, our drink,' he intoned. 'I'll certainly take you up on that offer.' Behind Grant's back he raised his thumb conspiratorially before saying goodbye to the headmaster and disappearing back through the door leading from the high-walled garden.

'Good to see you making friends with the other staff, Peter,' Grant enthused. 'Richard's one of our more senior staff. I'm sure he'll be able to help you with any aspect of life and work here at Langley Hill.'

'That's what I'm hoping,' Mason said.

55

'If my boss sees me I'll get the sack.'

Charlotte Stone stood beside the table inside the Cottage Loaf café, looking down helplessly at Frank Coulson.

'I need to speak to you, Charlotte,' Coulson explained. 'I saw the e-mails you sent to Amy just before she died. I saw the videos.' He sighed deeply, almost painfully. 'I know what happened. I need you to tell me why and how it happened.'

'Mr Coulson, I can't sit and talk to you,' Charlie said, looking over her shoulder in the direction of the counter. 'I'm not allowed to. I'm supposed to be working.'

'Have you had your break yet?'

She looked bemused for a moment.

'You're entitled to a break, aren't you?' Coulson persisted. 'Well, take it now. If anyone asks, tell them you're having your break. You're having a coffee and you're having it with me.' He looked up imploringly at her. 'Please, Charlie.'

She hesitated a moment then sat down at the table beside him. She put down her order pad, rolled up the sleeves of her tight white blouse and sat forward.

'What do you want to know?' she asked.

'Who's Andrew Latham?' Coulson enquired.

'He goes to Langley Hill, you know that posh boarding school just outside Walston.'

'How did Amy know him?' Coulson continued.

'Him and his mates they come into the town quite a bit, like a lot of those snotty kids do. Some of them are all right but they're a bit stuck up. Think they're better than us.' She smiled humourlessly. 'Amy and I were out one Saturday night. We were having a drink in a pub and Latham and some of the others came in and started talking to us.'

'Which pub?' Coulson interrupted.

'The Vine. Latham said he always goes in there. They have live music on Saturday nights.'

'I know the one,' Coulson interjected again. 'Was that the first time you'd met him?'

Charlie nodded.

'He seemed all right,' she went on. 'He was chatting to us and he had two girls with him, really pretty girls. They were dressed in designer stuff and they were telling us about their lives when they were at home and where they went for their holidays and all that. We thought it was great. Really interesting. Nothing like our lives.' She smiled thinly, almost sadly. 'They stayed with us all night, buying us drinks and that. We agreed to meet up with them there the next week. That was when Latham invited us to this party he said they were having up at the school.'

Coulson listened intently.

'He told us that they could do what they liked up there as long as they didn't disturb the teachers,' Charlie continued. 'So we went along.'

'What happened?'

Charlie hesitated, swallowing hard. She began picking

nervously at her fingernails, not so eager to make eye contact with Coulson any more.

'Charlie,' Coulson insisted. 'Was that when the video was shot?'

'No,' she said, quickly. 'Not that first time.'

'So tell me what happened the first time.'

'Me and Amy both had too much to drink,' she sighed. 'They had drugs there too. Coke and ecstasy. We took some.' She looked at him guiltily. 'We'd tried it before. Things happened. I mean, we were both off our faces.' She glanced down as if unable to look at him. 'Amy told me afterwards that she really liked Andrew Latham. She saw him two or three more times after that. Not proper dates but, well, you know.'

'She was sleeping with him?' Coulson stated, flatly.

Charlie nodded.

'He told her he'd let her meet his parents,' she breathed. 'That he'd take her on holiday with him, buy her expensive things. All that kind of shit. I couldn't believe that Amy fell for it but she really liked him.'

Coulson briefly clenched his fists under the table.

'So when was the video shot?' he asked through clenched teeth.

'I don't know. He invited us to another party up there but I couldn't make it, I had to see my nan that night – she wasn't well. I told Amy not to go but she really fancied Latham. She said she'd go on her own. That must have been when it happened. She would have done anything for him, Mr Coulson, and he knew that. He just took advantage of her. They all did. I'm really sorry.'

'It's not your fault, Charlie.'

They sat in silence for a moment then Coulson looked up wearily.

'What about the others?' he said. 'There were others

in the video and you said that Latham had two girls with him the first time you met him. What do you know about them?'

'Only their names. Sammi Bell and Jo Campbell. I don't know who the others were in the video.' Her voice tailed off. 'You'd have to ask Latham.'

'I intend to,' breathed Coulson.

They sat looking awkwardly at each other for a moment longer then Charlie got to her feet.

'I'd better get back to work,' she said, apologetically.

Coulson nodded.

'Just one more thing, Charlie,' he said as she prepared to walk away. 'I know you weren't there that night but do you think Latham was the one who made the video? I know he put it on the internet but do you know if he filmed it? If he actually held the camera?'

'That first time we went there they were taking photos too,' Charlie confessed. 'On their cameras and with their phones and that but Latham wasn't doing it. He took some pictures but that was it. Like I said, we were off our faces anyway, when they mentioned doing a video of us we were up for it but it wasn't Latham who brought the camera in. It was an older woman.'

'How much older?'

'She was in her thirties but she was really fit. Blonde haired and really slim. She didn't join in. She did whatever Latham told her to do.'

'And you don't know who she was?'

'No. She had quite a strong accent though. I think it was Irish. She was the one who filmed us that night.'

236

56

'And you found these in the cellar?' said Richard Holmes, slowly sliding each Polaroid back into the bundle he'd been handed.

'There's loads of stuff down there' Mason told him, sipping from his can of beer. 'It can't all be his. There's too much of it.'

Holmes, now more casually attired in a pair of brown cords, black leather loafers and a voluminous knitted cardigan over his striped shirt, nodded sagely and continued leafing through the pictures. He shifted position on the leather sofa, reaching for his wine glass.

'Well, I'm not an expert, my friend,' he murmured, his eyes still fixed on the images before him. 'Certainly not on the subject of animal killing. What the recently departed Mr Usher is doing with a butchered dog in his garden I have no idea.'

'Killing the dog's bad enough. I want to know who he got to take the picture. Any ideas? How well did you know him? Do you know who he was friendly with?'

'You mean do I know any of his acquaintances who

237

might have been happy to take photos of him standing over a butchered dog?'

'Yes.'

'We talked most days,' Holmes said, shrugging his shoulders. 'It's a little hard to avoid one's colleagues in such a closed environment, as you'll see, but I didn't know the details of his private life if that's what you mean. With him living here, he had more privacy than those of us who have quarters inside the school itself. He could have been up to all sorts and no one would have known.' Holmes leaned forward and spread some of the pictures of Usher out across the coffee table before him. 'You said you found some notebooks and papers too. Have you read them yet? I wondered if there might be any clue in those as to what was going on here.'

'I've looked through some of them but I couldn't find anything useful. It was all inconsequential day-to-day stuff. Nothing out of the ordinary.' Mason let out a long breath. 'Except for one thing. In several places in his notebooks, Usher mentions a name. William Bartholomew. Was that a teacher or pupil at Langley Hill?'

Holmes frowned.

'In what connection does he mention the name?' he wanted to know.

'There's nothing too specific,' Mason explained. 'But there's usually talk of money with the name.'

'It doesn't ring a bell,' he admitted at first but then he raised his eyebrows and nodded, a smile flickering across his lips. 'Unless he's talking about Abbot Bartholomew, God bless him.'

'Who's he?'

'Being a history teacher, my boy, I thought you'd have known.'

Holmes drained what was left in his wine glass and replaced the receptacle on the table. Mason refilled it immediately.

'Abbot William Bartholomew,' the older man went on, good-naturedly. 'He was burned in 1535, along with six of his companions.'

'It wasn't uncommon for priests or monks to be put to death in that time,' Mason offered. 'When Henry VIII ordered the dissolution of the monasteries any clerics who resisted were executed. But that doesn't explain why Usher would be mentioning a man in his notebooks who died during the Reformation. And why the connection with money?'

'Perhaps he'd heard about the treasure.' Holmes drank some more wine. 'Or the curse.'

'Now you are taking the piss,' Mason grunted.

Holmes shrugged.

'Abbot Bartholomew and his companions weren't executed by the agents of Henry VIII, they were burned alive by the people of Walston.'

'Why?'

'Bartholomew and his cronies were said to be alchemists.'

'They were trying to turn base metal into gold?'

'According to local legend, they succeeded.'

'So why were they burned?'

'Because they had a slightly different method to everyone else for achieving their aim. Supposedly, they used some kind of sacrificial blood ritual to produce the change from base metal to gold. The secrets of this ritual had supposedly been given to them by God Himself. Apparently it involved the torture and flaying alive of small children.'

'God recommending the slaughter of kids so that

239

priests can become rich,' Mason said, laughing. 'Obviously an example of God moving in a mysterious way.'

Holmes nodded, took a sip of his wine and continued.

'A number of children had gone missing from the local villages and Abbot Bartholomew and his companions were suspected. The locals stormed the monastery and apparently found the bodies of two dozen children hanging from the walls and ceiling of the monastery. All flayed. All with their throats cut and their hearts and entrails removed. They dragged the occupants of the monastery outside and burned them on the spot. Then they razed the place to the ground. Bartholomew and his followers belonged to some kind of order, cult for want of a better word, that believed people could be controlled by the strength of their libido. Manipulated by their sexual desire. Anyone with a particularly strong sexual urge could be controlled. The more powerful the urges, the easier they were to control. None of them ever had sex, naturally, because they were monks. They frowned upon it, not because they disapproved of its earthly pleasure, but because it took away their power. They achieved power through abstinence, if you like.'

'And they believed that?' Mason grunted.

'It's a noble belief,' Holmes joked.

'What about ley lines? The headmaster said the school was built on one.'

'On two to be exact,' Holmes corrected him. 'A confluence. Very unusual. But nothing to do with Abbot Bartholomew, I fancy. The poor old fellow can't be blamed for everything.'

'Like what?'

'There've been incidents over the years,' Holmes smiled. 'In and around the school. None of it conducive to the image of Langley Hill.'

'What kind of incidents?'

'When the school was being built there were a number of unexplained accidents involving the workmen here. Three were killed in a period of eighteen months. One reportedly went mad. Ghosts and apparitions were supposedly seen. More rumours. In the thirties, a number of local children went missing from Walston and a teacher here was blamed.'

'What happened to them?'

'No one knows. The bodies were never found.'

'They were murdered?'

'Rumours and gossip, my friend. During the war a stray German fighter plane crashed in the school grounds. The pilot got out safely but was supposedly caught and hanged from a tree in the grounds by a group of townspeople. They said he'd attacked and raped a local woman.' Holmes raised his hands. 'More rumour. More gossip.'

'What about the monks' treasure? The gold that Bartholomew supposedly made from base metal. Was it ever found?'

Holmes raised his eyebrows indulgently.

'A myth,' he explained. 'Nothing more.'

'So why would Usher mention it so many times in his notebooks?'

Holmes could only shrug.

'Perhaps he heard about it from another member of staff or one of the kids or even someone in the town. As I said, it's a well-known legend around here.'

'And the curse?'

'Stories passed down over the centuries say that Abbot Bartholomew cursed those who burned him. As the flames were licking around him he damned the villagers and all their descendants.' Holmes raised his hands to head height and wiggled his fingers in Mason's direction. 'Spooky, don't you think?'

'That still doesn't explain the dead dog in the picture with Usher,' Mason observed.

Holmes could only shrug.

'As I said, I have no idea what Usher got up to here,' he remarked. 'And to be honest, I don't really care.'

'Aren't you curious about his disappearance?'

'He didn't disappear, Peter. He left his job. Simple as that.'

'And what if it's not? What if there's more to it than that?'

'Then you are welcome to investigate what became of your predecessor. If you discover anything, I will be delighted to learn of your progress but I fear that there is far less to this situation than meets the eye.'

Mason exhaled wearily.

'You're probably right,' he conceded, tipping the last of the wine into Holmes's glass. He raised his own beer can in salute. 'Here's to Abbot Bartholomew.'

Holmes mirrored the gesture and both men smiled as they drank.

Outside, the wind whipped around the cottage and the first drops of rain began to fall.

57

It was after eleven by the time Richard Holmes left.

The portly English teacher teetered unsteadily up the path then made his way back up the driveway towards the school itself, ignoring both the rain and also Mason's offer of an umbrella.

Mason waved his new colleague off then locked the front door behind him, moving back through the cottage and switching off lights in his wake. He felt tired. It had been a long first day and he needed to get a decent night's sleep.

Before he retired though, he decided to return the boxes of photos to the cellar.

Good idea. Lock the bloody things away and forget about them.

He wandered through into the kitchen, dropping empty beer cans and wine bottles into the waste bin near the back door then he pulled open the hatch that led down into the cellar, flicking on the light that would illuminate the subterranean chamber.

He retrieved the boxes of photos from the sitting room, stacked them carefully on top of each other then made his way carefully down the stone steps into the cellar. He could hear the rain outside, beating down hard by now and, Mason thought, it was colder in the cellar than it had been before.

Just your imagination working overtime. All that bullshit about curses and mutilated kids.

He smiled to himself and replaced the boxes towards the far wall of the underground room.

He paused beside the other boxes that held Simon Usher's discarded belongings.

Move those too. Stick them out of the way so you won't be tempted to nose through them again. Just forget about Usher.

He bent down to lift them out of the way and noticed that the top one was open.

Just put it away. Close it and never touch it again.

There were several reams of paper inside. Letters. Bills. Circulars.

Christ, hadn't Usher thrown anything away?

Mason noticed that the topmost sheet of paper was headed and, despite himself, he read the heavy black letters.

WALSTON GENERAL HOSPITAL

Mason pulled the sheet from inside the box and scanned it.

'Notification of appointment,' Mason read aloud. There was a date beneath. 'What was wrong with you?' he muttered. He glanced down at the boxes, wondering if the answer lay within. He decided to find out.

58

Mason was lying on his back with just his pants on.

The girls were on either side of him.

Sammi to his right and Jo to his left. Both were dressed identically, clad in only white bras and white thongs, kneeling above him looking down expectantly. He felt their hands glide across his chest, stomach and thighs and the erection that was already pressing against the material of his pants grew even more prominent. Jo gripped it gently through the cotton as Sammi began to ease the garment from him. Mason lifted his hips to help her and she pulled the pants free, tossing them aside with a giggle.

Now totally naked he let out a deep breath as the two girls leaned forward and he looked longingly at them as they both ducked their heads towards his raging stiffness.

Their tongues met on his swollen penis head and he gasped as he felt the soft wetness caressing his tip, each tongue swirling around the bulbous end before gliding along his rock-hard shaft down towards his swollen testicles, then up again. They moved as one, a perfectly choreographed machine that existed only for his pleasure and he intended to enjoy every second of their attentions.

He allowed his hands to brush through their hair, one hand on each of them feeling the soft silkiness of the freshly washed manes beneath his probing digits. And all the time they licked and sucked at his throbbing stiffness with such fervour and expertise that Mason wondered how many times before they had performed such a ritual.

Jo held his penis, pushing it towards Sammi who fastened her soft lips around it. A moment or two of that ecstasy and Sammi raised her head, smiling up at him. Jo took him into her mouth, her tongue flickering over his throbbing tip while her lips engulfed him. He could feel light kisses on his thighs and hips then Sammi moved between his legs to lick at his scrotum and testicles, her long blonde hair caressing his flesh as surely as her mouth and fingers.

As Jo knelt beside him he ran his hand along her slender back, feeling the perfect smoothness of her young skin. Then his questing fingers moved further, sliding beneath the gusset of her white thong and slipping gently over her already moist sex. She sighed as he touched her, redoubling her efforts on his penis with her mouth and, for a moment, Mason thought he was going to lose control. The effect of these two girls upon him was incredible and he wanted to prolong this pleasure as long as he could.

As if a signal had been given, both girls knelt up and Mason watched as they kissed, tongues intertwining. Jo slipped Sammi's bra off to reveal her pert breasts with the nipples so pink and erect and then she reached back to repeat the action on herself so that her breasts too were exposed to his gaze. Mason reached up and cupped one in his hand, thumbing the stiff nipples one at a time.

Sammi wriggled quickly out of her thong and clambered onto his lap, gripping his penis in one hand, lowering her slippery cleft onto it with infinite slowness, wanting to tease him but also desperate to feel him inside her. Mason realised with delight that the girls were as desperate for release as he was.

Slipping off her own thong, Jo swung her slender leg over his face and lowered her glistening sex onto his lips, wanting him to taste her and he did so eagerly, lapping hungrily at her swollen clitoris. She gasped her approval loudly and pressed down a little harder onto his mouth.

Sammi began to move up and down on his penis, groaning her own pleasure as the sensations between her legs grew in intensity.

Mason reached up and held her breasts, squeezing and kneading the soft flesh, increasing her pleasure and she let out a loud gasp of pleasure.

It was stifled instantly as Sammi leaned forward and kissed her. The realisation that the two girls' mouths were locked together once again only served to intensify Mason's pleasure too and he grunted loudly as his own climax drew closer. He felt Sammi's muscles contracting around his shaft and felt her moving ever more rapidly upon him. She broke away from Jo's kiss to gasp her pleasure, now only seconds away from her orgasm. Jo too was panting continually as the furious passion inside her, coaxed closer by Mason's tongue, prepared to explode.

The moment came and Mason prepared himself for the ecstasy that was about to envelop him. His erection throbbed inside Sammi, his tongue lapped unceasingly at the swollen bud of Jo's clitoris and he heard them shout their pleasure, their slender young bodies shuddering as they climaxed.

Only then did he prepare to lose control, to pour his

247

fluid deep into Sammi. He was seconds from his peak, his heart pounding, his breath rasping in his throat.

And yet something stopped him from coming. Something prevented him from releasing his pent-up lust. As Jo lifted herself from his face he saw the third figure.

Kate Wheeler was standing naked at the bottom of the bed, her blonde hair unkempt, her slim body almost incandescent with desire. She had one hand between her slender legs, her fingers moving slowly over her clitoris. He wanted her next. He wanted her now.

She moved onto the bed between the two writhing girls.

Mason woke with a start.

He sat bolt upright in bed, the dream fading quickly from his mind.

He looked around him, almost expecting to see Sammi, Jo and Kate in the bedroom with him.

No such luck.

A dream. Pure and simple.

He looked down at his erection almost reproachfully.

A dream.

Outside, the wind was blowing. Howling around the cottage. The sound reminded him of mocking laughter.

59

Mason stood at the classroom window, gazing out across the vast playing fields, his gaze drawn to the football match that was going on in one distant section of the huge expanse of green.

But if his eyes were on the match, his mind wasn't. He hadn't slept much the previous night, unable to force away the thoughts of Simon Usher or, more particularly, of Sammi and Jo. He cast a wary glance at them as if fearing that they would somehow know the extent of his nocturnal flight of fantasy.

More secrets.

Behind Mason, the twelve class members worked away quietly and efficiently and the teacher finally made his way back towards his own desk where he sat down and regarded each of the pupils individually.

Sammi was sitting re-reading what she'd already written while Jo was hunched over her work scribbling away.

They don't look that much different to how they looked in your dream, do they? Except they're wearing clothes this time.

Mason tried to push the thoughts from his mind.

He concentrated on the other members of the class, gazing at each one in turn. He wasn't totally surprised when he saw that Andrew Latham was sitting with his hands clasped on his stomach gazing back at him.

'Have you finished, Andrew?' Mason asked.

'About five minutes ago, sir,' Latham answered.

'Then perhaps you could read the next chapter while everyone else finishes. Just so you've got something to do. Either that or you can come up here and clean this board for me.' Mason smiled.

'No thanks, sir,' Latham said, flatly.

'Just read the next chapter then.'

'I read it last night.'

Mason sucked in a breath.

'Then read the one after that,' he muttered.

'I have.'

'Then you won't mind me asking you some questions about it, will you?'

'Fire away,' Latham smirked. 'Fire away and fall back.'

Mason looked puzzled.

'It's a quote,' Latham told him. 'From a film called *The Long Riders*. Have you seen it, sir?'

'No, I don't think I have, Andrew.'

Some of the other pupils were now coming to the end of their essays and Mason could see pens being put down all over the class.

'It's a western,' Latham went on. 'So, it's history isn't it, sir? It's appropriate to this lesson.'

'We're supposed to be learning about Napoleon, not about the Wild West,' Mason reminded him. 'And certainly not about films. I don't think the headmaster would be very happy if he walked in and found me talking to you about films.'

'What sort of films do you like, sir?' asked Felix

Mackenzie. 'Do you like thrillers and horror films, that sort of thing?'

'Or romance and comedy?' added Jo Campbell.

'What about science fiction, sir?' Jude Hennessey wanted to know.

'I like all kinds of films,' Mason confided.

'What about porn films, sir?' Jo purred.

'That's enough,' Mason rasped, his words drowned by the laughter of the class.

'There's nothing wrong with sex, sir,' Jo continued.

There were some muted cheers from the rest of the class, silenced by a furious glare from Mason.

'What about sad films, sir?' Sammi Bell enquired. 'Films that make you cry?'

'You must have been sad when your daughter died, sir.'

The words hit Mason like a sledgehammer and, for brief seconds, all he could do was look blankly at Latham. The source of the comment.

'How do you know about my daughter?' Mason said, at last, his voice catching.

Latham merely smiled.

Mason took a step towards him, trying to control his temper but finding it difficult.

'How old was she, sir?' Precious Moore asked. 'I've got a little sister who's twelve and she's an absolute nightmare.'

'Be quiet,' Mason insisted, shooting a withering glance at the pale girl. He returned his attention to Latham who was still sitting there unmoved.

'I asked you a question,' the teacher snapped, his eyes still fixed on the youth. 'How do you know about my daughter?'

'Is it true then, sir?' Precious Moore added. 'Is your daughter dead?'

251

'What did she die of?' Felix Mackenzie wanted to know.

'Shut up,' roared Mason. 'All of you, just shut up.'

He stood before them, his face flushed, the veins at his temples throbbing ominously. Mason could feel his heart thumping so hard it threatened to burst from his ribcage. A heavy silence hung over the classroom and neither Mason nor any of the watching pupils was willing to break it.

'Don't ever mention my daughter again,' Mason finally breathed, his right index finger aimed at Latham. 'Never.'

The smile had faded slightly from the youth's lips but there was still defiance in his eyes.

'Now get out,' Mason added, turning his back on the class. 'The lesson's over.'

Precious Moore looked up at the clock above the blackboard and shrugged.

'There's still ten minutes before the bell, sir,' she bleated.

'The lesson's over,' Mason repeated.

One by one they filed from the classroom.

As he reached the door, Latham looked in Mason's direction and nodded.

'See you tomorrow, sir,' he said, quietly.

Mason didn't speak.

60

As Mason pushed a forkful of food into his mouth he gazed across the school refectory at the pupils who were having their lunch. There was a subdued, almost reverential quiet within the cavernous room, so different from what he'd always been used to as a teacher. However, as he cut another piece of beef, it wasn't the stillness within the refectory that was uppermost in his mind. He glanced around the room, one part of him hoping he didn't see Andrew Latham or any of the little group who hung around with him. The latest encounter had unsettled him and he was angry with himself for having allowed his temper to get the better of him in front of the class.

The question still bothered him though. How had Latham known about the death of Chloe? Was his business already common knowledge around the school? His past no more than a subject for gossip and idle chatter? How many people knew about his dead daughter? The headmaster and that was about it. How the hell had Latham discovered that painful part of his past?

Mason took a drink of water, wishing it was something stronger.

'Mind if I join you?'

Mason recognised the accent immediately and turned with a smile to see Kate Wheeler standing beside him.

Mason got to his feet and pulled the adjacent chair out for her, watching while she seated herself and set her food down.

'How's it going?' she asked him. 'Finding your feet?'

He nodded and finished chewing the mouthful of beef.

'You don't look too sure,' Kate offered, seeing how pale Mason appeared.

'A bit of a headache,' he told her. 'And that little bastard Andrew Latham.'

'I told you to watch out for him. What happened?'

'Another verbal clash.'

'He's testing you, Peter. He does that with every teacher.'

'Did he do it with you?'

She avoided eye contact but merely nodded.

'We should talk later,' she murmured.

'Where?'

'Dinner tonight at my flat?' She looked at him and smiled. 'We could have a drink first. There's some nice pubs in the town.'

'I thought you said we should take it easy for a week or two?'

'Well, seeing as I'm asking you let's call it quits.'

Mason smiled.

'There's a pub called the Vine,' Kate told him. 'You can't miss it. It's on the main road from here into town. I'll meet you there at eight. We can walk to my flat from there.'

'Invitation accepted. Thank you.'

'I hope that neither of you will object to the presence

of one much older and more feeble,' Richard Holmes said as he put down his plate opposite Mason and Kate.

They both smiled as Holmes joined them. He was wearing a dark-brown jacket and grey trousers illuminated by a bright-green knitted waistcoat and yellow tie.

'Richard, where do you get those waistcoats?' Mason asked.

'My sister used to knit them for me,' Holmes explained. 'Trouble was, she didn't just limit their distribution to birthdays and Christmas. Hence my inordinately large collection. Mind you, they are practical in the cold weather.'

'Where did your sister live?' Kate wanted to know.

'In Walston,' Holmes explained. 'I used to see her two or three times a week before she died.'

'Did Andrew Latham know about her?' Mason enquired. 'He seems to know every other bloody thing that goes on around here. Especially about the staff.'

Holmes looked briefly at Kate who met his gaze then looked away.

'He knew about your father,' Mason said to Kate. 'And he knew about my daughter too.'

'It's a very confined existence we lead here, I told you that before,' Holmes ventured. 'It isn't difficult for people to find out things about others if they're that determined.'

Kate touched Mason's thigh under the table and, when he looked at her, she shook her head gently.

'Little bastard,' Mason hissed, catching sight of Latham on the far side of the refectory.

'Forget him,' Kate urged.

Mason turned his attention back to his lunch.

'Can someone pass the salt, please?' he enquired.

No one did.

61

Mason was standing in the walled garden enjoying a cigarette when Nigel Grant approached him. The headmaster glanced disapprovingly at the cigarette Mason held then returned his attention to the matter in hand.

'I thought I'd find you here,' Grant exclaimed.

'I've not got a class until two, I thought I'd just clear my head,' Mason explained.

'That's fine, I didn't come here to check up on you, Peter. I've got some news that you will find relevant. It concerns one of your pupils.'

Mason raised his eyebrows.

'Andrew Latham,' Grant went on.

'What's he done now?'

'There've been problems with him for a while,' Grant began. 'Disobedience, disrespect and a growing feeling among the other teachers that he's, how can I put it, out of reach?'

Mason nodded.

'I will not allow disruptive influences such as Latham to flourish here at Langley Hill,' Grant said with an air befitting his authority. 'His behaviour could not be allowed to continue unchecked.'

Mason looked on expectantly.

'He's been expelled,' the headmaster went on. 'Effective immediately. He'll be off the premises before the end of the day.'

Mason took a step back.

'I only took him for a class this morning,' he said.

'I realise this has happened quickly but it's only the decision that has been taken swiftly. The thinking and reasoning behind it has gone on for many months. If he'd been allowed to remain here for much longer then his influence would have spread until it was out of control.'

'Have his family been informed yet?'

'Naturally. When they heard the circumstances they were in agreement with my decision. It won't be hard for them to find some other school to take him. Not with his intellect and with their money.'

'He was a clever kid.'

'But tainted.'

Mason frowned, surprised at the use of such an archaic word. He almost smiled until he saw the expression of anger set upon Grant's face.

'Tainted,' Mason repeated. 'Do the other teachers know?'

'Those whose classes he's in, yes. I informed them in the staff room earlier. That's why I came out here to find you. I knew you'd be here indulging your addiction.' He nodded in the direction of the cigarette.

Mason shrugged and took another drag.

'What reasons did you give his parents for his expulsion?' Mason enquired.

'The reasons I've just given you,' Grant told him. 'Does it really matter?'

'No, I suppose not. I was just curious.'

Grant glanced at his watch and prepared to retreat back inside the school.

'It's done now, Peter, it's over,' he said, curtly. 'He isn't the first pupil to be expelled and, unfortunately, he won't be the last. As I said before, I will not jeopardise the education of many children for the sake of one disruptive influence. The school is better off without him.'

He turned and left.

Mason was alone in the walled garden once more.

62

Mason guided the car into the tarmac area at one side of the Vine and switched off the engine. There were half a dozen other vehicles in the car park and the teacher checked his watch before swinging himself out from behind the wheel and walking towards the main entrance.

The pub was surrounded on three sides by trees that waved in the strong wind that had sprung up as afternoon had turned to evening. Now, with the time approaching eight o'clock and darkness having fully invaded the sky, the only light came from the windows of the pub and the dull sodium glare of the street lights that lit the main road leading into Walston itself. Mason shivered involuntarily as he walked, flipping up the collar of his leather jacket.

The Vine was a hybrid. The architecture was of the twenties as, Mason guessed, was the thick ivy that covered the stonework so comprehensively in places that it threatened to blot out the light from the windows. However, unlike most modern pubs, the Vine had not succumbed to the relentless torrent of gimmicks designed to pull in everyone from football fans to fruit-machine-playing youngsters. It had no widescreen TVs. It had just one fruit machine, a one-armed bandit that was a throwback to the sixties. There was a pool table but it wasn't used very often. Instead, the dart board was a more popular attraction. A more sedate game from a more sedate time. The Vine made few concessions to the electronic age and, despite this, it still attracted its share of younger customers (doubtless because of the hall at the rear of the building where live musicians performed three times a week) but, for the older inhabitants of Walston, it was something of an oasis of traditionalism among the plethora of plastic beams, micro-breweries and gastro-pubs that clogged the town itself.

Mason pushed open the main door and stepped inside, the warmth hitting him like a blanket. There was a small open fire blazing away in the grate to his left and he noticed several heads turn to inspect him as the occupants of the tables there glanced in his direction. Uninterested in him they continued with their subdued conversations and the teacher walked up to the bar, peering around for any sign of Kate Wheeler. He noticed that there was another bar through a set of thick red velvet curtains and he moved through into this smaller alcove.

There were two men sitting at the bar drinking, both of whom paid cursory attention to Mason as he walked in. The only other occupant of the bar, seated at a table close to a window, was Kate Wheeler.

She smiled happily at him as he walked across to her and she picked up her coat from the seat she'd been saving for him.

'I don't think anyone would have taken this seat,' she told him. 'But better safe than sorry.'

'I haven't kept you waiting, have I?' he asked.

'I've only been here a couple of minutes,' she assured him.

Mason leaned over and kissed her gently on the cheek.

She smelled of freshly laundered clothes, newly washed hair and a perfume that he couldn't identify but that he found captivating. That, combined with her perfectly made-up face and the tight black cowl-neck sweater she wore over equally skin-tight black jeans tucked into ankle boots, caused Mason to look admiringly at her for a moment. It was a gesture she wasn't slow to notice and she smiled broadly at him, enjoying the fact that the effort she'd put into her appearance had so obviously been appreciated.

'What can I get you?' he asked.

'Bacardi and diet coke, please.'

He nodded and walked back to the bar where a rotund, red-faced barmaid took his order.

The two men sitting at the bar took no notice of him as he waited for the drinks which he dutifully ferried back to the table.

'Cheers,' Kate pronounced and they both drank.

'I was going to get a bag of crisps but I thought I'd better not,' he told her.

'Don't you dare. Dinner's all prepared. As soon as we get back we can eat.'

Mason was aware of someone approaching their table. He didn't hear any footfalls or see anyone, he just felt the presence close to them.

He looked up to see one of the men who'd been sitting at the bar standing over them.

'You're from that school,' the man proclaimed, flatly.

Mason met the man's gaze and saw something burning in his eyes that looked like anger.

'Langley Hill,' the man repeated. 'I heard that you come from there.'

261

'That's right,' Mason explained.

'Both of you?' the man snapped.

Kate nodded and moved a little closer to Mason.

'We both teach there,' Mason told him. 'Why?'

'I need to talk to you,' the man said, pulling out a chair and seating himself opposite them.

'We're just trying to have a quiet drink,' Mason protested. 'I'm sure you understand.'

'I said I want to talk.'

Frank Coulson leaned forward menacingly.

63

Mason thought about telling Coulson to leave them alone but the determined look on the newcomer's face persuaded him to wait.

'Listen, I'm sure if you want to know anything about Langley Hill then we'll do our best to help you,' Mason began.

'There's lots of things I'd like to know about that place,' Coulson snapped. 'But, for the time being, you listen to me.'

The two teachers sat motionless while Coulson ran appraising eyes over each of them in turn.

'My daughter,' he said, his tone losing some of its venom. 'She died last week. Her name was Amy Coulson. She was seventeen.'

'I'm sorry to hear that,' Mason admitted. 'I lost my daughter too.'

Coulson fixed his gaze on Mason for a moment then continued.

'Amy killed herself,' he told them. 'Because of what was done to her by some of those little bastards up at that school where you both teach.'

'How can you be sure of that, Mr Coulson?' Mason ventured.

'It's true,' Coulson snapped. 'I spoke to one of the kids there on the phone. The one who caused it. Andrew Latham.'

Mason glanced briefly at Kate then returned his attention to Coulson's tortured features.

'He's about eighteen, this Latham kid,' Coulson went on. 'Spoilt, rich little fucker like all of those kids up there.'

'What makes you think that Latham caused your daughter to kill herself?' Mason asked.

'Because of what he did to her. He humiliated her. Tricked her into sleeping with him and then he filmed it and put the film on the fucking internet. That's the kind of kid you've got at that school of yours.'

Kate Wheeler moved a little closer to Mason, her heart thumping hard.

'What do you want us to do?' Mason asked, cautiously.

'I want to speak to Latham,' Coulson announced. 'I want to see that little cunt face to face and get him to tell me why he did that to my Amy.'

Mason nodded, placatingly.

'He was expelled today, Mr Coulson,' he said.

'That's not enough. He should be prosecuted for what he did to her. For what he made her do,' Coulson snarled, glaring at Kate who was eyeing him warily, the colour having drained from her cheeks.

'Do you know him too, this Latham kid?' Coulson wanted to know.

She nodded.

'Whatever you think he did to your daughter, Mr Coulson, I'm sorry,' she told the other man. 'And I'm sorry for your loss but my colleague is right.

264

Unless you've got evidence against Latham then there's nothing you can do. And he's gone now.'

Coulson looked evenly at her, listening carefully to each word.

'You're Irish, aren't you?' he stated.

'Don't hold that against me,' Kate said, falteringly, trying to force a smile to defuse the situation.

'And you teach up there, at Langley Hill?' he persisted.

'Yes,' she confessed. 'I don't see what my nationality has to do with what happened to your daughter though.'

The woman who held the camera had an accent. I think it was Irish.

Charlie Stone's words drifted into Coulson's head and stuck there like a splinter in soft flesh.

A strong Irish accent.

Coulson sat for a moment longer then he got to his feet.

'I won't let this go,' he said, menacingly. 'I want to talk to that fucking Latham kid and no one's going to stop me. If the police won't help me then I'll deal with it myself.'

He turned and walked out of the pub, slamming the door behind him as he left.

They both heard the roar of a car engine outside and Mason peered out of the window to see Coulson driving off.

64

Mason drained what was left in his wine glass and set the empty receptacle down on the coffee table before him.

He looked around the small sitting room where he was seated and smiled to himself. The meal he'd eaten had been delightful, the conversation had been good (once they'd both got over the meeting with Frank Coulson) and he could smell the pleasing aroma of coffee coming from the small kitchen behind him. He glanced around at the bookshelves covering three walls of the sitting room, his eyes also straying to some of the photos that shared space with the hundreds of paperbacks and hardbacks, DVDs and assorted other paraphernalia that was on display.

Mason hauled himself off the sofa and walked across to the nearest of the shelves. There were framed photos there. Some of Kate and, he assumed, of her family. Her image smiled back at him.

'Oh, no, not the photos.'

He turned as he heard her voice behind him.

Mason looked around and saw that she'd placed two

cups of coffee on the table by the sofa and was about to return to the kitchen.

'Sorry,' he said. 'I didn't mean to be nosy but I like the look of this one.' He held up a picture that showed Kate, he guessed aged around twenty-three, standing with two other young women, arms around each other. They were all dressed in bikinis and sporting suntans, beaming for the camera.

'That was taken in Italy,' she informed him. 'About two weeks after I got my degree. Myself and two friends went for a holiday there to celebrate.' She pointed to another blonde girl. 'That's Trisha and the dark one is Sasha.'

'Very nice,' Mason said, approvingly.

'Yes, they are, aren't they?' Kate said.

'I meant the photo,' Mason explained.

Kate smiled and shook her head then retreated briefly to the kitchen once again.

Mason replaced the picture and moved across to another. It showed an older man who was gazing un-smilingly back at the camera from a high-backed leather chair.

'That's my dad,' Kate informed him, solemnly, appearing at his side. 'It was taken about five years ago.'

'It's a good picture,' Mason told her.

'It just hurts to look at him there and then remember what he's like now.'

Mason nodded as he replaced the picture.

'I haven't got any pictures of my daughter on display in the cottage,' he said. 'But that doesn't mean I don't think about her. I hate old photos. I think that all they do is remind you of time you've lost that you can never get back.'

Kate squeezed his arm gently.

267

'Come and have your coffee,' she said and the two of them stepped back to the sofa and sat down.

'When was the last time you saw your dad?' he enquired. 'If you don't mind me asking.'

Kate shook her head.

'Of course I don't,' she told him. 'It was two days ago. He seems to be a little worse each time I see him and I know he's not going to get any better. The terrible thing is that I don't know how long he's going to be in the nursing home and it isn't cheap to keep him there.'

'How does Latham know about him?'

Kate ignored the question at first, more intent on sipping her coffee.

'I know he seems to know everything that's going on at Langley Hill but how did he find out about your father's illness?' Mason continued.

He studied her expression for a moment and thought he saw tears welling in her eyes.

'Kate?' he said, softly, reaching out one hand and resting it on her arm. 'How did Latham find out about your father?'

She exhaled almost painfully and looked straight at Mason.

'If it wasn't for Latham, my father would probably be dead by now,' she said, flatly. 'He pays for the nursing home where he is now.'

65

Mason was stunned.

For a moment he wasn't sure if he'd even heard Kate correctly.

'Andrew Latham pays for your dad's treatment?' he said, finally. 'But how? Why?'

'Because I can't afford it myself,' Kate told him.

Mason shook his head.

'I understand that,' he told her, agitatedly. 'But Latham? How did this all happen?'

She took a sip of her coffee then set the cup gently back on the table.

'I was desperate,' she breathed. 'I don't know how Latham heard what was wrong with my father but he volunteered the money.'

Mason listened intently.

'I said no to begin with, of course,' she went on. 'Apart from the complications and the conflict of interests and breaking God alone knows how many ethical considerations. I didn't want to be in debt to anyone. Especially not someone like Latham.' She licked her lips. 'But I took the money. I accepted his offer. I had no choice.

I love my father and I couldn't see him just left to die.
Left to shrink away.'

Mason nodded.

'I understand,' he murmured.

'I'm not sure you do,' she snapped. 'If someone had
offered you a way of saving your daughter wouldn't
you have taken it? Wouldn't you have done anything
to help her?'

'Yes I would.'

'And it's the same with my father. I know he won't
get better but at least he'll have the best care that money
can buy. Or should I say that Latham's money can buy.
And I'd do it all again if I had to.'

'How much did he lend you?'

'That's not important. The money isn't the issue, it's
what it can buy.'

'So you pay Latham back a bit at a time?'

She nodded.

'Who else knows about this?' Mason persisted.

'No one.' She sighed. 'Well, possibly Latham's little
group but I haven't told anyone else except you.'

'What about Simon Usher? Did he know about it?'

'What the fuck has it got to do with Simon Usher?'
she snapped. 'You're obsessed with him. Why would I
tell him?'

'Because Latham said you used to spend a lot of time
at his cottage. I just wondered.'

'Wondered what?' she cut in angrily. 'Wondered if I
was sleeping with him? Would it have mattered if I was?
He's gone now, isn't he? Anyway, why would you believe
anything that Latham said about me? Are you going to
trust his word over mine?'

'Kate,' Mason said, putting a hand out to calm her. 'I
just asked.'

She got to her feet and walked back into the kitchen out of sight. Mason ran a hand through his hair and exhaled wearily. Moments later, Kate returned carrying a bottle of Jack Daniel's and two glasses.

'I would have offered you more coffee,' she told him, slumping down on the sofa beside him once more. 'But I thought I needed something stronger.'

'I'm sorry,' he told her. 'I didn't mean to pry. I'm just telling you what Latham said. And hearing about you borrowing money from him was a bit of a shock too. What are you going to do now he's been expelled? How are you going to get the money to him?'

'I'll find a way,' she murmured.

They looked at each other silently for a moment.

'Truce?' he asked, his hands in the air in supplication. She nodded.

'If there's anything I can do to help, Kate,' Mason said.

'I'll manage. I have done so far.'

'And what if you can't? What then?'

'I'll be fine.'

She filled a glass and pushed it towards him. Mason hesitated a moment then took it and sipped at the liquor.

'Perhaps if we found Abbot Bartholomew's treasure you could pay Latham off,' he said, quietly.

66

It was Kate Wheeler's turn to look bemused.

She looked more closely at Mason's face, perhaps expecting to see the beginnings of a smile but there wasn't one.

'Abbot Bartholomew's treasure?' she murmured, her own lips finally curling into a grin. 'Who have you been talking to?'

'Richard Holmes mentioned it to me,' he admitted. 'So I did some checking of my own.'

'Peter, that's a legend. A ghost story. A local myth or whatever else you want to call it. Richard should have known better and so should you. He's winding you up. You know what he's like.'

'Abbot Bartholomew existed. He and his colleagues were burned alive for the ritual murder of some children.'

'That part of the story might be true but not the part about the fortune in hidden gold or him having found the secret of alchemy.'

'So you do know the story?'

'Everyone in Walston knows it. Certainly every kid. They grow up with it. But it's just hearsay.'

'What if it's not?'

'So you're telling me that a group of sixteenth-century monks found out how to turn base metal into gold and buried a fortune somewhere in the grounds of Langley Hill and that it's been buried there for more than five hundred years?'

'I spoke to Richard Holmes about it and I did some of my own research too.'

'So all of a sudden you're an expert on the myths and legends of Walston and its history?' she said, smiling. Mason watched as she poured herself another drink then held the bottle over his glass. He nodded and she added more of the amber fluid to what was already there. 'If I'm going to hear this I may as well be drunk. It'll probably sound more convincing.'

Mason pushed her good-naturedly and she giggled. He watched her as she pulled off her boots and drew her bare feet up onto the sofa next to her, her legs curled beneath her.

'I might as well be comfortable too,' she added. 'Go on then, tell me your story.'

'Oh ye of little faith,' Mason said dismissively. 'Sod you. I won't tell you what I found out. No. You can do what you like but I'm keeping the secret.' He reached for his glass and pretended to turn indignantly away from her.

'Tell me,' she urged, stretching her legs out before her towards him, prodding his thigh with her bare feet.

'No,' Mason insisted. 'I was going to let you know everything I'd discovered about Abbot Bartholomew and his mates but you're obviously too ravaged by cynicism to take me seriously.'

'Now you sound like Richard Holmes,' she told him, still poking him lightly with her toes.

273

Mason put down his drink and caught her feet in his hands, gripping them tightly. She wriggled without too much conviction, easing herself back against the arm of the sofa and flexing her toes as he began to gently massage the balls and soles of her feet with his thumbs.

'Want me to tell you?' he continued, still tenderly and expertly working on her feet.

'Only if you keep doing that,' she purred.

'You know the basic story about Bartholomew. About him and the other monks being burned alive for killing kids and about the secret they had.'

'Don't forget the curse.'

'I'm getting to that.'

She slid a little farther down towards him, her feet now resting on his thighs as he began to slide one index finger between her toes, softly teasing and pressing the tips of each one in turn.

'They were granted a treasure by their God,' Mason went on. 'By *their* God, whoever or whatever that was. Everyone thinks that treasure was an alchemical one and that they made gold by the sackful and hid it in the grounds of the monastery. Perhaps that's true. Maybe they actually did it.'

The smile faded a little more from Kate's face and she took another sip of her drink as he continued.

'And in return for that knowledge they had to offer something back to their own God,' he told her.

'Like what?'

'Blood. In the form of sacrifices. That's probably why there were kids' bodies hanging up in the monastery when the townspeople attacked them. That and their beliefs. This cult of theirs they had believed you could control people according to the strength of their desire and lust.'

'And you found all this out yourself?'

'I am a history teacher, remember. Research is supposed to be one of my skills.'

Kate held his gaze, flexing her toes as he continued to massage her feet gently.

'And you believe it? That people could be manipulated because they loved or lusted after someone or something?'

'I think Simon Usher believed it too. And I think that's why he disappeared.'

67

'He didn't disappear, Peter, he left.'

Kate shook her head and reached for her drink once again.

'You know those pictures I found in the cellar of the cottage,' Mason went on. 'There were a number that showed Usher standing over the carcass of a butchered dog. Killed ritualistically for want of a better word. Perhaps it was some kind of offering.'

Kate exhaled deeply.

'You're obsessed with what happened to Usher, you know that,' she breathed.

Mason pulled gently at the tip of her right big toe, running his index finger over the perfectly pedicured nail. She squirmed slightly but didn't withdraw.

'I spoke to Richard Holmes about it, about the photos and about Usher's disappearance.'

'And Richard agreed with you that Usher had found this treasure?'

'He saw the pictures I found. There were some of Usher taken in what looked like some kind of underground chamber. Richard said he thinks it might be one of the crypts under the main building of the school itself.'

'Richard shouldn't be leading you on,' she said, wearily.

'What if he's right? What if Usher had found something?'

'Like what? The secret treasure?'

Mason turned slightly to face her, the look on his face earnest.

'What if all this isn't just local bullshit?' he stressed. 'What if it's real? What if Usher really did find something in one of the crypts under the school?' He raised a hand to silence her. 'I know you don't believe it but just think about the possibility for a minute.'

'The possibility that Simon Usher discovered the source of some treasure that had been hidden by a group of sixteenth-century monks who had gained the secret of alchemy and believed that people could be controlled by the power of their sexual feelings? Is that the possibility you're asking me to consider? And that because he found this hidden treasure he disappeared? Just listen to yourself, Peter.' She smiled thinly, sat up and shuffled towards him on the sofa.

'Aren't you even a little bit curious about what happened to Usher?' Mason asked, her face now only inches from his.

'You know what curiosity does,' she murmured, putting down her drink and looking deep into his eyes.

'Only to cats,' he breathed.

They moved together as if a silent signal had been given, lips touching gently at first. Mason felt her hand on the back of his head, pulling him closer to her then their lips pressed together more urgently and he felt the warm wetness of her tongue probing against his. He responded willingly and leaned forward. Kate allowed herself to be pushed gently by him until her back was against the arm of the sofa. Mason looked down at her and was about to move forward when she raised her left leg, pushing her foot against his chest as if to prevent him from reaching her.

Mason saw the smile on her moist, slightly parted lips and he returned the gesture, holding her foot in both hands, drawing it towards his mouth. He took her big toe between his lips and flicked his tongue over the pad and then the nail of her toe. Kate sighed delightedly, her exclamations of pleasure growing louder as he repeated the same movements on each of her toes in turn before grabbing her right foot and doing the same again. Then he pushed her legs to one side and moved closer to her, his left hand sliding up beneath her sweater, gliding over the smooth skin there.

She arched her back and he pushed his hand higher, over her taut flat stomach and towards her breasts, his hand finally closing over the right one which was un-fettered by a bra. Mason squeezed gently, kneading the firm mound, his thumb rolling over her stiff nipple. Kate closed her eyes and pulled him closer, raising her head so that he could kiss her again. Locked together like that, Mason used his free hand to unbutton her jeans and she lifted her buttocks, using both her hands to push the black denim down, exposing the tiny white panties she wore.

Mason moved back slightly, gripping the legs of her jeans, tugging them from her shapely legs as she wrig-gled free of the clinging material. She moved towards him, sliding onto his lap, feeling his erection as she ground herself against his groin.

He had both hands beneath her sweater now, both breasts cupped tenderly in his eager hands. She was gasping loudly, moving more urgently upon him and

278

Mason pushed upwards to complement her actions. They remained locked together by their kiss, tongues darting feverishly in and out of the other's mouth, sometimes gliding over each other. A thin, silvery trickle of saliva ran down Mason's chin and Kate wiped it away with one index finger before resuming the kiss.

Mason grunted as he felt her hand gliding across the front of his trousers. She gripped his engorged penis through the material then pulled back until she slid off his lap and onto the sofa once again, pushing herself away from him with her feet. He gasped in frustration and moved towards her but, again she raised one foot and pressed the sole against his chest, keeping him at bay. She shook her head slowly.

'Wait,' she whispered, breathlessly.

Mason looked lustfully at her, seeing her slide her right hand over the smooth material of her panties, her index and middle fingers pressing against the cotton that encased her mound. Still fully clothed and now desperate to touch her, Mason once again tried to move nearer to Kate but she shook her head, her fingers now disappearing inside her panties.

Mason could see them moving within the flimsy garment and she smiled, her breathing growing more ragged.

Mason was transfixed.

She opened her legs a little wider, the motions of her fingers now more rapid. Kate saw him looking at her and it was as if his inaction was a spur to her. She slipped her left hand down to her thighs, massaging the smooth flesh there as her fingers continued to push and caress more urgently inside her panties. Mason too was breathing heavily now, his gaze moving back and forth from Kate's face to between her legs. He put one hand on her outstretched right leg and she allowed him to rest his palm on her knee but nothing more. He moved his fingertips in tiny circles on the soft flesh there but dared not slide them higher. Instead, he looked at her face as she began to gasp loudly.

She had both hands inside her panties now, one covering the other, creating more pressure on her sensitive labia and clitoris. The muscles in her thighs and calves were taut, her whole body beginning to stiffen. Mason realised she was moments from reaching her climax and he watched intently as she surrendered to the feelings coursing through her body.

He would have given anything to be able to touch her, to caress her taut body but he knew that he could do nothing but watch as her pleasure reached its height. He was surprised when she stopped, withdrawing her fingers slowly from between her legs, holding them up for him to inspect. Mason could see the moisture glistening on the digits. Breathing heavily, she pushed her fingers towards his face and he leaned forward, sucking them into his mouth to taste her. She smiled lustfully at him and moved towards him.

The ringing of her mobile phone caused her to turn momentarily.

'Leave it,' Mason urged. 'They'll ring back if it's important.'

But she'd already picked up the mobile from the coffee table and was checking the identity of the caller.

'I've got to answer it. It's the nursing home.'

68

'If you don't want me to have it then that's fine but I'm asking you as a favour, Andy.'

Frank Coulson stood in the sitting room of Andy Preece's farmhouse looking intently at the younger man.

'Frank, you're not asking to borrow a hammer or a fucking drill,' Preece reminded him. 'You want to borrow one of my shotguns. I think I'm entitled to know why. If anything happens while you've got it, I'm the one who's going to get it in the neck from the law.'

'Nothing's going to happen.'

'So why do you need it?'

'There's a squirrels' nest under the eaves of the house. They're driving me nuts. I think there's a family of the bloody things.'

'So call Rentokil.'

'It'll be quicker if I take care of it myself.'

'At this time of night?' Preece enquired, looking at his watch. 'You're not going to be able to see them in the dark, are you?' He smiled.

'I'll take care of it in the morning,' Coulson assured him.

Preece hesitated a moment then shrugged and walked through into the kitchen to a dark wood cabinet close to the back door. He took some keys from his pocket and unlocked it, seeing that Coulson had followed him and was standing respectfully behind him, his eyes fixed on the cabinet. Preece opened it to reveal what looked like a metal filing cabinet within. He selected another key and prepared to open the second of the two containers.

'Did you ever find out what happened to your sheep?' Coulson asked, conversationally.

'I told the police,' Preece informed him. 'I even showed them the carcasses but they didn't do anything.'

'Who did they think it was?'

'They hadn't got a clue. Useless bastards.'

He unlocked the metal cabinet and opened it up to reveal three shotguns and several boxes of ammunition. Preece ran his eyes over the weapons then selected one and handed it to Coulson. It felt heavy in the older man's grip and he hefted it before him, raising it to his shoulder and squinting down the sight.

'That's a Beretta,' Preece informed him. 'Twelve bore. It should do the job.' He placed a box of shells on the kitchen table then closed and re-locked both the cabinets. 'Just watch out for the recoil. It kicks.'

'Thanks, Andy, I appreciate this,' Coulson told him, holding the weapon before him. He stuffed the ammunition into his jacket pocket.

The two men regarded each other silently for a moment.

'How's Maggie?' Preece asked finally. 'Is she coping?'

'No, not really. Sometimes I wonder if she'll ever get over it.'

'Losing a kid must be bad enough, Frank, but not the way Amy died.'

282

Coulson nodded.

'And what about you?' Preece added.

'It wouldn't do for both of us to give up, would it? What would Amy think?' He tried to force a smile but couldn't quite manage it. 'I'd better go.'

Preece walked him to the front door where they shook hands and then the farmer watched as Coulson climbed into his waiting car.

'Be careful with that shotgun,' Preece called, waving his friend off.

Coulson didn't reply. He swung the car around in the muddy yard and headed back towards the main road.

69

'At least let me drop you off,' Mason said as he watched Kate Wheeler pull on her clothes, her face still flushed.

She didn't answer him, merely continued dressing as quickly as she could, finally stepping into her boots.

'It might not be anything serious,' Mason offered, aware that his words of encouragement were both strained and also wasted.

'They wouldn't ring if it wasn't serious,' Kate countered, snatching up her keys and heading for the front door of the flat with Mason in hot pursuit.

'What did they say?' he wanted to know.

'Just that there'd been an incident, they wouldn't say any more.' She slammed the door of the flat and locked it. 'You go back to the school. I'll be fine. I can get to the nursing home on my own.'

'Don't be bloody stupid. Come on. You can direct me.'

They hurried across to Mason's car and he started the engine, stepping on the accelerator and guiding the vehicle out onto the road. It was quiet on the thoroughfares of Walston and he drove as quickly as he dared, aware that Kate's agitation was growing by the minute. Nevertheless, she gave him directions tersely enough and within less than ten minutes, he was pulling up outside a set of tall iron gates set into white-painted walls that protected a short driveway leading towards a three-storey brick building with a newly tiled roof. A plaque on the wall beside the right-hand gate announced, Durnford House, Care Home.

Mason guided the car into position and Kate scrambled out of it without waiting for him to open her door.

'Do you want me to come in with you?' he asked.

'No, there's nothing you can do anyway,' she told him.

'I'll wait here and take you home.'

'No, Peter, just go. I'll speak to you tomorrow.'

She slammed the car door and before he could say anything else, she had disappeared through the black-painted main door into the building, the door closing behind her. Mason waited a moment then guided the car away from Durnford House back onto the main road.

As Kate Wheeler walked into the hall of the building she let out a deep breath, glancing around her at the lobby with its reception desk and prettily papered walls. There was soft music playing gently in the background, piped into the reception from somewhere in the rear of the building. An unattended computer was perched on the dark wood desk straight ahead of her, the screen displaying an electronic fish swimming slowly back and forth like the resident of an electric aquarium. As ever, Kate was reminded more of the lobby of a hotel than of a place of care and healing.

She walked across to the desk, wondering where everyone was. Surely, even with the clock on the wall behind the reception showing 11:05 pm someone should be on duty. There were closed wooden doors to her right and left and an open archway to the right of the

285

reception that she knew led through to the residents' rooms beyond.

It was from this archway that Richard Holmes emerged.

He was smiling.

70

Mason didn't realise he was being followed until he was less than two minutes from the main gates of Langley Hill.

Ordinarily, the fact that another car was on the road behind him would have been of complete indifference to him, especially as he had other things on his mind. Nine out of ten times he wouldn't have even been aware of another vehicle tracking him but, on roads as quiet as those around Walston, it wasn't too difficult to spot. The fact that one of the pursuing car's indicators was broken also made it more conspicuous.

Mason continued to drive at an even pace, wondering if he was mistaken about the other vehicle. Once he'd satisfied himself that he was indeed being pursued, he then wondered who it might be. And why? These considerations tumbled through his mind with the same irregularity as those about Kate Wheeler. Thoughts about her father. The look of fear on her face as they'd arrived at the nursing home and also, despite himself, the sight of her in her flat. Mason, no matter how hard he tried, couldn't push aside his feelings of lust for the woman.

He felt a little twinge of guilt that he'd been so frustrated at her having to leave when she did.

It's not her fault her father's ill, is it? Perhaps you'd rather she'd have stayed behind and spent the night with you instead of checking on her only living relative.

He would ring her later he promised himself.

To see how her father is? Or to see if she wants you to drive back to her flat?

He shook his head, irritated with himself. There were more pressing matters to be considered at the moment.

The presence of the vehicle following him suddenly came to the forefront of his mind once again.

He checked his rear-view mirror and saw that the car was still behind him. It was keeping back a hundred or so yards, its driver obviously convinced that the night and the poorly lit roads around the town were aiding his anonymity.

On Mason's right there was a lay-by and he slowed down and suddenly swung the car across the road and into it, leaving his engine running, waiting to see what the other car would do.

It swept past him, barely slowing down and Mason watched as its tail-lights disappeared behind a tall hedge that framed the road on one side.

Mason frowned, his eyes still fixed ahead, wondering if the other car was about to turn around and come back towards him but he saw nothing. He sat behind the wheel, drumming agitatedly on the plastic, wondering what his next move should be.

He could hear the wind blowing ever more urgently through the roadside trees, bending and shaking the branches every now and then. A piece of twig, broken loose by the strong gusts, came free and ricocheted off his windscreen. Mason sucked in a deep breath, startled by the impact. He turned off his own headlights and sat in the blackness, looking ahead for the other car. Surrounded by the night and the increasingly blustery wind he remained still, wanting to melt into the gloom. Not wanting to see the other car come back in his direction. He tried to swallow but his throat was dry.

He just wanted to be back at his cottage now with the doors and windows locked. Shut away from the night and from whoever might have been following him. He looked at the dashboard clock. It was 11:34 pm.

Mason waited more than five minutes before he restarted the engine, flicked on his headlights and then jammed the car into gear again. He swung it out onto the road, heading for Langley Hill.

If the car had been following him then it seemed the driver had tired of the game because there was no sign of the other vehicle anywhere. Mason squinted more closely into the rear-view mirror, wondering if the driver had decided to follow him with his lights off or adopted some other tactic to make his presence less conspicuous. But there was nothing on the road except himself. Maybe, he mused, it had been some kids trying to frighten him. Some local kids enjoying their idea of a game. Someone he'd inadvertently cut up in town wanting to teach him a lesson. By the look of it, whoever had been on his tail had finally tired of the game.

Mason shook his head.

On your tail? Where do you think you are? In a bloody detective film?

He saw the gates of Langley Hill up ahead of him and swung the car between the two pillars. The stone eagles that perched atop either one regarded him with blind eyes as his car swept beneath them. Mason guided his vehicle up the driveway, flicking his headlights on to full beam so they could cut through the night.

The car that had been following him was parked in some bushes about fifty yards further down, well hidden now and with the driver sitting in darkness watching intently.

71

Mason parked his car next to the cottage and glanced around him in the darkness for a moment before heading towards his front door.

The wind that had been building gradually that evening was now whipping frenziedly through the trees, the branches waving madly, some of the lower ones slashing at his face when he passed. He selected his front door key and was about to push it into the lock when he heard movement away to his left.

He spun round, certain that he saw a dark shape in the trees but unable to pick it out in the gloom. Mason stared into the impenetrable night for a moment longer, his heart beating faster, then he unlocked the front door and stepped inside.

The envelope was lying on his doormat.

Mason closed the front door behind him and stooped to pick it up, turning it slowly in his hand. There was no stamp and no address. All that it bore was his own name scrawled on the front in a hand that he didn't recognise. It had obviously been pushed through his letterbox earlier that evening.

He walked through into the sitting room, flicking on lights in his wake, still holding the envelope. Finally, he flopped down onto the sofa and exhaled deeply. As curious as he was about the envelope, his first inclination was to reach for the phone and call Kate Wheeler and he flipped open his mobile and called her number.

No answer. Perhaps she was still at the care home. For one awful moment he wondered if her father might have died. Mason tried once more then finally left a message on her voice mail telling her to ring him back no matter what time she got home.

He put the phone down and returned his attention to the envelope.

The writing was large but untidy, letters scrawled the way a young child would produce them and Mason frowned as he opened the envelope. Was this a practical joke perpetrated by some of his new pupils?

He pulled the sheet of paper from the envelope and opened it out to inspect the contents.

SCHOOL LIBRARY
LOOK IN THE DESK
Please help me.

And that was it. That was all of it. Mason inspected the paper more closely, noticing that there were dark smudges on the sheet. He looked more closely, rubbing one index finger over the marks. The first of them resembled dried earth. The other was congealed blood. He was sure of it. But it was what was written at the bottom of the page that transfixed him.

SIMON USHER

Mason swallowed hard and shook his head. This had to be a trick. He thought immediately of Andrew Latham's little group. Were they even now laughing at the thought of their prank? And yet, Mason mused, this seemed very basic for Latham's cronies. There didn't appear to be much cunning or much craft about it. He regarded the note once more and got to his feet, deciding that he wanted a drink.

'What does it say?'

The voice startled him and he spun round.

'The note, what does it say?'

Frank Coulson took a step out of the kitchen, the shotgun held firmly in his grip.

72

'How the hell did you get in here?' Mason snapped, the colour draining from his face.

'The lock on your back door wasn't hard to break,' Coulson told him.

Mason took a step back, his gaze flickering from Coulson's face to the yawning double barrels of the shotgun.

'Just take what you want and get out,' the teacher instructed.

'Give me a break,' Coulson said, dismissively. 'If I'd come here to rob you I wouldn't have hung around for a fucking chat, would I?' He sat down in the nearest chair, the shotgun resting across his thighs.

'What *do* you want?' Mason asked, some of the fear leaving his voice to be replaced by curiosity.

'Where's the girl?' he wanted to know. 'The one you were with tonight?'

'She's not here.'

'So what does the note say?' Coulson persisted, nodding in the direction of the piece of paper that Mason still held.

The teacher took a faltering step towards him and handed him the note, watching as Coulson ran his gaze over it. Just for a second he wondered if it would be possible to jump at the man and wrestle the shotgun away from him but the thought passed as quickly as it had appeared.

'What are you going to do?' Coulson said, finally, dropping the note onto the sofa beside him.

'About what?'

'About the note.'

'Why the hell should I tell you?'

Coulson lowered the shotgun so that it was aimed at the teacher.

'Because I'm pointing a fucking gun at you,' he breathed. 'And I know that name. Simon Usher. He lived here before you, didn't he?'

Mason nodded.

'I know this is a small town but does everyone know everybody else's business around here?' he muttered.

'That kid Andrew Latham that I mentioned earlier, is he up at the school now?'

'He's been expelled. I told you that. What do you want to do? Check his room?'

Coulson got to his feet.

'That's not a bad idea,' he agreed. 'Come on.'

'Come on where?'

'To the school. You're going to find Simon Usher and I'm going to talk to Latham about my daughter.'

'I told you, he's been expelled,' Mason snapped. 'He's not even there.'

'There are kids up there who were his friends. I'll talk to them. I want to know why he killed her.'

'He didn't kill her, she committed suicide.'

'Because he forced her to,' Coulson said through clenched teeth. 'Just like he did the others.'

Mason frowned.

'What others?' he murmured. 'What the hell are you talking about?'

Coulson let out an almost painful breath.

'Switch your computer on,' he sighed, nodding in the direction of Mason's laptop. 'I'll show you.'

73

Mason had no idea exactly how long the two of them had been sitting in front of the computer. All he knew was that the information he'd been given by Coulson during their vigil before the glowing screen had made his head spin and also ache. There were five pictures on the screen, each one accompanied by a short article telling of the accidental deaths of those on display. Mason looked again at the names.

ROBBIE PARKER
CALLUM WADE
HOLLY PRESTON
SARAH TINDALL
AMY COULSON

'Something like this happened in Wales a year or so ago,' Coulson said, rubbing his own face as if to keep himself awake. 'A group of kids made some kind of suicide pact. Ten or twelve of them topped themselves within a year and the police said it was all down to this one particular website, encouraging them to do it.

Giving them information about the best ways to kill themselves.'

'And you think that Andrew Latham and his friends set up something similar here in Walston?' Mason muttered. 'Why would he do that?'

'Because he's a twisted little fucker who gets his kicks by messing with other people's heads.'

'That much you could be right about,' Mason conceded. 'But what had he got to gain by causing five teenagers to kill themselves?'

'I don't know. I don't know how the little bastard's mind works, do I? All I know is that if it wasn't for him my Amy would still be alive.'

'Why's it taken you until now to do something about it?'

'I couldn't go to the police about Amy's death. There didn't seem to be anything suspicious about it. What would they have investigated? They would have told me that she just killed herself because of the stuff Latham put on those websites about her. Those videos that were taken.'

'How do you know it wasn't because of those?'

Coulson shook his head.

'She was a good kid,' he said, quietly, lowering his gaze. 'And she was a strong-minded girl. We were a close family. We could have worked it out. No matter what she did. No matter what he filmed her doing.' Coulson swallowed hard, his hands clenching into fists.

'And she knew the other four kids who killed themselves. You're sure of that?'

'She went to school with them. They were all around the same age.'

'So how come the police haven't treated these other deaths as suspicious? Five teenagers all commit suicide within the space of three weeks and the law isn't interested?'

'No investigation was made into these suicides and, if it was, then nothing was found that the police thought was worth pursuing.'

Coulson didn't answer, he merely hefted the shotgun before him.

'And why come to me with this information?' Mason went on.

'Because you're here. But you're not one of them. You're an outsider. How the fuck do I know? You're in the job that Simon Usher was in. I need someone to get me inside that school. You can help me if you want,' he breathed. 'If not then keep out of my fucking way but I'm going to find out one way or another what's been going on at this place.'

Mason regarded him evenly for a moment, not doubting for one second the sincerity of his words.

'What about Simon Usher?' he said, quietly. 'Do you think the note's for real?'

'Why don't we find out?' Coulson breathed.

Mason nodded then headed off briefly into the kitchen. When he returned he was carrying two large torches. He handed one to Coulson who flicked it on, testing the powerful beam.

'Come on,' Mason said. He glanced at his watch and saw that it was approaching 12:55 am.

74

The gaunt edifice of Langley Hill private school loomed into view as if it had risen from the earth itself, propelled from the depths by giant thrusting hands.

Coulson slowed his pace slightly as they emerged from the trees that had previously masked the buildings from them. The school was momentarily illuminated by moonlight as the gathering clouds rolled back high above them and the cold white glow shone down on the monolithic structure. Mason noticed his companion falter and glanced in his direction, ready to ask him what was wrong but Coulson seemed to recover his composure and the two of them walked on.

There were only two or three windows lit within the school, yellow pinpricks of light against the gloom.

'What if they see us coming?' Coulson asked, his eyes fixed on the school.

'The kids should all have been in bed for over two hours and so have the staff,' Mason informed him.

They were less than a hundred yards from the main entrance by now and Coulson looked up at the large stone gargoyles that stood sentinel along the edge of the roof. They seemed to be staring hungrily down at him and he shifted the shotgun from one hand to the other.

They pressed on until they reached the huge, ornate main doors to the building. Mason stepped up to the panel beside them and keyed in a code. There was a loud click and he pushed the nearest one. It opened and the two men stepped inside the stone-floored hallway.

Coulson looked around him at the stairway that led up to a galleried area above. To his right and left there were archways that snaked away into long corridors.

'Come on,' Mason urged, tugging at his arm. 'We'll go to the library first.'

Coulson followed him off to the left, relieved when the bare stone was replaced by carpeted floor. The thick pile muffled the sound of their feet as they hurried along the corridor. Paintings lined the walls on both sides. Portraits and landscapes. Former headmasters and teachers and scenes of Walston through the years. There was even a painting of the Queen on view. Coulson regarded it reverentially as he passed.

'Here,' Mason hissed, urging him towards a set of dark wood double-doors. The teacher slapped at a panel of light switches just inside, snapping on switches. Brightness swelled inside the room, banishing the gloom and illuminating everything before them.

The two of them stepped through the doors into a room with a high vaulted ceiling and shelves that seemed to tower to the roof itself. There were more shelves on the floor of the huge room, arrayed with an almost military precision into rows that looked as if they formed some kind of maze. Every one of them heaving and creaking with books of all shapes and sizes. The musty smell of old paper filled the air.

301

'The note said to come to the library,' Mason reminded his companion.

'And then what?' Coulson demanded.

Mason didn't answer. At the far end of the library there was a large mahogany desk on a dais belonging to the librarian. It was towards that he moved.

Coulson hesitated a moment then followed him, moving as quietly as he could across the polished and lacquered wooden floor.

Mason had reached the desk by now and he scanned the items upon it. Apart from a couple of plastic trays, some pens and an angle-poise lamp there was nothing. He began opening the drawers, not even sure what he was looking for.

'This is crazy,' snapped Coulson.

Mason pulled open the last of the drawers.

There were two Polaroid photos within and he plucked them from the drawer and held them before him, his hand shaking.

'What is it?' Coulson snapped, snatching the photos from him. He could see that the first showed a man about the same age as Mason.

'Is that Simon Usher?' Coulson demanded.

Mason could only nod.

The second picture showed someone they both knew.

'Isn't that the woman you were with tonight?'

Mason tried to swallow but his throat felt constricted.

'Yes,' he whispered. 'It's Kate Wheeler.'

'I don't understand this. Why leave the photos here? It's as if whoever left it wanted it to be found.'

'Someone wanted me to be here in this library tonight, didn't they? Why else would they push that note through my door? It makes sense they should want me to find the photo as well.'

'Where were they taken?' Coulson wanted to know, jabbing a finger at the pictures

Mason looked more closely. Usher was standing with his back to a brick wall but the stonework was chipped, crumbling and looked old. Ancient almost, Mason thought. Kate Wheeler was standing against the same background, her face pale, her eyes wide with fear. Exactly how long ago it had been taken Mason had no idea but he could see that Kate was wearing the same black cowl-neck top and black jeans that she had sported that very evening.

'I can show you where it was taken.'

The words echoed around the huge library and both Mason and Coulson spun around in the direction of the sound.

Richard Holmes walked slowly towards them.

75

Coulson instinctively raised the shotgun but Mason put out a hand and gently pushed the barrels down.

'What are you doing here, Richard?' Mason wanted to know. 'What's happened to Kate? Who's got her?'

Holmes shook his head.

'Who the hell are you?' Coulson wanted to know.

'My name's Richard Holmes. I'm a teacher here.'

'Who put the note through my door?' Mason interrupted, pushing in front of Coulson.

'I don't know,' Holmes insisted. 'Probably the same person who sent me mine. The same person who's got Kate.'

'Was it one of the kids?' Mason went on, growing increasingly agitated.

'I said I don't know,' Holmes told him. 'Just like I don't know what's happening with Kate. Someone left me a note: that's why I'm here.'

'I want some fucking answers,' snapped Mason.

'So do I, Peter,' Holmes hissed. 'But you've got to come with me now. There isn't much time.'

Mason looked at Coulson then both of them followed

the older man towards the library exit, hurrying to keep pace with him despite his bulk.

'Do you want to tell me what the fuck is going on here?' Coulson rasped, grabbing Mason's arm.

'I don't know,' the teacher told him, tugging free. He increased his pace and caught up with Holmes. 'Where are we going?'

'To the chapel,' Holmes told him. 'If I'm right, the only way into the tunnels is through an entrance beneath the altar. I'm sure that's where they're being held.'

Mason's head was spinning.

'Tunnels?' he murmured.

'I told you, there's a network of tunnels running under the school that have been there for centuries,' Holmes informed him. 'By the look of the brickwork in that picture, Usher's down there somewhere.'

'And Kate too?' Mason enquired.

Holmes could only nod.

'So Usher isn't missing? He never disappeared?' Mason went on. 'He's being held somewhere too? Who the hell by?'

'If I had to guess, I'd say Latham's group. This might even be some kind of revenge for his expulsion.'

'This is insane,' Mason snapped. 'Why don't we just call the police?'

'There isn't time,' Holmes insisted, speeding up. 'Even now we might still be too late.'

Mason grabbed the older man's arm and tugged hard to stop his progress.

'What do you mean too late?' he rasped. 'What do you think they're going to do, kill them?'

Holmes didn't answer.

The trio continued hurriedly through the school, moving as quickly and soundlessly as they could. When

305

they reached the corridor that led to the chapel Holmes leaned against the wall, sucking in laboured breaths. He pressed one hand to his chest, his face pale.

'Are you all right?' Mason asked, seeing the obvious distress that the other teacher was in.

'You two go ahead,' Holmes urged. 'I'll catch up. I need to get my breath.'

'But how are we going to find Usher and Kate?' Mason demanded.

'Once you get below ground there's only one way you can go,' Holmes informed him. 'Keep walking until you find them. Go, I'll catch up.'

Mason glanced at Coulson who nodded.

They left Holmes slumped against the cold stone wall, still sucking in air and Mason pushed the chapel door open, relieved when it didn't creak. Their footsteps echoed as they hurried across the cold stone floor, Mason glancing around at the ornately carved stalls and pews and at the pulpit that towered ahead of them. Coulson looked at the stained-glass windows that bore so many figures, all, it seemed, gazing intently at him as he followed Mason down the central aisle of the chapel.

Three stone steps led up to the chancel and a few paces beyond it the altar. Mason inspected the heavy woven cloth that covered the altar, pulling at it as if it were a tablecloth.

'What are you doing?' Coulson whispered, lowering his voice in a gesture of almost unconscious deference.

'Holmes said the entrance to the tunnels was behind the altar,' Mason reminded his companion. 'There's nothing behind it but stone wall, it has to be underneath.'

He stepped back, inspecting the flagstones around the altar, prodding each one with the toe of his shoe.

The third one tilted slightly as he put pressure on it.

306

'Here,' he said, dropping to his knees. 'Help me get this up.'

Coulson hesitated a moment then joined the teacher who had managed to slide his fingertips beneath the large slab of stone and was lifting it, surprised at how easily it came free.

'Slide it your way,' Mason hissed and they both put all their efforts into shifting the slab sideways. 'Hold it for a minute,' the teacher instructed, reaching for the torch he'd put down.

As Coulson took the strain, Mason flicked the torch on and shone the powerful beam into the gap under the flagstone that the men had opened. He played the light over the area beneath and caught sight of something glistening below.

'There's steps down there, Holmes was right,' he murmured.

Coulson grunted and pushed the slab the remaining foot or so to expose the hole completely. There was a loud, echoing thud as the stone was laid down and both men stood up, looking towards the door of the chapel in case their intrusion had been heard by other ears. Satisfied that they were still undiscovered, they knelt down beside the entrance once more.

'It must have led to a priest hole or something like that,' Mason mused. 'Some kind of escape route for the priests here hundreds of years ago. Either that or it leads down to the crypts.'

'Are we going down?' Coulson wanted to know.

Mason hesitated a moment, aware of a powerful smell that was rising from the freshly opened hole. Finally he nodded.

'After you,' Coulson said, cryptically.

He watched as Mason edged his way through the hole,

stepping carefully on the stone stairs beneath, careful to avoid the slippery parts of the stonework.

'What about the other guy?' Coulson said, looking towards the chapel door.

'He said he'd follow us,' Mason reminded his companion.

Coulson merely nodded and followed Mason down into the enveloping gloom, switching on his torch as he went. The twin beams cut through the darkness.

'Jesus,' Coulson coughed. 'It smells like something died down here.'

Mason said nothing but merely continued his descent towards the bottom of the stone steps. He reached the final one and waited for Coulson to join him.

Both men found themselves in a narrow tunnel, the floor of which was wet and, Mason noticed, in places was merely wet earth. The tunnel stretched away in front of them, so long that their torch beams couldn't pick out the end of it. They both looked briefly at each other then Mason strode off, leading the way. Exactly what he was leading the way to he had no idea.

76

The two men guessed that they must have walked at least two hundred yards along the stone corridor before they came to the end.

It opened out into a T shape with identical walkways leading to both the left and the right. Mason paused, unsure of which direction to take.

The smell that had assailed their nostrils from the time they entered the underground tunnels was stronger now and Coulson coughed. The sound reverberated through the subterranean passages.

'Which way?' he urged.

Mason swallowed hard.

'This way,' he indicated, taking the left-hand path.

'How can you be sure?'

'I can't. What do you want to do, split up? Take the chance we don't find each other again down here? We don't know how far these tunnels go.'

Coulson considered the options then nodded, following the teacher as he stepped to the left and began walking once more, the torchlight cutting through the gloom ahead of them.

'What is that smell?' Coulson remarked, again wincing at the intensity of the odour.

'We're twenty or thirty feet underground,' Mason reminded him. 'It could be anything. Rotting vegetation. Dead animals. How the hell do I know?'

'Whatever it is it's getting worse.'

Mason aimed his torch at the wall of the tunnel nearest to him and noticed that there was something dark stuck to it. He reached out and pulled gently at the matter, rolling it between his fingers.

'Silk,' he said, quietly. 'From a jacket or sweater. Someone has been down here.'

'How can you be sure?' Coulson snapped.

'I can't but what's your explanation?' Mason challenged.

Coulson also inspected the material, dropping it to the floor of the tunnel. He stepped ahead of Mason, playing his own torch over the ground they walked on.

There were several shallow puddles ahead and, somewhere beyond the reach of the torch beam, he could hear something dripping. A steady rhythmic plop of liquid into liquid. He increased his pace slightly and Mason had to hurry to keep up with him.

The tunnel turned slightly to the right and they followed it. There were several large metal grilles in the walls and ceiling and Mason wondered if they were part of some kind of ventilation system. He tried to work out which part of the school they were now beneath. The kitchens possibly? However, in such impenetrable gloom, he wasn't sure of his bearings. He wasn't even certain that they were still beneath the school by now.

The two men moved on, treading through deep puddles as they did so, both of them cursing under their breath as freezing water lapped against their ankles. And still, the fetid stench filled their nostrils and throats.

'Stop,' Mason said, suddenly freezing where he stood.

Coulson looked quizzically at him and was about to say something when he too heard it.

A low moan echoed through the tunnels. It was unmistakably human in origin.

Mason swallowed hard.

'Come on,' he said, quietly.

The moan was followed, seconds later, by another sound. A guttural, mucoid rasping that filled the tunnels and bounced off the dripping stonework like a warning.

'What the fuck was that?' Coulson said, breathlessly.

Mason could only shake his head.

Coulson stopped dead, shining his torch back in the direction from which they'd come.

There was only silence now.

Mason walked ahead, moving his torch slowly from side to side, the beam now picking out another junction ahead.

'Which way?' he murmured aloud.

'Right,' Coulson offered. 'And no, I don't know if that's the way we're supposed to go. I just want to get out of here.'

'We came down here to find Kate and I'm not leaving until I find her,' Mason told him.

'Then we'd better fucking find her and quick.'

77

'It's getting narrower,' Mason exclaimed, aware that the tunnel walls were now much closer together. He reached up with his free hand and found that he could touch the roof of the stone corridor easily too. He pulled at the wet brickwork, slightly alarmed when a large portion of it came free. It fell to the ground with a loud thud.

'We'll have to go back,' Coulson urged, glancing behind him, the light from his torch swallowed up by the subterranean blackness.

They both turned, hurrying their pace as they made their way back the way they'd already come, passing the junction from which they'd emerged.

It was from that tunnel that another sound issued.

A loud, wet noise that Mason thought sounded like soggy bellows being rhythmically pumped. Along with the sound came a blast of noxious air, so vile and powerful that it made both men recoil.

'Keep moving,' Mason coughed, pushing Coulson before him.

They moved as quickly as they could, almost managing

to jog down the tunnel now, desperate to be as far from the sound and the vile smell as possible.

They splashed through freezing water, Coulson almost stumbling. He shot out a hand to steady himself and hurried on, keeping pace with Mason, almost colliding with him. The shotgun scraped against the stonework and Coulson gripped it tightly to stop himself from dropping it.

'The tunnel's sloping downwards,' Mason exclaimed, almost slipping over on the wet floor.

Coulson seemed less interested in the contours of their underground domain than he was in the increasingly loud noise that was filling the tunnel behind them. He turned and waved his torch behind him but could see nothing. When he looked back in Mason's direction once more he could see that the teacher was squatting down, examining something on the tunnel floor in front of him.

Coulson joined him and Mason pointed at the object before them.

It was a man's shoe. There was fresh mud on it.

'First the silk, now this,' Mason echoed. 'Looks like we're going in the right direction.'

As they walked on they were both aware of the heavy silence that had settled in the tunnel. Only the sounds of their own laboured breathing filled the stone shafts now. The unidentifiable rasping that they had heard all too many times was now absent.

Mason raised a hand to halt his companion.

The tunnel was silent again.

Coulson merely nodded slightly, urging Mason forward with a gentle shove in the back.

'Let's keep moving,' he insisted.

Mason nodded and did as his companion advised.

He recoiled slightly as a large cobweb brushed against his face and he pulled the thick strands from his hair as he walked on, noticing something about twenty yards ahead of them. He held a hand out to halt Coulson, raising his finger to his lips when he noticed that the other man was about to speak.

Mason switched off his torch and pointed towards what he'd seen.

There were two lights flickering in the darkness ahead of them. Both men advanced towards the pinpricks of luminescence and saw them grow slowly from small points into fuller flares.

On either side of the tunnel, placed carefully on fallen brickwork to keep them out of the water on the muddy floor, were lamps. The sickly yellow glow they gave off reminded Mason of dying candles and he moved closer to inspect the sources of light.

Both the lamps were plastic. Very similar to the kind of battery-powered lights used for camping purposes. Mason wondered how long ago they'd been placed there.

He was still wondering when Coulson walked a couple of steps ahead of him, indicating more of the dull points of light.

There were more lamps set up along the rest of the tunnel. Mason counted at least twelve of them.

Coulson switched off his torch and jammed it into his belt, gripping the shotgun with both hands now as he walked forwards. The lamps gave off enough light for both men to move with reasonable sure-footedness.

'Who put these here?' Coulson murmured but Mason could only shake his head. He was more concerned with what the lamplight had uncovered.

Propped against the tunnel wall less than ten yards ahead of them was the body of Andrew Latham.

78

Mason advanced slowly towards the corpse, followed now by Coulson.

For a second, Mason wondered if the boy might still be alive but, as he leaned over the figure he knew that was impossible.

Even in the dull light of the lamps, Mason could see that the boy's flesh was pale, almost white but it was puckered around not just the mouth, eyes and nose but everywhere. Latham's body looked as if it had been left in warm water for a very long time, the flesh pruned and crinkled. Mason reached out one tentative finger and touched the dead boy's cheek.

It was as dry as a bone. The corpse looked mummified. Shrunken, as if all the internal organs had been sucked out and discarded but Mason could see no wounds on the corpse. Apart from its dried and shrivelled state it was untouched. There were no cuts, bruises or abrasions anywhere to be seen on it.

'He looks like he's been down here for years,' Coulson murmured, transfixed by the sight of the body.

Mason exhaled and nodded almost imperceptibly.

'Who could have done that to him?' Coulson continued.

'I don't know,' Mason breathed, stepping away from the body. 'Come on, we've got to move on. We've got to find Kate.'

Coulson shook his head.

'Whatever killed him is down here with us,' he snapped. 'And I don't want to end up like him. You want to find the girl, you go on.'

'And what are you going to do?' Mason rasped, gripping the other man's arm. 'Find your way back through these tunnels? Make your way out and go and fetch the police?' He glared into Coulson's eyes. 'If we stay together we've got a chance. If we separate we might not get out of here alive.'

Coulson met his gaze and held it.

'What are you going to do?' Mason went on, his voice now little more than a whisper.

Coulson shook loose of the teacher's grip and nodded.

'We go on then,' he grunted. 'But if I see a way out of here I'm taking it. You want to stay down here and find your fucking girlfriend that's your business. I'm getting out as soon as I can.'

'Understood,' Mason intoned then pointed in the direction he felt they should go.

There was a large hole in the right-hand wall of the tunnel. The brickwork looked as if it had, over the course of many years, simply disintegrated. There were several large cracks in the ceiling too, some of them leaking mud like blood seeping through tears in overstretched skin. Large lumps of stone were scattered across the tunnel floor and Mason looked warily at the ceiling, shining his torch nervously over the rents.

Mason ran his hand over the wall and another piece of stonework simply fell to the ground.

316

There was a loud groaning sound and both men froze. Moments later there was a rumble and they both felt the ground shudder slightly beneath their feet.

Coulson steadied himself against the nearest wall and felt vibrations coming through the stonework as if someone on the other side were hammering it.

A lump of stone the size of a fist fell from the tunnel roof, missing Mason by inches.

'Jesus Christ,' Coulson gasped. 'The roof's falling in.'

They ran as fast as they could, happy to be swallowed by the gloom, wanting only to be away from the lumps of rock and stone that were starting to fall all too numerously. Mason shot a terrified glance behind him and one horrific thought filled his mind and would not budge.

We're going to be buried alive.

He ran, no longer caring whether or not Coulson was with him. He was unconcerned by the darkness and the stench and the mud that gripped his feet and slowed his pace. He wanted only to be out of this vile subterranean labyrinth. He wanted only to see daylight and to smell fresh air again and not inhale this fetid stink of corruption and decay.

Coulson slipped, fell and dropped the shotgun as another large chunk of the ceiling slammed down, accompanied by some thick clods of mud. He scrambled to his feet, paused a second and almost bent to pick up the weapon but his fear overcame all other instincts and, instead, he hurled himself forwards towards a curve in the tunnel. As he hit the wall his torch went out.

Mason shot his own torch beam behind him, trying to see the extent of the collapse but, as Coulson dived forward he slammed into him, almost knocking him flat and dashing the torch from his grasp.

Blackness enveloped the two men totally.

Mason dropped to his knees, desperate to find the torch again.

The tunnel collapse he had feared had not happened and for that he was grateful but the loss of the light, however meagre, was almost as intolerable. He felt his hands slide through freezing mud that grasped as high as his forearms and he crawled like a blind man, searching for the torch.

Coulson flicked on his own torch again and the beam illuminated Mason's terrified, mud-spattered face.

The teacher looked up briefly at his companion then felt something familiar beneath his probing fingers and he tugged the torch from the glutinous ooze beneath him, pressing frantically at the on/off switch.

The light came on but it was only through a thick film of slime. Mason wiped as much as he could from the plastic, relieved that the beam of light once again cut through the darkness. He stood up, his heart hammering madly against his ribs.

Coulson put a comforting hand on his shoulder and Mason nodded as if to signal that he was regaining control.

'Come on,' Coulson said, stepping away from the fallen debris.

Mason followed him, aware that the ground beneath their feet was now more solid.

He shone his torch down and saw why.

Both of them were standing on damp wood.

That realisation was eclipsed a second later as the wood splintered beneath their weight.

They both fell.

79

Mason slammed into the rock with an impact that tore the breath from him.

He rolled over clutching his right side, convinced that he'd shattered at least one rib. When he breathed, a sharp pain bit into his side and chest and he groaned as he rolled over. He couldn't see a hand in front of him in the gloom but he realised that he and Coulson had fallen no more than ten or fifteen feet through the floor of the tunnel above.

Coulson.

Where was his companion, he wondered? He'd fallen at the same time and Mason had heard his scream of shock and terror as the tunnel floor had swallowed them. Where he was now, however, Mason had no idea.

'Coulson,' he whispered into the darkness.

No reply.

Mason crawled a couple of feet in the darkness and called the man's name again.

This time it was met by a low groan.

'Here,' Coulson breathed.

Mason scrambled in the direction of the voice, dragging himself through the freezing wet mud.

Coulson was propped up against a rock, one hand pressed to his head, his body shivering.

'Are you all right?' Mason grunted.

'I think I've broken my ankle,' Coulson slurred. 'I can't move it.' He sounded like a drunk.

'You're going to have to,' Mason sighed. 'I'm not leaving you here.'

'Just get out, leave me here. Send help when you get out.'

'It might not be broken,' Mason insisted, digging into his pocket and pulling out his lighter. He flicked it on, holding the flame up to illuminate his companion.

Coulson's left leg was extended before him and Mason could see that his foot was twisted at an impossible angle but it wasn't the broken ankle that was concerning him. It was the damage to Coulson's skull.

Mason held the lighter higher, the sickly yellow light illuminating the full extent of the damage.

'What are you looking at?' Coulson slurred and, at last, Mason realised why his speech was so distorted.

There was a hole in the back of Coulson's skull the size of a tennis ball and through it, Mason could see a greyish-red matter bulging from the hole in the other man's skull. He realised with revulsion that it was brain. Coulson's eyes rolled briefly upwards in the sockets and he tried to speak once more but, this time, no words, just a stream of blood poured from his mouth. Rivulets of the dark fluid were oozing from his nose too.

'Oh Christ,' Mason murmured, unable to keep his reaction in check.

Coulson's head flopped backwards, his tongue lolling from his mouth.

'Coulson,' Mason hissed. 'Stay awake. I'll get out. I'll get help.'

It was already too late.

'Come on,' Mason said through gritted teeth. He held up his lighter once again in an attempt to see where they were. It looked as if they'd fallen into a culvert of some kind, two of the sides were smooth, the other two were bare rock. Mason glanced upwards to the wooden slats they'd crashed through then held the lighter away from him once more.

The flame was flickering, blown by a strong breeze. Buffeted so much he feared it might go out.

'There's air blowing into here from somewhere,' he mused. 'I'm guessing from outside.' He nodded in the direction of the breeze. 'We should go that way. We can get out.'

Coulson looked blankly at him.

'I'll lift you,' Mason said. 'Try and get up.' Even as he spoke he realised how ridiculous his words sounded. Coulson was hovering very close to unconsciousness and, for all the teacher knew, to death. The possibility of him standing up, let alone walking out of this subterranean labyrinth, was out of the question.

'I'll go on,' Mason insisted. 'I'll send help. I promise.'

Coulson said nothing. His eyes were already closed.

Mason waited a moment longer, listening to the low, guttural breathing of his injured companion then he began walking.

The lighter grew hot in his hand the longer he held it and, more than once, he had to flick it off and stand still in the darkness until the metal cooled enough to allow him to use it again.

As he walked, he was becoming more and more convinced that his trek was futile. His mind was filling with one unshakeable conviction. That he would never see the surface again. That he would wander helplessly in the gloom below ground until he simply couldn't walk any longer. Then exhaustion would overtake him and finally hunger and thirst. He would, he was convinced, die in this monstrous place.

He was still considering that appalling fate when he saw the torch beam shining in his direction.

It was fifteen or twenty yards away, bright and welcoming. A beacon in the gloom.

'This way,' a familiar voice boomed, echoing off the culvert walls. 'Come on.'

Mason shuffled forward.

Richard Holmes stood in the middle of the wide culvert, waving the torch back and forth.

'I told you I'd catch you up,' Holmes said, conversationally. 'Come on, let's get out of here.'

80

'How the hell did you find me?' Mason wanted to know as they struggled on.

'That's not important now,' Holmes told him. 'All that matters is that we get out. Where's Coulson?'

'Back there,' Mason confessed. 'He's dying. He fractured his skull when we fell.' He allowed the words to trail off.

'We can get him help.'

Mason nodded.

'It's like a maze down here,' he offered. 'If you hadn't found me I'd have been dead. Andrew Latham is back there too. He's dead.'

Holmes pressed on, shining the light ahead of them along the culvert.

'I said Latham's dead,' Mason repeated.

'Let's get you out of here first,' Holmes insisted. 'Tell me everything when we've reached the surface.'

'What about Kate?' Mason demanded.

Holmes didn't speak.

'Kate?' Mason persisted.

'This leads to a central hub,' Holmes told him. 'It's like

323

a sewage pipe. We can get out once we reach it. Then we can get help.'

'We found a shoe and a piece of cloth,' Mason informed the other teacher. 'And there were lanterns in the tunnel above. As if someone had been down here before us. Like they were trying to leave a trail for us.'

Again Holmes remained silent.

'Not far now,' he said, finally, pointing to a curve in the pipe.

'Is Kate down here?' Mason asked, more forcefully.

'We need to get you to a doctor,' Holmes said. 'Then we can call the police.'

'Richard,' Mason insisted. 'Where's Kate? If she's down here I want to know. I want to know if she's safe.'

'She's fine,' Holmes told him.

'You've seen her then?'

'She'll be waiting,' Holmes assured him.

'How can you be so sure?' Mason challenged, gripping the older man's arm and dragging him back.

'Trust me,' Holmes said, flatly.

The men moved on once more. Mason was aware of light at the far end of the culvert. Welcoming yellow light that banished the darkness the closer they got to its source.

'Thank God,' Mason breathed.

The light was brighter now. So bright in fact that Mason was forced to squint when he looked towards it but, as his eyes became accustomed to the fierce white luminescence he grew aware of its source.

There were dozens of torches ahead of him. Each one held by a different person.

He noticed that one was held by Nigel Grant. The headmaster was smiling happily as he played the beam over Mason and Holmes. The others were being held by members of staff, every one of them shining the bright lights at the newcomers.

Kate Wheeler held hers too.

Holmes quickened his pace and walked across to join his colleagues, turning his own torch beam on Mason.

'What the fuck is this?' Mason murmured.

'A gathering, Peter,' Holmes told him.

'We've been waiting for you,' Nigel Grant added.

'It's like a welcome committee,' Kate Wheeler offered.

Mason shielded his eyes as he looked towards the teachers gathered in front of him.

'I don't understand,' Mason said, warily.

'We didn't think that you would,' Kate Wheeler told him.

'It isn't an easy thing to understand,' Nigel Grant added.

'And it doesn't matter that you can't fathom the reasons, Peter,' Richard Holmes added. 'Some things are better left as mysteries.'

Mason took a step backwards.

'Tell me what's happening,' he called.

'This is almost over, Peter,' Kate Wheeler told him. 'For us and for you. But it has to be this way.'

'We need you,' Nigel Grant told him.

'For what?' Mason gaped.

'You're not like us,' Holmes offered. 'You're an outsider. You're different. You don't belong here and so you're more acceptable. More potent.'

'I don't know what the hell you're talking about,' Mason rasped.

'Does it really matter?' Nigel Grant said, a note of condescension in his voice. 'You're here now, just as we intended.'

Mason looked even more vague.

'You came here because we wanted you to,' Grant continued. 'To this school, to this town and to this place.'

'And now to where you stand at this very moment,' Richard Holmes added.

'Where's Simon Usher?' Mason asked, his voice catching.

Kate Wheeler laughed and the sound echoed within the subterranean chamber. It was a noise as grating as fingernails on a blackboard and it caused the hairs on the back of Mason's neck to rise. When it was joined by that of a number of others, he felt as if his ears would burst from the sound.

'What's going on?' he roared.

'I suppose it's only fair that you know,' Richard Holmes told him. 'Before this is all over you'll know everything.'

'Tell me now,' Mason demanded.

Kate Wheeler moved towards him and Mason, in spite of himself, went to meet her.

She was smiling as she reached for him. Mason shook his head, wondering why she was holding a hypodermic needle in one hand.

He felt a cold pinprick in his left arm as she ran it into his muscle then stepped back.

'What's going on?' Mason babbled, his head spinning.

Kate stepped away from him. Still smiling.

He saw the lights of the torches moving closer as the watching teachers advanced upon him. Mason tried to move away but it was as if the darkness inside the tunnel had flooded into his brain. Everything before him blurred then disappeared.

He blacked out.

81

From the smell that clogged his nostrils and the darkness around him, Mason knew that he was still underground when he woke up.

He opened his eyes slowly, aware instantly of the pain in his head and also of something clinging to his wrists and ankles. He tried to move and realised immediately that he was bound. Exactly what he was bound to he wasn't sure but, as he slowly raised his head he could see that he was firmly secured to a large wooden table, held captive by thick ropes around his ankles and wrists. More rope had been fastened around his chest then beneath the table to ensure there was no possibility of him freeing himself.

As his vision cleared a little more he could see that there were figures standing around him. He recognised three of them.

'If you untie me now I'll leave,' Mason said, his voice a mixture of anger and desperation. 'I'll walk away from here. From the school, the job. Everything. I won't tell anyone what's happened here.'

No one spoke.

'This is fucking ridiculous,' Mason shouted, his voice

echoing off the walls of the subterranean chamber. He strained madly against the ropes for a moment but then fell back helplessly, aware that they weren't going to budge, only too certain that he was trapped.

'Tell me what's happening,' he said, breathlessly. 'Why am I here? Why are you doing this to me?'

'The obligatory explanation before the final resolution,' Richard Holmes smiled. 'Usually so necessary in great works of fiction.'

'For God's sake,' Mason sighed.

'God has very little to do with this, Peter,' Holmes continued. 'Not your God.'

'Just stop talking in fucking riddles and tell me what's going on here,' Mason pleaded.

'It's hard to explain,' Holmes went on. 'At least in terms that you'd understand or in words that wouldn't sound preposterous.' He sucked in a deep breath. 'It probably relies on you accepting truths that, previously, you would have dismissed as idiotic. Perhaps even lunatic.'

Mason shook his head and exhaled almost painfully.

'Are you going to kill me?' he asked.

'No,' Holmes told him. 'We are, or we were, instrumental in bringing you to this place which will be the site of your death but we will not physically take your life ourselves. Something else will do that.'

Mason tried to swallow but his throat was as dry as chalk.

'What do you mean?' he croaked.

'You will die tonight,' Holmes told him. 'But not at our hands. It will be something more powerful than us that ends your time here.'

'Like what?'

'It's difficult to find the words to describe it, to be honest,' Holmes offered, cheerfully.

Mason closed his eyes tightly for a second.

'Did you kill Simon Usher too?' he asked, quietly.

'He came here,' Kate Wheeler explained. 'The same way you did. He came because he wanted to. We didn't make him. He came looking for the treasure of Abbot Bartholomew and, in a way, he found it.'

'It's all a matter of free will,' Holmes added. 'There had to be a sacrifice.'

'Sacrifice?' Mason gasped.

'I couldn't think of a better word,' Holmes said, almost apologetically. 'Sacrifice. Offering. Gift, if you will. It all amounts to the same thing. You're our gift and in return we will receive something we all need. Something we all cherish.'

'Gift to who?' Mason demanded. 'Who's going to give you what you all fucking want so badly?'

'We don't really have a name for it,' Nigel Grant interjected. 'We never have.'

'Someone once called it a guardian,' Kate Wheeler told him. 'That seemed quite a good name.'

Mason shook his head again.

'All those stories about Abbot Bartholomew and his treasure that you heard,' Holmes cut in. 'They were true. He and his colleagues were given a secret. A treasure. But it wasn't the kind of treasure that can be counted. Not gold or silver. It was something more powerful than that. It was a power that could reverse what had gone before. Change things that had happened. It could heal. It could restore. It could even give life back to those who no longer had it. As long as the offering was made. Life is all about desire, whether it's for money, fame, health or love but the need for sex is the greatest and most potent of all. The lust for lust if you like. That's what Bartholomew and his associates knew and that's

329

what we've come to learn. The stronger the desire, the easier someone is to control.'

'You're fucking mad,' Mason said, dismissively. 'All of you.'

'That may be but we have our beliefs and we stick to them,' Holmes told him.

'And what about the kids in Walston who killed themselves?' Mason grunted. 'Were they offerings too?'

'That was Latham's doing,' Kate Wheeler told him. 'He knew about the guardian. He knew that those with the strongest desires could be controlled most easily and he abused that knowledge. He took lives for his amusement. He didn't give them as offerings. He manipulated those kids. Twisted their minds with their own desire until they killed themselves.'

'So you killed Latham because he betrayed your little cult?' Mason snapped.

'He was an initiate who exceeded his position,' Grant offered. 'He had no right to do what he did. He had to be punished. The guardian punished him.'

'There was no other way,' Holmes insisted. 'Who knows what goes through the mind of a teenager? He wanted too much power too quickly. He couldn't handle it. He showed no respect. So we brought him down here and he paid the price for his insolence.'

'They say youth is wasted on the young,' Grant chuckled. 'So are certain kinds of knowledge.'

'And you believe you can control this thing, whatever it is?' Mason snorted, the bravado in his voice fading.

'No, no one can control it. We worship it,' Kate Wheeler added. 'We give it what it needs so it repays us with the things we crave the most.'

'At the beginning we thought that simply causing an affront to God was enough. Desecrating churches, killing

330

animals and things like that. Then we came to understand it more and realised that lives were required. Animals
were tried,' Holmes added, wearily. 'Horses, dogs, sheep,
cats. But they're not enough. They're sufficient if one
only wants to be free of a disease or an impediment but
they're not powerful enough offerings to allow the
restoration of life. Only the offering of a man satisfies
the cravings of the guardian fully. And once given, we
are repaid.'

'And how many people have you murdered in the
name of this thing?' Mason snapped.

'We haven't killed anyone,' Holmes reminded him.

'What about Usher?' Mason demanded.

'We offered him,' Kate explained. 'But he was ill.
Cancer. The guardian wouldn't accept the offering. It
won't accept anything impure. We left him down here.'

'He died down here,' Richard Holmes added.

Mason could feel his body shaking uncontrollably now
and he didn't care if the others could see his fear.

'Please let me go,' he said, his voice cracking.

'No,' exclaimed Kate Wheeler without a shred of
emotion in her voice. 'It's almost over now, Peter, and
we can't go back. Not now. We've all got too much to
gain. Next time it may be my turn and an offering will
restore my father's health but it isn't my turn. Not this
time.' She stroked his head gently, the tone of the voice
softening.

'So whose fucking turn is it this time?' Mason rasped.

'What would you want, Peter? If you had the chance
to change anything that had happened in your life what
would it be?' Kate purred.

'I'd want to see my daughter again. I'd want her back.
Alive,' Mason breathed.

'Then your death will be worthwhile, Peter.'

Mason heard the new voice and he twisted around madly to locate its source.

It came from behind his head and he couldn't twist his neck enough to see who spoke the words although he recognised the voice immediately.

'I waited. Now the waiting is over and what I've wanted so badly will come to pass. She'll live again,' said the voice. 'Chloe will live again.'

The figure stepped into view, standing between Kate Wheeler and Richard Holmes, looking down at him with a beatific smile.

Natalie Mason reached out and gently touched his cheek.

82

He couldn't speak.

Mason looked incredulously up at his wife but the words he wanted to say simply wouldn't force their way past his lips.

'She'll live again because of you,' Natalie announced. 'Your life for hers. Wouldn't you have given that before? Why not now?'

'You knew about this from the beginning?' Mason gasped. 'You knew everything?'

'I knew about the cult,' Natalie informed him. 'I'd been searching for some way to get over the pain of Chloe's death. I found out about them. I spoke to them and they explained the situation and the possibilities. I had to believe them, Peter. My belief was all I had. I waited my turn and now my time has come.'

'Oh, Jesus, Natalie,' he said, imploringly. 'Think about what's happening here. This is bullshit. They're all fucking crazy. Chloe is dead and nothing can bring her back. Certainly not this.'

'I have to believe them, Peter,' his wife crooned, still stroking his face gently. 'They're all I have now.'

Kate Wheeler put a comforting arm around Natalie's shoulder and guided her away from the table where Mason was held. He writhed frantically against the ropes that restrained him.

'It's time,' Richard Holmes told him. 'We have to go.'

Nigel Grant nodded affably in Mason's direction as he left. Richard Holmes stood looking down at Mason, his face expressionless.

'Please,' Mason croaked. 'Let me go.'

'It's too late now, Peter,' Holmes told him.

'And what if it doesn't accept me?' Mason said, defiantly. 'What if this thing comes looking for you or Kate or Grant or any of the rest of you?'

'It won't.'

'How can you be sure?'

Holmes took a step back.

'It won't,' he repeated then he turned and walked briskly away.

Mason was alone in the chamber.

He strained madly against the ropes, not caring that the hemp cut into the flesh of his wrists and ankles. He continued like that for fully thirty seconds then he simply slumped back onto the table, his heart hammering, his breath rasping in his throat.

He lay there motionless for another moment or two then tried again but still the ropes didn't slacken.

Mason wondered if there was any way he could turn the table over. Perhaps, if he could flip the heavy piece of furniture somehow he could get out. But how to do that? He began rocking back and forth with increasing violence. The table didn't budge. It was far too heavy. He had no other ideas. He was clueless. There seemed no way out.

Mason lay still, sucking in the dank air, his head spinning.

334

Then he heard the sound.

Far away to begin with. It was the noise he'd heard in the tunnels earlier. The wet bellows wheezing. And it was growing closer.

Mason tried again to free himself.

Come on. Think. There has to be a way off this table. A way to slip these bonds.

The wheezing was much closer and it was accompanied by a loud sucking sound. A sound like something very large slithering over damp earth. The rank odour he'd come to know so well was also more intense.

'Please help me,' he whispered, not knowing who the words were directed at. Perhaps at God. It seemed that no one else could help now.

Mason twisted his wrists frantically, not caring when the flesh there split and blood oozed over the table. He kept straining, desperate to free himself.

And all the while, the vile sucking sound filled his ears. The stench clogged his nostrils.

He tried to tell himself that this wasn't happening. That it was a trick of his mind. Some monstrous dream that he'd wake from any second.

It couldn't be real.

It couldn't.

'Help me,' he said, aloud, his voice echoing inside the chamber.

The noise was very close now. Whatever was making it was in the chamber with him.

'Help,' he shouted. 'Please help me.'

There was desperation in the words.

The stench was so strong by now that he almost retched. Whatever was with him must be only feet away but he couldn't turn his head to see it.

It was just as well.

83

It was getting cold.

The wind that had been growing in strength all afternoon was now blowing strongly across the beach. It brought with it the scent of the sea and also the threat of rain. Dark clouds were gathering far out above the steel-grey water and a small boat was making its way back to shore before things got too rough.

Natalie Mason looked up and saw seagulls dipping and diving against the increasingly turbulent backdrop. She shivered as the breeze whipped around her then she took a final sip of her tea, got to her feet and walked towards the sea wall.

The tide was a long way out and there was nothing but sand six or seven feet below.

Somewhere out by the water's edge she could hear a dog barking. As she looked more closely, she could see two children throwing a stick for the animal to chase. It scurried happily back and forth between them, each child petting it as it reached them. Natalie smiled and continued along the seafront, pausing to brush some strands of hair from her face.

The beach was more or less deserted except for the children down by the water and a couple who were walking arm in arm over the sand. Natalie liked it like that. When it was quiet. She had more time to think and she appreciated the stillness. Only the far-off crashing of the waves on the beach broke the solitude.

She headed for the jetty that stuck out into the sea like an accusatory finger, the water lapping around the rusted metal struts that held the structure up.

There was a single figure on the end of the wooden promontory and Natalie walked towards it.

When she got ten yards away she called once but the figure didn't turn. It was peering out to sea, towards the growing banks of dark cloud and the diving seagulls and the little boat.

Natalie moved nearer, her feet tapping out a tattoo on the wood of the jetty as she walked towards the figure ahead of her.

The figure didn't turn. It seemed more interested in the seagull that had landed on the parapet of the jetty and was sitting there motionless.

Natalie saw the figure extend a hand towards the bird as if to welcome it and the gull left its temporary perch and dropped down close to the figure.

Natalie hesitated, slowing her pace as the figure moved towards the gull. The bird seemed unconcerned and merely let out a squawk. The figure knelt close as if inspecting it.

The speed of the movement was incredible. The figure grabbed the gull by the neck in one hand and stood up instantly. The gull flapped its powerful wings once but the reflex was stopped as its head was torn away by the figure's other hand. The body jerked involuntarily, the wings flapping again as the bird's body was tossed away over the parapet of the jetty into the dark water below.

Natalie stood motionless, watching as the figure looked at the ripped-off head of the gull, holding it for a second longer before hurling it into the water in the same direction as the body.

Natalie closed her eyes briefly then sucked in a deep breath that was tinged with the taste of the sea.

At last the figure turned, nodded, then scampered back towards her.

Natalie scooped the figure up into her arms, smiling broadly as she felt the embrace returned so warmly.

'Come on,' Natalie beamed. 'Let's get home before the rain starts.'

She looked at the figure's hands and saw that there was some blood on them. Natalie reached into her coat pocket, pulled out a tissue and wiped the crimson fluid away, stuffing the rag back into her pocket.

Chloe Mason smiled back at her, reaching for her hand as they walked back down the jetty.

They were still halfway along it when they felt the first spots of rain. Laughing, they began to run, wanting to reach shelter and escape what threatened to be a downpour.

Natalie pulled the bloodied tissue from her pocket and tossed it into a waste bin as she passed.

This wasn't the first incident of the kind she'd just witnessed. There'd been a dog, a rabbit and several other birds. She didn't know why. She didn't want to know.

It was, she told herself, a small price to pay for having Chloe with her again.

The rain fell more heavily now, large cold droplets hammering down from the threatening clouds but to Natalie and her daughter it didn't really seem to matter.